Mayfield's Last Case

Other Books by Graham Sutherland

To Brian:
Do enjoy your retirement.
All best wishes
Graham Sutherland

Mayfield's Last Case

Part Three of the Warwick Detective Trilogy

Graham Sutherland

Spiderwize

Mayfield's Last Case
Part Three of the Warwick Detective Trilogy

Spiderwize
3rd Floor
207 Regent Street
London
W1B 3HH

www.spiderwize.com

ISBN: 978-1-908128-33-1

To

Mo, Claire, Jo, Ally, Clara and Seren.

PROLOGUE

Gettysburg, Pennsylvania …July 3 1863

Lieutenant Silas Whiting paused, and took another swat at the host of flies buzzing around him. He knew it was a pointless exercise, as they would soon return.

The sweat was running into his aching eyes, and making them sting. His eyes, along with his back and most of his body, ached enough already without this extra discomfort. And he could not remember when he had last slept. Next he selected a relatively less filthy part of his apron, and rubbed his hands on it, which removed some of the blood on them. He knew from experience, there was little or no clean water to be had just at the moment.

Having wiped the sweat from his forehead, with the back of a hand, he rubbed it on the seat of his trousers, blinked a few times and returned to his work. However, Silas knew he was fighting yet another losing battle, in trying to deal with the steady stream of wounded men being brought into the field hospital.

When the Civil War had started in America, Silas was still in his first year at medical school. However, after listening to one of Abraham Lincoln's anti-slavery speeches, he had not needed very much persuasion to join the Union Army Medical Department as a lieutenant. He was welcomed with open arms, in spite of having only had the most basic training.

Suddenly there had been a great need for doctors, regardless of how little experience they might have. That would come quickly enough on the battlefields. Luckily, Silas was a quick learner.

He had to be.

Medical science was not always appreciated by many people. In normal times, trainee doctors could expect to undergo an apprenticeship of two years, which would include little or no practical experience. For many young doctors, the war now gave them the chance of getting that much needed experience, and was the reason many of them, including Silas, enlisted. After the war, provided they survived, these doctors could become leaders in the field of medicine.

Gettysburg was not his first major battle. Silas had been at 2nd Bull Run, Antietam and Fredericksburg, the year before, as well as several other lesser clashes.

'He's gone doc,' said his assistant, interrupting his thoughts.

Silas looked down at his patient, and quickly checked the man's pulse. It was not that he doubted his assistant, but a doctor was required to make sure. Already he was gaining the reputation of being a dedicated doctor, who would save lives whenever he could. But, as he expected, in this case he could find no pulse, which given the state of the man's injuries was not surprising.

'Let's have the next,' he instructed.

Automatically he looked down as the wounded soldier was put on the table. He saw the man was wearing a butternut grey uniform, and he was clearly one of the enemy soldiers. But here, in the field hospital he treated all wounded men the same, regardless of which uniform they wore.

Silas had lost count of the days this campaign and final battle had been going on. It was now at its height, and his field hospital, one of several, was much in demand. To call it a hospital was an exaggeration, as it was really nothing more than a large tent, attached to the rear of a ruined warehouse.

The medical staff employed in the tent, were unaware of the passing of time. Their work was continuous. In the background, they were all aware of the cannons firing almost non-stop, interspersed with the rattle of musketry.

Some of the casualties which they treated bore evidence of hand-to-hand fighting, with close-up bullet and bayonet wounds. When it ended, the battle would have claimed more than 50,000 casualties. Death and maiming had no respect for loyalties or uniforms. His new patient needed an arm amputating.

When Silas had first started in the Medical Corps, the skill of the few existing Army surgeons was often called into question. They had to seek advice from their civilian counterparts, prior to amputating any limbs. It was an impractical situation, which had been dictated by there then being less than ninety surgeons in the entire Union army. Times had moved on.

Silas gave his instructions and the operation was completed very quickly. He had become very proficient at this type of surgery, acting on his own initiative, rarely having the luxury of being able to obtain a second opinion. Once the operation was completed, the patient was removed into the ruined warehouse, which housed what were loosely called beds. In due course they would be moved to hospitals in much safer areas.

To call them beds was another exaggeration. They were often not much more than blankets which had been laid on the bare floor. Occasionally there might be some straw mattresses, or whatever could be salvaged from nearby houses. These were either given freely by their owners, or taken on promise of suitable compensation being made, at an unspecified time in the future.

For the most part, the casualties were beyond caring, either because of their pain or as a result of the anaesthetics they had been given. Likewise, they were fairly unaware of the additional treatment they were given by various nurses. They were women volunteers, who had started out with little or no experience. Initially they had not been welcomed by the army, but they still persisted in coming to help. They too had learned very quickly.

As a team, Silas and his two assistants worked well. Each one respected the skills and abilities of the others. Silas was always ready to listen to their advice, although they needed to give it to him less and less now. In return, he enjoyed their respect for the humane and, whenever possible, kindly way he treated his patients, regardless of which uniform they wore. The same could not be said for some doctors.

'Lootenant! Go and take half-an-hour,' growled Captain Crowley, who had suddenly appeared.

For a moment Silas thought about disobeying his senior officer, but he did not argue. Taking off his bloodstained apron, he made his way out of the hospital, and into the night outside. It was a relief to breathe in fresh air…that is if the heavy pall of smoke and gunpowder fumes, which were everywhere, constituted fresh air.

He had not been aware of daylight going, and of the lamps being lit in the hospital. It was not a peaceful evening. Guns were still firing, with their flashes lighting up the sky, although the sounds seemed to be dying out. Silently, he breathed a short prayer for the battle to end soon.

Even as he stood there, another team of sweating horses pulling an ambulance arrived, bringing in more wounded men. Their pitiful cries added to those of the wounded, already in the overfilled hospital.

Making his way to a nearby pump, Silas worked the handle, glad it still functioned. Putting his head under the flow of cold water, he then washed his hands. It was a blessed relief to feel the cold water run through his hair, and down his neck. He only stopped the flow when the water was no longer tinged with blood.

Next he visited the latrines. Their stench encouraged nobody to linger. He did what he had to do, and quickly returned to the fresh air and had another wash under the pump.

Unlike some of his colleagues, Silas was a firm believer in hygiene, and he washed whenever he could, but it was not always easy. In the operating theatre, he tried to wash after each operation, but a chronic shortage of water, usually caused by the lack of anyone to fetch it, often made such luxuries difficult or even impossible.

'Coffee Lieutenant?'

Silas turned and saw a young woman holding out a steaming mug towards him. He inhaled its aroma from where he stood, and it smelled good.

He saw she was of medium height, but tending to be a little on the tall side, slimly built with her hair piled under a mob cap, from which a few stray brown strands escaped. Her face was drawn, and it showed the familiar signs of exhaustion, which were prevalent everywhere he looked. Silas knew he looked similarly weary.

In the dim light he saw there were stains on her clothing, which he could not identify, but guessed, rightly, they were blood. He assumed she was a nurse.

'Thanks,' he said and took the mug gratefully. Moving to a nearby wall, he sat down and sipped the coffee. It tasted good, and he savoured the enjoyment of it trickling down his throat. She sat alongside him.

'Is this your coffee?' he asked guiltily.

'Yes, but don't worry,' she grinned in reply. 'I've got a friend in the canteen, and can soon get another one.'

They talked for a while, mainly about the war and what they hoped to do after it had finished.

'Lootenant!' roared an all too familiar voice. 'I said half-an-hour. Not the whole damned night!'

Silas finished the coffee in a single swallow and smiling, handed the mug back to his companion. 'Duty calls. And thank you once again.'

'My pleasure,' she replied, and watched him walk back into the hospital, before climbing down from the wall.

Smiling to herself, she realised she had not even asked him his name, although she knew who he was. All of the nurses did. With his light brown hair, brown eyes and boyish face, he appealed to many women, especially those who had become nurses during this conflict. They would be envious of her when she told them about their meeting. It did not matter he had not asked for her name.

She made her way into the nearby bushes. The latrines were strictly for the men, but even if they were not, the stench was enough to put her off using them. Adjusting her skirts, she made her way back on to the path.

'Oh! Hello,' she said, recognising the familiar figure standing before her.

The young nurse gasped in surprise and pain, as the scalpel was thrust into her stomach, and wrenched upwards. Through a maze of pain, she was vaguely aware of her hair being pulled back, exposing her throat. The scalpel severed her carotid artery, and she was mercifully dead within seconds.

Pausing only to drop the scalpel nearby, the figure turned and walked back towards the field hospital.

★ ★ ★

In the early morning light, Provost-Sergeant Cornelius Lake looked at the body of the murdered nurse. He was not remotely interested that the day promised rain. Neither was he interested in the rumours, which were filtering through, to the effect the battle was over. Robert E Lee, and his Confederate Army, were in full retreat. It was certainly much quieter, with only sporadic shooting.

Although no stranger to violent death, he was appalled at the wanton viciousness of the attack on the nurse. He asked himself, as he had done before: Wasn't there enough death and destruction on the battlefields, without senseless murder being added to it? Hadn't somebody had enough of killing?

Cornelius knew his captain would not be too interested, and would insist it was a job for the local police. But that argument would not deter Cornelius. This was the fourth such death he had encountered. The others were at 2nd Bull Run, Antietam and Fredericksburg. Yet this one was different. Unlike the others, this woman was a nurse and not a hooker, which was one of the names now being given to whores.

Already he had discovered she was Martha Maudsley, a volunteer nurse, trying to do her bit for her country. He knew her parents had yet to be told. Luckily that task would be carried out by someone else. It would be bad enough to discover your daughter had been killed by enemy action. But in this case, it was much worse. She had been killed, apparently, by someone on her own side.

A search of the area had soon recovered a bloodstained scalpel, which Cornelius believed to have been the murder weapon. And that its discovery only served to strengthen his suspicions that someone from the field hospital was responsible for the murder.

The other victims had all been found close to field hospitals, with bloodstained scalpels nearby. And their injuries seemed to have been inflicted by someone who had some medical knowledge. Or if not, the killer had to have access to medical equipment. But who was their killer?

As he thought, Captain Ventry was not particularly interested. He listened whilst Cornelius unfolded his theory.

6

'Even if you're right,' he replied at length. 'The army's so short of medics that I couldn't possibly agree to you arresting one.'

Cornelius began to object.

But Ventry silenced him. 'I'm sorry, but the lives of our boys are more important than those of a few hookers.'

'Martha Maudsley was not a hooker,' protested Cornelius.

'Makes no difference,' continued Ventry. He held his hand up as Cornelius began to protest again. 'No. Listen to me!' he commanded. 'Gather all your evidence and be patient. When this damn war's over, then you can go after your man. For now, I'll give you forty-eight hours.'

Deep down Cornelius knew his captain was probably right. There was a continual shortage of doctors in the army. But after the war…that would be different.

He went and took a final look at Martha's body.

'I'll get you, you bastard, no matter how long it takes me,' he vowed.

CHAPTER ONE

The visitor, Warwick, England...March 1867

'Come in!' instructed Police Superintendent John Mayfield, when he heard the knock on his office door.

'Apologies for bothering you, guv'nor,' said Constable Harry Barlow. 'But I've got a young gentleman who wishes to speak to you.'

John looked up from his writing.

'He says he's a Doctor Silas Whiting, and he sounds a bit foreign,' continued Harry, as he handed John a visiting card.

John sat back. Harry's brief description of the man meant nothing to him, but the name did. Could he be connected somehow to Kate Whiting? Possibly it might be a coincidence, but he did not believe in them.

His memory went back to Kate Whiting, as she was called then in those heady days, when he first came to Warwick.

He would never forget them, or Katherine, as she now liked to be called. Or, she did when he had last seen her. How could he forget them?

That had all happened over a quarter of a century ago, and it was now 1867. Her husband had been called Silas, whom he knew was long since dead. How time had passed.

'I can't say I know the man, but show him in. I'll enjoy the break from doing all this paperwork.' John waved a hand at the pile of papers on his desk.

A few moments later, Harry Barlow reappeared. John saw he was accompanied by a well-dressed young man, who seemed to be in his mid-twenties, although his eyes, streaks of grey hair, and the lines on his face, made him look considerably older. He was carrying a small leather case.

'Dr Whiting, guv'nor,' announced Harry. Then he stopped and looked first at John and then at his visitor.

'Is there something else?' queried John. 'If not, perhaps you would be good enough to make us some tea.'

'Er no, guv'nor: I'll get the tea,' replied Harry, but he still kept looking at the other two men, before he hastily withdrew.

'Mr Mayfield, I'm Dr Silas Whiting,' John's visitor held out his hand.

John took it, noticing how his visitor had an American accent. 'How can I help you?' he added. By now his mind was in a whirl. Silas Whiting? It was too much of a coincidence. He must be connected to Katherine.

His visitor grinned. It was a friendly face, which John thought would go down well with his patients, especially the ladies. The man's face looked familiar, but it did not particularly remind him of Katherine.

'If you'll forgive me, sir, for the intrusion,' the visitor replied. 'It's purely a social call. I believe you once knew my mother and she asked me to look you up, whilst I was here in England.'

'Katherine? Katherine Whiting?' John asked, both amazed and a little flustered. 'Good grief. After all these years! How is she?'

'She's fine, sir. Absolutely fine. She keeps very good health, although, when she thinks I'm not looking, she wears spectacles for reading. And she's got a few grey hairs, but then so have I. But woe betide anyone who mentions them.'

John chuckled, and produced his own spectacles from the top of his desk, and rubbed his own grey hair. 'I know the feeling.'

Whilst he was still tall and slimly built, John had been only too aware of the passing of the years. In spite of his spectacles, his steely eyes had lost nothing of their intensity, and he still had a good head of hair. But he was conscious of the fact he was starting to slow down, and on some days, he found the prospect of retiring to be quite inviting.

Both men laughed.

So this was Katherine's son. John wondered who the lucky man was who had married her. It might have been me, he mused, if only things had been different. Certainly this young man was a credit to his parents. For a moment he studied Silas, liking what he saw, yet thinking once more how there was something familiar about the young doctor's looks. No doubt he would soon discover the identity of the boy's father.

'She asked to be remembered to you. That is if you remembered her.'

'How could I ever forget her?' For a few moments he relived the last time they had met. If only things had been different. 'What's she doing with herself now?'

'She's a very successful businesswoman, who inherited grandfather's steel business when he died. Then during the war, although she refused to be a profiteer, she still made a vast amount of dollars. Much of it she ploughed back into the community and funded the military hospitals where I worked, and offered all sorts of aid to the returning soldiers.'

'Who did she marry, after Silas died?' asked John hesitantly, not quite sure he wanted to hear the answer.

'No-one sir. But I think there's a man in her life somewhere, although I've never met him. She keeps him a close secret.'

John did not know to react to that answer.

Further conversation was stopped by the arrival of Harry Barlow, who came into the office, carrying two mugs of tea. Once again he stopped and stared at the two men and then withdrew. As he did so, Silas looked in the mirror that hung on the wall behind John's head.

He stopped suddenly, his face paling.

'What's the matter?' asked John and turned to look in the mirror.

It only took him a moment to study his face, alongside that of his visitor's, to realise why Harry Barlow had stared. Now he knew why he thought his visitor's face was familiar.

Both their faces were alike.

Quickly John crossed to his office door. He opened it and called. 'Constable Barlow! I do not want to be disturbed.'

'Yes guv'nor,' came the reply.

John returned to his visitor and saw the friendly look on his face had gone. It had been replaced by one of anger and puzzlement.

'When were you born?' John asked.

'October 19th 1843.'

Quickly John calculated, although he did not need to do so. It was obvious Silas was his son.

'You're my son,' he said weakly.

'It would appear so,' was the taut reply. 'I was always told my father, who I was named after, was dead. But now I find I've got a secret father, who has wanted nothing to do with me, for all these years. No wonder mama thought it was time you were made to face up to your responsibilities.'

'That just isn't true,' John shook his head sadly. 'I never knew I had a son until now.' He shook his head in total bewilderment. 'Believe me. I never knew.'

A look of uncertainty passed over his son's face. 'Somehow, I'd like to believe you,' he said. 'But, why should I?' He sat down. 'I just don't know what to believe.'

'It's as big a shock to me. Harriet couldn't have any children although we both wanted to. Now I find I have a son.'

For a while neither man spoke.

'I could almost believe you.' Silas broke the silence. 'But why should I?' John noticed his voice had softened a little, and he had the opinion, rightly, that his son really wanted to believe him.

'Mama would have known you were my father, so why didn't she tell you or me?' he continued accusingly.

John thought for a moment. 'It's a long story,' he announced. 'And it's one I've never told anybody else, not even Harriet, my wife. But I think it's time to break that silence.'

He stood up and walked across to his safe. Selecting a key from his fob, John unlocked it and opened the door. Then he took out an envelope, which had browned with age. Closing the safe, he walked back to his desk, and sat down. He put the envelope on the top of his desk, but made no attempt to open it, or give it to Silas.

'I'll show you this in a while, but first let me tell you what happened.'

Silas listened in silence, whilst John told him about Kate and Silas Whiting, and young Edward, and their involvement in the James Cooper case.

'When I said good-bye to Katherine at Coventry railway station, all those years ago,' John continued, 'I thought I would never see her again. But I was wrong.'

CHAPTER TWO

London...mid-February 1843

John had been called to London, to testify in a lengthy fraud trial. It was scheduled to take three or four days, and related to a case in which he had been involved before he moved to Warwick. As the trial was due to start on the Monday, he went to London the night before.

He had hoped to use the visit to see his parents, but they were both away. After a quiet night, he presented himself at the Old Bailey the next morning. To his surprise, he found the trial was not listed to be heard that day, or at any other time during the coming week. After asking several barristers about it, he was finally directed to William Booth QC, who was obviously discomforted to see him.

'The Whittaker fraud trial?' he mumbled. 'Er...er...um: hasn't anyone told you?'

'Told me what?' John replied tartly. 'I've come for the trial, which I was told would start today. But I cannot find out where it is happening.'

'That's just it. You should have been told. It's off.'

'Off? Off? What do you mean *it's off*? I've come all the way from the Midlands.'

'As I said: it's off.'

'So you keep saying. When will it be heard?'

'It won't. There's been a deal. You know how it is.'

'No. I don't know how it is!' John was struggling to keep his temper. Why wouldn't this man give him a straight answer?

'Let's just say,' Booth lowered his voice and looked around. 'Let's just say,' he continued, satisfied nobody was close enough to hear him. 'He's been very useful to the Government. Chartists. You know. All the charges have been dropped. Just go home and forget about it.'

Much as it grieved him, John could appreciate the growing Chartist problem would probably be grounds enough for his case to be dropped, especially if Whittaker was now helping the Government.

However, knowing Roger Herbert Devereux Whittaker as he did, John had little doubt the man had convinced the Government of his sincerity. After all, he was an accomplished, plausible, and very convincing fraudsman. Just how sincere he was, the Government would have to find out. John doubted they would actually find his information that useful.

If he was honest with himself, John quite liked the man, and in many ways he was glad not to have to testify against him, especially as his victims had all been in banking. But that was not the point. He had come to London on a fool's errand, and he was far from happy about it.

'But I've arranged to be here for the week.'

'Oh, don't worry about that. Take some leave. Go back at the end of the week.' Booth smiled. 'No doubt you'll enjoy yourself here in the Capital. It's far different from Warwick.'

'I know. I used to work here! Remember?'

Booth ignored his reply. 'Your Watch Committee will know all about it by now.' He consulted his pocket watch. ''Fraid I've got to dash. You'll have to excuse me.'

Before John could reply, Booth had gone and moments later, he was deep in conversation with another barrister. He did not look back.

John stormed out of the court, and returned to his overnight lodgings, where he changed out of his uniform, hastily repacked his clothes, and made his way to the *Belle Sauvage Inn*, to catch the next coach back to Warwick. His wife Laura would be pleased to see him back so soon.

She had seemed so edgy when they parted the previous day. He had asked what was wrong, but she would not tell him, but hinted at a surprise. Although he could have taken the train, John preferred to travel by coach. But it seemed so did everyone else; there were no seats available until later that night.

Leaving his luggage at the inn, John went back towards the centre of the city, at a loss to know what to do. He was so wrapped up in his thoughts, he failed to see a carriage stop at the kerbside, and the young woman who descended from it. She failed to see him and they both collided.

John was the first to recover. Taking off his hat, he put out his hand to steady her. 'I'm so dreadfully sorry...' he began. But his voice tailed off as he saw the look on her face.

It was not the anger he expected, but a warm smile of recognition. 'Why, Mr Mayfield,' said Kate Whiting.

'Kate...Kate...Whiting?' he stammered.

He barely recognised the attractive, smartly dressed, sophisticated young woman standing in front of him. She was a far cry from the foundry worker he had first met. True, she had been smartly dressed when they had parted on Coventry railway station. But that was nothing to how she now looked.

'Kate Whiting?' He stammered again.

'Actually,' she smiled back at him. 'Kate's gone. It's Katherine now.'

They just stood looking at one another remembering their last meeting.

'How are Silas and young Edward?' he asked, at a sudden loss for something else to say, but was saddened, yet excited to see her face fall.

'Both gone: cholera.'

'I'm so sorry.'

'It happens,' she shrugged. 'But at least they were able to enjoy a few months free from poverty, thanks to you.'

Katherine had given John an immense amount of help in running a big counterfeiting gang to justice. It was when he had first come to Warwick. She had done it at some considerable danger to herself. Afterwards, John had made sure she benefited from the very substantial rewards offered both by the Bank of England and the Royal Mint.

During their brief association, they had fallen in love. The problem was, she was already married.

'And you? Did you marry your Harriet?' she continued.

'No,' John shook his head sadly. 'She was lost at sea, but now I'm married to Laura.' He had been tempted to say he was single, but he had never lied to her, and did not want to start now.

Never lied to her! Never lied to her! He hardly knew her!

'What are you doing here?' he asked.

'It's not a long story,' she replied. 'Come.' Taking him by the arm, Katherine led him into a nearby hotel.

Her touch still caused a ripple of electricity to go through his body, and he went willingly with her.

Over coffee, she explained how she had heeded the advice, from the Bank of England, on how to invest her reward money. Coupled with the advice she had received from John's recommended solicitor, Katherine had made a small fortune in just a few weeks.

Tragically, her husband Silas and son Edward had died before they could all fully enjoy the benefits of it. Silas had never discovered the truth about her involvement with James Cooper, and she was very relieved at that. How could she have told him about the way that man had used her? Although she had done what he wanted for her family's sake, Katherine was always scared Silas would find out. And if he had done so, just how would he have reacted?

But he had never found out.

Having had a governess for her mother, Katherine had inherited a thirst for learning. Now she had the money, she had used it wisely and improved her education, absorbing knowledge like a sponge soaking up water.

Also, she had been able to trace her real father back to America, where he was a successful steel manufacturer. She had written to him, via her solicitor. Her father was a widower with no children, and he welcomed the chance to get to know his unknown daughter. Although he had asked all manner of searching questions about her mother, she was able to answer them. Katherine had now disposed of her rented house and she had come to London, for a few days.

'He's asked me to go and join him, in America, and I sail on Friday. So I thought I'd spend a few days in London, before I go. But what are you doing here?'

John told her about his trial fiasco, and not being able to get a seat on the coach.

'Does that mean you don't have to go back straight away?'

'Well, yes. Apparently, it seems I'm on extended leave.'

'Then John: why not stay here in London? You're from these parts and I really would like to see some of the sights before I sail. Will you show me around?' As she spoke, Katherine put her hands on his.

Her touch removed any lingering doubts he might have had.

'Put that way, madam,' he smiled. 'How could I possibly refuse?'

Later that evening, after a busy round of sightseeing and a visit to the theatre, they enjoyed a late supper, before he escorted Katherine back to her hotel. During the day they had swapped histories and were now very comfortable in each other's company.

Finally they arrived back at her hotel.

'Would you be so kind, sir, to see me safe and sound up to my room?' teased Katherine. 'Who knows what perils might await me on the stairs.'

'It would be my pleasure, my lady,' he replied in the same tone.

They stopped at her door.

'I need my room checking, as well, just to make sure it is safe for me to sleep in,' she continued.

He only hesitated for a few seconds.

On opening the door, the first thing he saw in her room, was his luggage, which he had left at the *Belle Sauvage*. She smiled at the surprised look on his face.

'You weren't thinking of sleeping anywhere else, were you?' she asked innocently, raising her eyebrows. 'And I have it on very good authority, that there is no accommodation available anywhere in London, tonight.'

He opened his mouth to protest, but she put a finger to his lips. 'Say nothing, my darling,' she breathed, her breath warm on his cheek. 'You've no idea how long I've waited for this moment.'

'Oh but I have,' he replied hoarsely. 'Ever since the day I first saw you.'

'Forgive me, Laura,' he said to himself, as he felt Katherine's eager fingers begin to undress him.

The next three days were among the happiest both of them had ever experienced. Their first lovemaking had only settled a basic need in them. After that, they indulged in tender and passionate lovemaking, satisfying to both of them.

But all too soon, Thursday night was upon them.

Katherine had told John she sailed at 5 p.m. on the Friday, and she would need to be at the docks soon after 3 p.m. After an early supper, they retired to bed, where they made long lingering love. They both realised the hour of her sailing was drawing ever nearer. As they sat in companionable silence, Katherine opened a bottle of champagne.

'Forgive my back,' she asked John, as she turned to the dressing table and poured out two glasses.

She gave one to John and kept the other herself.

'To us,' she smiled and raised the glass to her lips.

John took a mouthful and frowned. 'That tastes a little strange,' he said.

'You're imagining it, my darling,' she smiled and raised her glass again. 'Drink up!'

He took another swallow.

All at once John felt a wave of tiredness flow over him, and his eyes began to close. He barely had time to put his glass down, before he fell into a deep sleep.

Sometime during the night, he heard her say tenderly, 'goodbye, my darling.' But in his sleepy state, he thought she had said 'goodnight.' At the same time he felt something warm and moist fall on his cheek, as she kissed him.

'Goodnight,' he muttered in reply.

When John awoke, the sun was shining into their bedroom. From force of habit, he reached out to touch her, but she was not there. Also, her side of the bed was cold. Sitting up, he looked at his watch, and was horrified to see it said 2.20 which he knew had to be in the afternoon. Where was Katherine? She was due at the docks in less than an hour.

As he swung his legs out of bed, he noticed all her clothes had gone. Then he saw the envelope, which was addressed to him. John tore it open, took out the letter, and began to read.

My Dearest, Dearest Darling John

This is the hardest letter I have ever had to write. I beg you, please don't think too badly of me.

I'm afraid I lied to you. My ship sailed at 5 o'clock this morning, so by the time you read this, I shall have been at sea for several hours. You were quite right about the champagne tasting strange. It contained a powerful sleeping draught. Please don't think I enjoyed doing it. I didn't.

You see, I fell in love with you, the very first time I saw you in Warwick, which was before your kindness to Silas and Edward. You did that because you are a compassionate man.

Why did I lie to you?

In the past few days, I have come to love you more than I ever thought it was possible for any woman to love a man, and I know you came to love me just as much. I also know if I had asked you to, you would have left Laura and come to America with me.

Somehow, I didn't think that was right. I know your first love was Harriet. After all, she saved your life twice, and I realise how much you miss her, even with Laura as your wife.

There is no way I could have come back to Warwick. The scandal would have ruined you. And, even if I had come back, I'm not certain just how safe my life would have been. James Cooper did have some friends.

Also my Darling, Warwick needs you. You have the town's interests at heart. After the Cooper years, the town needs stability, and you are the one man who can provide it. Warwick does not need another scandal.

At heart I am a coward. I could not bear to tell you this after the wonderful time we have just had. One look at your face, and all my resolve would have vanished. So I think this is the kindest way. (Here the writing was smudged. John correctly surmised it had been caused by her tears).

So please, please forgive me, my Darling, for doing this to you. I will not give you a forwarding address, as I know I could never resist any entreaty from you for us to meet again.

However, should the time ever arise, when you desperately need me, as a matter of life or death, then all you have to do is contact Mr Wilkins at the Bank of England, or his successor. He will know how to contact me. But please only do this if it is really necessary.

My Darling, my cab will be here in the next few minutes, and there is so much more I would like to say, but I cannot do so.

I firmly believe we will meet again one day. Please, please forgive me for what I have done, but I have done it for you. I can never love another man as much as I love you. Be strong, my Darling, for both of us.

Go back to your Laura. She does not deserve to be hurt like this. Who knows, she will probably give you the children you want.

Look after Warwick.

I will never ever forget you or ever love another man.

Please forgive me, my Darling. I love you so very much.

> *Yours only, now and forever*
> > *All my dearest love*
> *Katherine*

The last words were smudged again by her tears. Now John realised, she had said *'goodbye'* to him last night, and not *'goodnight.'*

John paused in his narrative, and he handed Katherine's letter to Silas to read.

'You're only the third person to have read this,' he explained. 'And that includes me and your mother. Not even my wife, Harriet, has seen it.'

CHAPTER THREE

A bad time

John waited patiently whilst his son read the letter. At last he finished.
'Is Harriet, your wife, the same woman mama refers to?' Silas asked.

John nodded. 'Yes. She survived the shipwreck and finally made it back to Warwick.'

'But did you not try and chase mama?'

'Oh yes. I went straight to the docks, but as she said, her ship had long since sailed. I wanted to go after her, but I had to come home first, and get some money for the passage. And...' John paused. 'And I would have to explain everything to Laura, as I was determined to leave her and go to America. I didn't think I'd have any problem being a policeman over there. But...'

'Why didn't you?' prompted Silas, slightly accusingly.

'Because when I got back here, Laura was brimming with excitement. She was pregnant and I couldn't possibly leave her. Perhaps if I'd known your mama was also pregnant...' He faltered. 'Laura lost the child, a few weeks later.'

Silas said nothing.

His mind was in a whirl. Everything was happening too quickly. Suddenly he had found he had a father, whom he had accused of having ignored him. Although, in view of the letter he had just read, this would appear not to be the case. Somehow, the fact his father had kept that letter all these years, supported his story of really loving his mother.

'And Laura miscarried again,' added John.

'You say you are married now to Harriet? What happened to Laura?'

'She was murdered along with her unborn child,' John's reply was very quiet, and a hard look came over his face. 'Whoever did it came close to killing me at the same time. I was only saved by the quick thinking of one of my men, and my very good friend Dr Thomas Waldren.' John paused.

Silas could sense the suppressed anger in his father's voice, and he waited, knowing there was more to come.

'And to my everlasting shame,' continued John, eventually, through tight lips. 'We have never found their murderer. It was supposed to be someone taking revenge on me. We think it might have been a woman. She wrote to me and talked about revenge, and taunted me for killing her love. But that might not have been true. Whoever this person is, or was, he or she drove Harriet away from me, and I suppose I married Laura because she happened to be there.'

John told Silas about meeting Laura, and how they had become lovers. But Harriet had always been, and always would be his first love. Yet he still hoped the day would come when Laura's killer would be brought to justice. But as so many years had now passed, in all probability her killer was long since dead. At times, he had still felt remorse for having betrayed her, when he had his affair with Katherine. And yet, he found he now had a fine son, from that time. Somehow, he felt that made his betrayal seem less serious.

For several moments father and son just looked at each other; neither knowing what to say.

'I'm so sorry I doubted you, father.' Silas was the first to break the silence. 'Can you ever forgive me?' He suddenly felt a real wave of affection for this man, whom he now knew to be his father. And he was glad he had misjudged him.

'Of course,' smiled John. 'You and I have a lot of catching up to do. Though God knows what I am going to tell Harriet. Ironically, she came back to Warwick that very evening when Laura was murdered.'

Any further comments were interrupted by an urgent knocking on John's office door. 'Come in!' he called.

Harry Barlow put his head around the door. 'Apologies for interrupting you, guv'nor. But there's been a serious accident in the Market Place. The gaol van has overturned, trapping its driver underneath.'

'Have you sent for a doctor?'

'Yes. But Dr Waldren's out of town and so's Dr Delany. We're still trying to find another one.'

John remembered.

Thomas had taken Harriet to London. Her health had been deteriorating for some weeks. She was losing weight and coughing up blood, and Thomas had taken her to see a specialist in London. Privately, as he confided to John, he was very worried about his niece.

'You say you need a doctor?' Silas asked the constable.

'Yes sir. We do. Warder Johnson's badly hurt. He's trapped by a leg.'

'Then, I'm your man. I'm a doctor. Let's go!'

Waiting only to pick up his leather case, Silas followed John up into the Market Place, where a small crowd had gathered. The two men pushed their way through, and Silas knelt beside the injured man, who was clearly in a great deal of pain.

Silas opened his case, and John saw it contained numerous medical instruments and some bottles. Quickly selecting a scalpel, Silas cut through the man's trouser leg. A horrified gasp came from some of the spectators as they saw a broken piece of bone protruding through the skin.

'Please sir! Please sir, don't take my leg off!' pleaded Charles Johnson. 'I'll lose my job if you do. And I've got a family to care for.'

Silas smiled. 'Don't worry, I think I can save it.'

'YOU think YOU can save it?' A stern voice came from behind him. Both he and John turned to see Dr Thomas Waldren glowering at Silas. 'How can you make such a diagnosis, sir? Are you a doctor?'

'Actually I am,' replied Silas, coolly, but firmly. 'Dr Silas Whiting, at your service, sir.'

John thought about intervening on his son's behalf, but somehow he felt the young man was managing all right on his own.

'And just how old are you, sir?' sneered Thomas.

'I'm twenty-four, sir.'

'Twenty-four? Twenty-four? Twenty-four? You can only just have left medical school, if you're not still there. And just where did you acquire all that extensive knowledge, to enable you to make such a vital life and death decision? Perhaps when you've been a doctor for as long as I have, then you can make such promises,' sneered Thomas.

'By spending three years in the field hospitals on the battlefields of North America, where we treated three out of every four of all casualties by amputation. There was less risk of infection that way. At the same time, we learned how to repair many of those damaged limbs, and combat some of the infections. We learned a lot in those days, especially when there was major battle raging all around us.' Silas paused, and looked at Thomas straight in the eyes.

Thomas opened his mouth to speak, but Silas continued relentlessly.

'But when we did save their limbs, all that happened was the poor soldiers were sent back into the mincing machine of death once more. It was usually kinder to turn them into cripples.'

'My dear sir,' spluttered Thomas at last. 'I apologise to you unreservedly. If you can save this man's leg, then I will be both proud and pleased to assist you. I'm Thomas Waldren and my surgery is at your disposal.'

As Silas returned to his patient, Thomas began issuing instructions. Then he turned to John. 'Remember you're dining with us tonight.'

As he spoke, Thomas kept looking from John to Silas, who was working on the injured man. Clearly he had noticed how similar they were in looks.

Minutes later, Silas had splinted Warder Johnson's legs together, and he was on his way to the Harriet Foxton Hospital. Thomas had watched Silas at work, and he was very impressed by the younger man's skill. John watched the doctors follow their patient, talking as if they were old friends.

Suddenly John was overwhelmed with an immense pride in his son. Then the realisation hit him. Undoubtedly Silas would be invited to join them for dinner. Although Thomas had said nothing, the look on his face showed he had worked out the relationship between them. This made it all the more important for him to explain to Harriet first.

But it was not to happen.

Soon after returning to the police station, John was fetched out to a serious warehouse fire, in the Saltisford. Fortunately it was by the canal, so there was no shortage of water. However, by the time he could leave the scene, John was late in arriving at Thomas and Sarah's house.

He had not had the chance to speak to Harriet. Not only did he need to explain about Silas, but he desperately wanted to hear about her visit to the London specialist. Whilst he hoped for the best, Thomas had warned him, it was unlikely to be good news.

John had been horrified to find she was regularly coughing up blood. When he mentioned it to Thomas, who was also Harriet's uncle and her doctor, it confirmed his worst fears.

Thomas had been secretly treating her for several weeks, but to no avail. Today's trip to London had been a little bit of subterfuge on everyone's part. Officially she had gone with Thomas and Sarah to do some shopping. In reality, Thomas had taken her to see a specialist. He had told John in confidence what was really happening.

Knowing Harriet's strong will, John had gone along with the deception, but now he was desperate to find out how she had fared. Then, as if that was not enough, Silas had arrived on the scene.

As Redman opened the door, at the Waldren household, John saw by the look on the butler's face that he too had made the connection between him and Silas.

On being shown into the drawing room, John saw Harriet already happily engaged in conversation with Silas. She looked up as her husband arrived, and smiled knowingly at him.

As both Harriet and Sarah were tired from their trip to London, it was not a late night. Silas had already been invited to spend a few days with Thomas, and to keep an eye on Warder Johnson. The operation had been successful, and both doctors held out high hopes for his full recovery. They would continue drinking and talking until late into the night.

John was pleased to see the earlier animosity between them had gone. He would be glad of the excuse to leave early, and get Harriet on her own to find out how she had fared.

And he had plenty of explaining to do.

As John prepared for bed, Harriet asked the question he knew she would ask and which he had been dreading.

'And just how long, my love, have you known you had a son?'

'Since about half-past two this afternoon.' John looked at her, and replied sheepishly.

Harriet burst into peals of laughter: laughing as only she could, although she was obliged to stop, when a coughing fit started. Once it had finished, she smiled at John. 'Well?' she asked.

For the second time that day, John told about his visit to London, and his meeting up with Katherine Whiting. When he had finished, he gave her Katherine's letter to read.

Harriet read it slowly. By the time she had finished, her eyes were brimming with tears.

'Oh my love, my love,' she cried. 'What a fortunate man you are, to be loved so much by Katherine that she sacrificed all for you. I was right to consider her to be a serious rival.' She sniffed and rubbed her eyes.

'I think...' she continued. 'I think I could have coped with Laura as a rival. But Katherine would have been a very different story.'

'My love,' John interrupted her. 'Never mind Katherine. You have always been and always will be my first love. It's because I thought you were dead, that I even allowed Laura to come into my life.'

'I know,' she said, gripping his hand. 'And Silas is absolutely charming: just like his father.' Her face fell. 'And you're going to need all of his love soon. I have something to tell you.'

'Yes, I know.' John felt cold. 'I know the real reason for your going to London today. Please, don't be angry with Thomas for telling me, but I've known about it for quite a while.'

'Oh!' she visibly relaxed. 'I'm so glad he did. If you only knew how difficult it has been, these past few weeks keeping it a secret from you. And you knew all the time.'

Then the tears ran down her cheeks and she bit her bottom lip. 'Oh my darling. There's nothing they can do for me.' Her voice came as a whisper. 'At the most, I've got a few weeks to live: but not very many.'

John opened his mouth to speak, but she put her finger on his lips, just like Katherine had done all those years ago. 'No my darling,' she breathed. 'Don't say anything. Just hold me.'

CHAPTER FOUR

Harriet and Silas

For the next few days, Harriet seemed to be the same, with no obvious signs of deterioration in her health, and John's hopes rose, but not for long. All too soon she began coughing more frequently, fetching up blood. She noticeably began to lose weight and energy, and now spent much of the time resting.

Silas was a regular visitor, both as a doctor and John's son. Thomas had invited him to stay on for a while and help out in the hospital. The young American had agreed, and he stayed with Thomas and Sarah for a while, before taking some rooms at the rear of the hospital. John had quickly confirmed their suspicions about Silas, and they happily treated him as his son.

Meanwhile, Silas had grown a full beard in order to disguise his obvious relationship to John. This was much to Harriet's amusement. John was adamant he was not ashamed to admit the young doctor was his son, but Silas thought his father had enough to worry about, as he struggled to come to terms with Harriet's imminent death.

Silas spent as much time as he could with her. Any lingering doubts he might have had about John not marrying his mother, were soon dispelled. He quickly learned just how highly Harriet was regarded by everyone, as was his father. In her turn, she told him as much as she could about John. However, she was a little surprised at first, just how much he knew already.

'That's easy to explain,' he chuckled. 'Mama, as you know, came from here, and she still has the local newspaper sent to her every week. She likes to see what's happening in her old town. And she used to make me read it as well. I must admit, I never had any idea that the John Mayfield, who appeared in it so often, was my father.'

Inwardly Harriet smiled at his answer. She quickly realised there had to be more to it than what he had just told her. Although, she accepted that he thought it was the truth.

In her turn, Harriet told him about her marriage to Edmund: his death and her subsequent meeting with John. Then came their quarrel: the shipwreck, her wanderings with the bushmen along the Skeleton Coast, her rescue and finally being reunited with John at the time of Laura's murder. Silas particularly liked the story of her return to England.

Having finally found a ship going to England, in mid-1844, Harriet had managed to bribe her way on board to cook for the crew, as she was unable to pay her way as a passenger. She had given the captain her golden wedding ring as the bribe, which was not worth much, but it was all she had left to remind her of Edmund. It was a high price for her to pay, but she wanted desperately to get back to England, and to John.

On her way to the ship, Sergeant Willie McEwan and the rest of his troop, whom she had saved in the desert, escorted her. Just as she was boarding the ship, he gave her a small package.

'Don't open this until you're somewhere on your own,' he cautioned, tapping the side of his nose with his right forefinger. 'Let's just say one of my men won it at cards. He plays regularly, and yon ship's captain's not as good a cheat as he likes to think he is.'

When she opened the package later, Harriet wept. Inside it was her wedding ring, from Edmund: the one she had given the captain. How Edmund would have laughed at the irony of it. He had been a successful, though honest card player.

Harriet had experienced a hard time in Walvis Bay, after her rescue. She had originally been cared for by Bushmen, whilst in the desert. They had treated her well, believing her to be some sort of goddess with her golden red hair. Consequently they had made no effort to take her back to civilisation, and only abandoned her when they encountered Willie McEwan's military patrol.

They were short of food and water, and they had expected to die in the desert. Having spent several months in the desert with the Bushmen, and in the Australian Outback prior to that, Harriet had learned much about survival techniques. Using those skills, she had helped the patrol to survive, and they had taken her back to Walvis Bay.

But here she was treated as an outcast both by the officers and their wives, because she had lived with the Bushmen. They snobbishly dismissed her claims that she had been treated properly by them. In their opinion, she had loose morals, and was a disgrace to her class. The fact the Bushmen had saved her life, and she in her turn had saved the soldiers, was of no interest to them.

It was a view which was shared by all the administrators and their wives. None of them would acknowledge her. The Governor's wife, reluctantly, gave her an old cast-off dress, as a dubious act of charity. The dress was very much worn out, and it was really nothing more than the woman adding insult to injury, by giving it to Harriet.

Yet the ordinary soldiers and those wives who had been allowed to accompany them, took her to their hearts. She had saved their men's lives and for that alone, they were very grateful.

In return for their kindness, Harriet had given Sergeant Willie McEwan and his men, some of the stones which she had found. She thought they could be uncut diamonds, and asked him to have them examined and shared out amongst his troop, if they were of any value. On the day she finally sailed, the whole little troop, plus their wives and children, but minus their officer of course, had escorted Harriet to the ship.

Tearfully she took her leave of them as they escorted her on board. In complete violation of their standing orders, they had each saluted her as they parted company.

Some of the sailors had seen Harriet come on board and they liked what they saw, and thought they would have some fun with her during the voyage. They drew lots for the first one to try his luck. Hardly able to believe his luck, the winner went in immediate search of his quarry.

The sailor found her in the small galley and he quickly manoeuvred her into a corner, locking the door behind him. Rape was clearly on his mind. She saw him leering at her, and felt his rancid, foul smelling breath on her face, as he fumbled with the belt on his breeches. Harriet made no attempt to resist, although it was obvious what he had in mind. As his breeches fell round his ankles, he was fooled into believing she would not resist. His hands grabbed at her breasts.

Suddenly, he yelped in pain, and drew back.

Harriet had thrust the barrel of her revolver up his right nostril, where the foresight ripped into the flesh. He pulled back, his nose bleeding copiously, his face flushed with pain and anger.

But then he stopped, and his mouth went very dry.

Her revolver was pointed straight at his face. And, he realised, it was not wavering. Clearly this woman was not afraid of him, and she obviously knew how to handle her revolver.

'Pull your breeches up!' she commanded.

The man did as he was told.

'Now, let's get one thing clear, shall we?' Her voice was quiet, but full of menace. 'Am I right in thinking the offence of rape still carries the death penalty out here?' It was a bluff on her part, as she did not know. She assumed he also did not know.

He nodded miserably.

'This is what we're going to do,' smiled Harriet. It was a very icy and humourless smile. 'You will tell anyone who asks that you had a little accident and injured your nose. I won't say anything.' She paused. 'But you can also let it be known, if you or any or your shipmates ever try a trick like this again, I'll blow your balls off, and then report you to the captain. Understand?'

The man nodded thankfully, holding a rag to his bleeding nose.

'You wouldn't be the first man I've shot, who fancied his chances with me. Now go!'

Gulping, and still holding his bleeding nose, the sailor beat a hurried retreat. He did not have the slightest doubt she meant what she said.

Throughout the remainder of the voyage, Harriet had no further problems with any other of the crew. As an added bonus, she was a good cook, and they enjoyed her meals. It was late in 1844 when they finally docked in London.

Harriet could not wait to go ashore, and get back to Warwick. But first, she needed some money. Whilst she still had Edmund's wedding ring hanging around her neck, that was only to be pawned for a real emergency.

Without wasting any time, she left the ship, and started walking through the approaches to the Docks, and made her way to the City, where she hoped, she still had a bank account. Normally it was not the type of journey she would have made, alone and on foot, in the early winter morning. But she had no money for a cab, and still had her revolver.

As another bonus, she had long since abandoned the dress the Governor's wife had given her. It was threadbare and falling apart when she was given it, so it was no loss to her. Still wearing seamen's clothes, she fitted in very well with her surroundings. Nobody paid her any attention.

It had only just passed 9.00a.m, when Harriet climbed the steps to the main entrance of her bank. But here she was stopped by an officious uniformed porter, James Palmer.

'This entrance is reserved for clients of the bank,' he snapped, barring her way.

'That's what I am.'

'Oh yes? Dressed like that?'

'It's a long story. Please I wish to see Mr David Bradley?'

'And who shall I say is calling?' came the sarcastic reply.

'Mrs Harriet Foxton.'

The porter's eyes widened, in disbelief. 'Oh yes, my lady! Certainly my lady. Dressed as a man! Oh and where is your wedding ring, pray?'

'What's going on Palmer?' Another voice spoke behind Harriet, and she turned to look at the speaker.

'Good morning, Mr Bradley. This...this...person...calls herself a Mrs Foxton, and maintains she wants to see you, sir.'

'Mrs Foxton? Mrs Foxton?' queried Bradley, looking at her intently. 'Is it really you?' Moments later, his face broke into a welcoming smile. 'By God it is you. We all thought you were dead.'

'It's a long story, Mr Bradley. But do I still have an account here?'

'Of course you do. Without any definite proof of a client's death, the account is held open for seven years, before being closed. You're well within that time limit.'

He led the way into the bank and into his office. 'You look in need of some refreshment,' he added. 'Can I get you some tea, or coffee? Or breakfast even?'

'Yes please to tea, and breakfast would be appreciated. It was too early for breakfast when my ship docked.'

Several minutes later a much chastened Palmer appeared with a pot of tea, some china cups, saucers, milk and sugar. It was all served up on a silver tray. Ten minutes later, he re-appeared with ham, eggs, and toast for Harriet.

Whilst she ate, Harriet related all her adventures to Bradley. He was horrified to hear how she had come from the docks on her own. And he was even more horrified, when she told him about her suspected uncut diamonds.

She handed him one to examine.

'I think you could be right,' he said after examining it very closely. 'But I'm not the best person to ask. However I do know just the right person to ask for a definitive answer. If these are uncut diamonds, then you could be sitting on a small fortune.'

Bradley issued more orders, and a diamond merchant was summoned. Whilst waiting for his arrival, Bradley arranged for a dressmaker to call. When she did, he left Harriet with her to make arrangements for some proper female clothes. He also purchased a first class train ticket for her return to Warwick, later that afternoon.

When Rupert Jordan the diamond merchant arrived, Bradley took him into his office, and introduced him to Harriet. For nearly an hour he examined all the stones she had brought back with her. Finally he put down his magnifying glass. Putting his elbows on the desk, he rested his chin on his interlaced his fingers and studied Harriet.

'Well Mrs Foxton. I've examined these stones, and…' His face fell. 'I suppose Bradley here has told you they were worth a small fortune. Is that right?'

Tears of frustration welled up in Harriet's eyes. She had carried those damned stones everywhere. And now it turned out they were worthless. Miserably, she nodded.

'Well, he's wrong.'

As Jordan's words slowly sank in, Harriet was concentrating on them so much, she missed the sudden change in his voice and surreptitious wink to Bradley.

'Yes. He's wrong. They're not worth a small fortune. In fact, they are worth a considerable amount of money.' He paused and shook his head. 'At present, I could not even begin to put a value on them. That will have to wait until they have been cut and polished.'

He reached over the table and shook Harriet's hand. 'You are now an extremely wealthy young lady.'

The rest of the morning passed in a haze for Harriet, as she struggled to come to terms with her good fortune. It made all that time in the desert worth it. How she would love to find a way of letting that dreadful Governor's wife know what had just happened.

Harriet was not normally a vindictive woman. Perhaps when she was ready, she would send the woman a guinea, which was more than the dress had been worth. Eventually, she had another dress made, as near to the same pattern as she could remember, and sent it to the woman. She never received any acknowledgement which did not surprise her.

As she neared Warwick, in the train, her mind was in absolute turmoil. There was no way she could let Thomas and Sarah know of her return; assuming they were still alive. The thought brought her up with a start.

And what about John?

Her darling John: the man she had been stupid enough to leave just to test him, to see if he would chase after her. She learnt, shortly before the shipwreck, that he had come after her, but bad weather, and a coach losing its wheel, meant he had missed her, and her ship had sailed long before he arrived at the docks.

For several long minutes she thought about the letter she had given to her uncle. In it she had intimated she would not be coming back and he should tell John to look for someone else. Coupled with her being reported lost at sea, might have meant John doing just that. What would she do, if he was already married?

Might he have married that Whiting woman, even after the scandal at the Assizes? Harriet knew there was no way that woman could ever have come back to Warwick. But what if John had gone after her, and he was no longer in Warwick?

At last she arrived back in Warwick and made her way to Thomas and Sarah's house, only to discover her beloved John was likely to die, having been poisoned.

She had sat and nursed him whilst he was unconscious, and fighting for his life. Once she realised his wife, Laura, was now dead, Harriet stayed with him, day and night. As he slowly recovered his health, she had the difficult job of telling him about Laura and their unborn child. Nobody else, apart from Thomas was allowed to do anything for John, during this period. She did it all.

After a decent interval had elapsed, she and John had married, and moved to a large house in Jury Street. It was a very happy marriage, in spite of her not being able to have children. John had always taken the blame for that upon himself. But with the arrival of Silas, Harriet knew it was not true. In fact she had known the truth, long before Silas arrived.

In the months that followed her return, Harriet had set up various charitable trusts. One of these was the founding of the Harriet Foxton Memorial Hospital. It started when the house next door to Thomas's house became vacant. She bought it, and turned it into a hospital. As more houses came up for sale, she added them to the complex. The hospital now housed twenty beds, and had saved many lives since its inception.

Another trust involved her purchases of land, in and around Warwick and Leamington. With the income from here, many needy people in the town were helped, especially during hard winters.

Now she was confined full time to her bed, knowing she and John would not have very much longer together. She had made all manner of financial arrangements for her charitable work to continue after her death.

In the short time she had come to know Silas, Harriet had come to love him as she would have done her own son. And just when he came into her life, she had discovered she would soon be losing hers. Fate can be very unkind.

By comparison, his life had been quite as exciting as hers, but in a different sort of way. He had served, and lived through a bloody civil war, and come close to being killed, on more than one occasion.

Silas had become interested in medicine at an early age, and he went to medical school in late 1860, where he was a quick learner. Then the war started.

When it did, the Northern army boasted of having just 30 surgeons: 83 assistant surgeons and later, a mere 2,000 voluntary nurses. They soon had a great need for many more. Any medical student, with only the minimum of knowledge and experience, was willingly and gratefully accepted into the Army Medical Department of the day. Silas had needed no urging.

He was appalled at the general filthy state of the hospitals. Then there was the rivalry that existed between the regular army doctors and the volunteers, such as himself.

In his many letters home to his mother, Silas complained about the filthy state of the hospitals, and the inhuman way in which many of the troops were treated. Katherine had used much of her own money in equipping field-hospitals and helping crippled discharged soldiers. She was still doing it when Silas was finally discharged from the army.

He was emotionally upset by all the suffering he had witnessed and been unable to alleviate. Consequently, he found it impossible to settle down. It was Katherine's idea for him to travel to Europe, and perhaps go to England.

Ever since Silas could remember, Katherine had told him about Warwick, where she used to live. She knew John had lost Laura, but in the same edition of the *Warwick Chronicle*, she heard about Harriet's return from the dead. So she was not surprised to hear they had finally married.

Silas had needed very little encouragement to go to Warwick. Katherine knew he would call on John, because she asked him to. Unless he was blind, there was no way John could fail to see Silas was his son, or to be correct, their son. She wanted them to meet, not out of malice, but because she thought it was time for Silas to discover his real father. Also, she hoped, it would distract him from his war memories.

Unwittingly, in doing so, she would expose him to very grave danger.

It had worked better than she could have hoped, although she would not know about Harriet's health until Silas wrote and told her. When he did, she knew it would be good for John to have his son with him at such a difficult time.

Although Harriet had been her rival, Katherine's heart went out to John. Somehow, she felt his love for Laura, whilst strong enough for them to marry, was nowhere near what he had felt for Harriet. He would be devastated when she died. For a while she thought about writing to him, but she remembered that was not the arrangement.

He would have to contact her first.

CHAPTER FIVE

Difficult days

Charlotte Goodwin, always known as Lottie, was not having a good night. There had been a race meeting in the town that afternoon, which should have resulted in her getting plenty of trade, but for some reason, it just did not happen. In some respects, Lottie was grateful, as she did not desperately enjoy being a whore, but she had to live. Although, with luck, she hoped, she would not have to sell her body for very much longer.

She had made the acquaintance of a young stranger soon after he arrived in town, and he had taken an interest in her. Whilst she attended to his sexual needs from time to time, he was encouraging her to give up whoring, and get some proper employment elsewhere.

To help, he had started teaching her how to read and write. Now, whenever they met, he continued with her lessons. As her education improved, Lottie was getting quite close to abandoning the street life, although it was with mixed feelings.

For the most part, her clients were reasonably well-behaved. She especially liked the young man who was giving her lessons, and she would have liked to have known him better. But she knew that could never happen, no matter how much the idea appealed to her.

He more than made up for the occasional man who preferred to give her a good beating, rather than pay for her services. Whilst she would miss some of her regulars, these others she would not.

Lottie had been with her tutor that evening for another lesson. He had his own rooms close to the hospital, and he was most impressed by how much her reading and writing were improving. As she left him, it was a late spring evening, which had gone a little chilly, and he had lent her a scarf, which she promised to return on her next visit.

Now she moved up to her normal area, by St Mary's church, looking for some customers. The only men she had seen were already accompanied by women, some of whom Lottie knew. Undoubtedly the cold evening was probably deterring any potential customers.

It had started becoming a little foggy, as happens sometimes on such an evening, so Lottie decided to call it a day, and moved slowly down Church Street. As she walked by the edge of the churchyard, she thought she heard someone trying to attract her attention. She stopped, and listened.

'Psst! Psst!' The sound came again, from behind her, actually in the churchyard.

She turned and could just make out a figure, wearing a top hat, who beckoned to her. Clearly he wanted what she had to offer. Happily she went towards him, and into the shadows. Then she stopped. It was dark in the churchyard and she did not know who she was going to meet in there. But it was where she often took her customers, and she needed some money.

No doubt had she asked her tutor for some, he would have given it to her. But that would have seemed like begging to Lottie, so she decided to take a chance. Lifting her skirts, to keep their hems off the grass, she followed the figure onto the grass and going under the trees, she went further into the darker depths of the churchyard.

Joseph Garner, the gravedigger, known to all as Joe, did not feel very well. He knew it was his own fault. Perhaps it was not entirely all his fault. If only he had not decided to go out for a few drinks with some old friends, the previous night. But he had.

The evening began reasonably, but all four men were former soldiers, and they began reminiscing about their time in the Crimean War. After that, one drink had led to many others, as they re-fought old battles.

They had finished so late, that Joe was too scared to go home and face his formidable wife's wrath. There was only one place where he dared to go, and he had made his way into St Mary's churchyard, to sleep in his hut, for what remained of the night. He had to dig a grave later that morning, and soon convinced himself it was a good excuse for not going home.

Now as he shouldered his spade, and made his way blinking into the sunlight, Joe cursed the drinks he had consumed the previous night. Whistling tunelessly, he made his way to where he had to dig the grave. His head hurt, his stomach was churning, and he knew he had to find a privy fairly soon.

Passing a small clump of trees, near the path, he saw what looked like a female's shoe lying by a tombstone. Curious, he went to take a closer look. As he did so, Joe saw the toe of another shoe nearby, just poking out of a bush. He picked up the first one, and went to pick up the second one.

Using his spade to push the bush aside, he took a closer look, and soon wished he had not done so.

He saw there was a foot still in the shoe. Investigating further, he discovered, as he now expected, the body of a young woman. Going further into the bushes, he saw the area was covered in blood, as was the dead body.

Joe took a closer look at her, and immediately regretted it. Although Joe was no stranger to death, both in his current job and his earlier military service, he was not prepared for what he saw, on this particularly pleasant and sunny morning.

Her body had been ripped open, along with a huge gaping wound in her throat. It reminded him of some of the bodies he had seen on battlefields, but never in his worst nightmares did he ever expect to see them here. The sight was too much for his already weak and suffering stomach.

Leaning over another tombstone, he was violently sick.

John was in his office, trying to concentrate on some reports which needed his attention. He was now spending very little time in his office, normally only an hour or so each day before returning to be with Harriet.

She was weakening by the day, if not by the hour. Silas and Thomas had done everything they could to make her as comfortable as possible. But they all knew she only had hours left to live. As he stood up and prepared to go home, John heard running feet, followed by the police station door being thrust open.

Instinctively he knew it could only mean trouble.

He waited impatiently as a babble of voices came from the public counter. Soon Harry Barlow appeared at his office door.

'Guv'nor,' he announced without any preamble. 'It seems we've got a murder in the churchyard.'

'Which one?'

'St Mary's.'

'Right. I'm on my way. Get Dr Waldren, then find Inspector Harrison and Sergeants Perkins and Young, and have them meet me there.'

Stopping only to collect his uniform cap, he followed Joe Garner into the churchyard. Although Joe had warned him she was not a pretty sight, John was aghast when he saw how Lottie had been killed. As he stood there, Thomas Waldren arrived.

'Dear God!' he breathed. 'What sort of person could do this?' Thomas shook his head in total disbelief, as he knelt beside her body, on a patch of grass which was relatively blood free.

'I don't suppose it could have been an animal, could it?' John asked forlornly.

Thomas peeled back part of the girl's dress, and shook his head. 'No. These injuries have been caused by a very sharp instrument, such as a scalpel. Oh no! Look!'

He pointed to the heavily bloodstained scalpel lying nearby. Turning back to the body, he looked much closer at the injuries. John said nothing, as he had an idea of the way Thomas's mind was working. At length he stood up.

'I hate to say this, John. But I think you are looking for someone with medical knowledge. The only good thing is that she doesn't appear to have been raped. You can see her skirts are still well below her knees. And provided her throat was cut fairly early on in the attack, she wouldn't have suffered very much.

'What's that?' John pointed downwards.

Thomas knelt down again, and studied the dead girl's right hand. Clutched in it was a piece of material.

'It looks like she might have pulled this from her attacker.' He hesitated.

'Why do you hesitate?'

'If she died almost instantaneously, I don't see how she would have the time to pull this material away'

John felt a gentle tug on his sleeve.

He turned and was relieved to find Inspector Mathew Harrison standing there. Mathew had been John's deputy ever since his first arrival in Warwick. He was a very capable officer who had started as a sergeant, but had been promoted a few years ago, when John's establishment was increased to twelve officers, one inspector and two sergeants. His sergeant had been the obvious choice for inspector.

Mathew had always been well-built, but now his once dark hair and beard were greying. His two sons were a sergeant and an inspector in the adjoining Warwickshire Constabulary. Harriet had always enjoyed a special relationship with Mathew, ever since they had fought side-by-side, and rescued John from being killed. She always called him her *comrade-in-arms*.

Sergeant Samuel Perkins stood alongside him. He was another of John's original men. Samuel or Sam, as everyone called him, was still tall, and he had remained extremely fit. Unfortunately, a clue to his advancing years was his losing more hair than he cared to admit. Whenever possible, he kept his helmet on. However, his still babyish looks, although now somewhat lined, belied his physical ability, as many had discovered to their cost. Only once had he come close to being bettered in a fight.

Some years ago, a gang of ruffians had come to the Races, from Birmingham, with the sole intention of giving Sam a beating. He had arrested one of their members at the previous meeting, and they wanted their revenge. Armed with cudgels and alcohol induced courage, they had surrounded Sam. Even with his formidable fighting ability, Sam realised he could not win, but he was determined to give a good account of himself, before he went under.

Help arrived suddenly from an unexpected source, as Pa Morgan and three of his boys stood alongside Sam.

The Morgans were a hard fighting family, who indulged in regular petty criminal activity, usually fighting after they had taken a few drinks. Over the years, they had fought a few times with John and his men, and usually lost. They had a particular respect for Sam's fighting ability, and bore the scars to prove it. Yet, as a family they never bore any grudges, and enjoyed a love/hate relationship with the police.

'You'se can bugger off back to Brum,' snarled Pa Morgan.

'Piss off, you silly old sod!' came a ribald reply, as they launched their attack.

It was a brief, but very bloody affair, which resulted in seven of the attackers being knocked unconscious. The last one standing was held by Luke and Isaac Morgan, whilst their father spoke to him, as if speaking to a child.

'We take care of our own here,' he snarled, prodding the other man in the chest, emphasising every word he spoke. The man winced. It might only have been a prod, but it hurt his broken ribs.

'You'se not wanted here. So I'll tell you'se just once more. Bugger off back to Brum! If you'se comes back again...' Pa Morgan continued, emphasising his point by prodding the man in the chest. He left his threat unfinished.

Later that night, when Pa Morgan and his boys went into the *King's Head*, they found a crown had been left behind the bar for their drinks. Sam always paid his debts.

Sam's daughter, Ruth, and Lawrence, one of his twin sons shared their mother's artistic skills, both with paints and cameras. His other twin son, Jethro, actually the eldest by a few minutes, was studying medicine in London. Sam and Lucy, his wife, believed Thomas and Sarah had sponsored him, but in fact it had been Harriet who had provided the money. As the three officers and their wives were firm friends, she had not wanted to cause any embarrassment by openly admitting to providing the finance.

'John. Please go home,' said Mathew gently. 'There's little you can do here, and Harriet needs you more than we do. I promise to keep you informed of any developments.'

John started to object.

'Please John. Go home to Harriet,' Mathew insisted.

Deep down John knew he was right. He nodded to his fellow officers and Thomas. After standing for a moment looking at Lottie's body, he shook his head in total dismay and disbelief, and walked home. It was not far. His house in Jury Street backed onto the churchyard. Minutes later, he was home.

Silas met him, and John could see it was not good news.

'I'm so sorry, father. But I don't think Harriet will be with us for very much longer. I feel it's only a matter of a few hours now. I'm so desperately sorry.'

The tears began to trickle down his face. 'I can mend broken bodies, and even some broken minds. But I'm a useless doctor who's powerless to help her. It's so grossly unfair.'

Father and son held one another for several moments.

'And do you know what's so particularly unfair?' he continued. 'I feel cheated by not having had the opportunity to really know her.' Silas paused. 'I must tell you this. I would not change my mother for anything, but if I had to, then I would have chosen Harriet without any hesitation. I can see why you married her and never went back after my mother. Now go to her.'

Silas walked away sniffing back his tears. John had remained dry eyed, albeit with a lump in his throat. He was more than a little affected by what Silas had just said.

Pausing to regain his composure, he made his way into Harriet's bedroom. He was appalled to see how pale and shrunken her face had become, in just the short time he had been away.

'Hello my love,' she greeted him wanly, and took his hand. But there was no strength in her grip.

John sat with her for the rest of the day. He did not need to be a doctor to realise she would not see the night out.

When it grew dark, Harriet asked for just one lamp to be lit. John moved his chair even nearer to her.

'No my love,' she spoke in a whisper. 'Come into bed with me and hold me.'

John did so, noticing how weak her voice had become.

'Talk to me my love. Remind me about how we first met and all those adventures we had.' She snuggled closer to him, and he put his arm around her.

John told her about that night in Warwick, when she first arrived and how he had made such a fool of himself. Then of his embarrassment to discover she was Thomas and Sarah's niece. He spoke about their adventures in the James Cooper affair, and how she had saved his life.

'Will you open the window for me, please my love?' she asked at one stage. 'It's such a lovely night.'

John got out of bed and did so. For a moment he gazed out at the beautiful, still and clear night, then he returned to bed. He was aware she was now breathing very shallowly. She kissed him gently just before she fell asleep. John closed his eyes, but he did not sleep.

He was only too well aware of the belief that an open window, where someone is dying, helps the freed spirit to escape.

Suddenly John felt a soft touch on his cheek, just like a hand caressing it. He opened his eyes immediately and, although he could never be sure afterwards, saw or at least thought he saw a shadow pass him, and flow out through the open window. Turning, he spoke to Harriet, but she did not reply.

There was a gentle smile on her face, which now did not seem to look so gaunt and drawn. He knew then it had been her departing spirit which had caressed him, as she departed through the window.

His darling Harriet was now at peace, and free from pain.

He never knew how long he held her slowly cooling body, with his mind totally numb. In due course he was aware of the sun shining through the window and of Silas coming in, and gently, but firmly, parting them.

Silas attended to everything, ably assisted by Sarah, Margaret Harrison and Lucy Perkins. The women would not allow anybody else to attend to Harriet's body.

Mathew and Sam came, and they began to plan the funeral, which they all knew would be a big event, and had to be done properly. And there were many people who needed to be informed. It was here where Robert Andrew was so useful.

Robert was the last of John's original men, who had lost the full use of his left hand after being stabbed whilst trying to make an arrest. As chairman of the Watch Committee, Thomas Waldren had ensured he was kept on the Force, albeit in a clerical position.

Thomas felt it was the least he could do, as Robert had received his injuries whilst saving his life. Initially he had paid Robert's salary, until he persuaded the Watch Committee to take over the responsibility. It rewarded Robert for all his loyalty, and also freed up John's men from much of their paperwork.

As a clerk, Robert was very adept at collating all manner of information about crimes and travelling criminals in the area. He also had a similar system for retaining other important information, which he collected both from other forces and newspapers. As an added advantage, he had a very good memory and was a valuable source of information.

It was whilst taking a brief respite from writing, and advising all manner of people and organisations about Harriet's funeral, that he noticed an advert in the *Warwick Chronicle,* which was the local newspaper.

NOTICE *is hereby given of our intent to offer help to fallen women, to enable them to better themselves.*
RESIDENTIAL EDUCATIONAL COURSES *will be held, to enable these women to read and write. Once a minimum standard has been obtained, we will*
GUARANTEE *to find employment for each successful* candidate. *These courses will be run **entirely free of charge**, as* **THE SOCIETY FOR THE PROPER EDUCATION OF FALLEN WOMEN** *operates by way of public subscription.*
FOR FURTHER INFORMATION *please apply to the Reverend Mordeccai Carew and Mrs Madeline Pascoe, The White House, Birmingham Road, Warwick.*

Robert's first thoughts were how sad these courses had not started the week before. If they had, then poor Lottie Goodwin might still be alive.

She had soon been identified as a local prostitute, and that was all the progress they had been able to make in trying to find her killer. To be strictly correct, Harriet's death had taken precedence, although their enquiries into the murder were still continuing.

Then Robert saw the address. The White House!

Memories came flooding back. It was where James Cooper had lived, and run his criminal enterprises. When Cooper's empire all fell apart, Robert had spent quite some time at the house collating evidence. As far as he knew, none of them had ever gone back there. His guv'nor certainly had not wanted to. He had faced death twice at that house.

After the Cooper affair, the house had remained empty for several months. After that, it had enjoyed a succession of owners, none of whom had stayed there long. They did not like the atmosphere the house radiated. Robert checked his records and found the house was owned by someone in London, and was being leased out. It had been empty now for a few years. He made a note in his records and told Mathew on his return.

CHAPTER SIX

A New Beginning

The morning of Harriet's funeral was bright and sunny, which completely belied the mood in Warwick. Since her death, John had been besieged by numerous visitors coming to pay their last respects. They were in addition to the scores of letters he had received. In fact, he had been glad of their distractions.

Now he sat in his drawing-room, waiting for the hearse and the undertakers to arrive. Thomas, Sarah, Silas, and Lucy Perkins sat with him. Nobody was talking, as they were each wrapped up in their own grief and thoughts.

John looked up as the door opened and Sam came in. He was immaculately dressed in his best uniform, complete with white gloves. Sam nodded and John stood up and left the room.

An undertaker had arrived to screw down Harriet's coffin lid, and John wanted to take his last farewell of her. He accompanied the man upstairs, but asked him to wait for a few moments. The undertaker fully understood.

John went first to another room, and returned with a bunch of red roses. They had been grown in a nearby hot house. Nodding to the undertaker, he entered the bedroom. Moments later Margaret Harrison came out. She had been sitting with Harriet.

Since her death, Harriet's body had not been left alone. Her friends had all taken it in turn to sit with her. With tears in her eyes, Margaret smiled wanly at John, and touched him gently on his arm. He went into the room and closed the door.

Looking down at the body, she was still his Harriet and always would be. She lay there, peacefully, as if she was asleep. Her long golden red hair was draped over her shoulders. He put the flowers on her breast, and kissed her one last time.

'Goodbye my darling. I know we'll meet again. But until we do, may God keep you, in his loving care.'

He took a last look at her, and left the room.

The undertaker went inside. Margaret, who had waited, took John's arm and escorted him downstairs into the drawing-room. Still nobody spoke.

John's eyes went, automatically, to Harriet's portrait, hanging over the mantelpiece. Undoubtedly it was Lucy's very best painting. No matter where you stood in the room, Harriet's eyes followed you. The smile on her face was so lifelike. Contrary to the accepted custom of the day, none of the pictures or mirrors in the house had been covered or draped in black.

Some of the older visitors to the house, no doubt, would have been scandalised. But Harriet had been such a vibrant person, and she had insisted there was to be no lengthy period of mourning for her. John had been only too happy to go along with her wishes.

There came a gentle tap on the door, and Sergeant Caleb Young entered, also wearing his very best uniform. He was not one of John's original men, but had been one of his first replacements. It was thanks to his quick actions that John had survived the attempt to poison him; an act for which Harriet could never thank him enough.

'I'm sorry, guv'nor,' there was a catch in his voice. 'But, it's time to go.'

They all stood up and waited by the open door. The pallbearers slowly came downstairs with Harriet's coffin, and paused for a moment in the hallway. When everyone was ready, Caleb opened the front door, and the sad procession moved forward slowly.

John followed immediately behind Harriet's coffin, flanked by Silas and Thomas. If anyone wondered why the new doctor should be walking with John, they kept their thoughts to themselves. Sarah, Margaret and Lucy followed. They knew the practice of women following hearses was not usual, but they too were not worried by convention. Just like their men folk, they had all been very good friends.

Behind them came Seth Walters, who was John's chief servant, and Redman, leading a mixture of servants from both John's and the Waldren's houses. Even after all these years, nobody in the Waldren household, or elsewhere, knew Redman's Christian name. Other servants had stayed behind to safeguard the house, and prepare for the massive influx of mourners, who were expected after the funeral.

As the sad procession left the house, Mathew and Sam took up their positions, just in front of the coffin. But, as they did so, two wagons rolled to a halt outside the next door house, which was to rent. They had approached from the Stratford direction, which meant passing in front of the hearse, before they could stop. Quite clearly they appeared to be preparing to unload.

Sam, who was nearest, broke away from the procession, and strode towards them. His white face was a mask of fury. The people who saw him maintained they had never seen anyone look so angry. At the same moment, a gig appeared from the other direction, stopped, and a smartly dressed woman climbed down.

She quickly looked at the scene of the funeral, and her hands flew to her mouth. Gathering her skirts, she ran back to the wagon drivers and instructed them to return later. They did as instructed.

'I'm so dreadfully sorry,' she gasped to Sam, shaking her head. 'I had no idea. I'm so, so sorry.' Turning on her heel, she returned to her gig, climbed on board, turned it round, and followed the wagons.

Sam nodded brusquely and returned to the cortege. Two of John's constables stood by the hearse. As Harriet's coffin arrived, they stood smartly to attention and saluted. They remained in this position as her coffin was gently transferred into the glass sided hearse. This was drawn by two black horses, with matching plumes and harness.

The funeral bell began to toll at St Mary's church.

When all was ready, Mathew and Sam moved to the front of the hearse, and led the way up Jury Street. The hearse and the procession of mourners followed them. John acknowledged his constables in a desultory fashion.

Only when the chief mourners had all passed by, did they end their salute. Moments later, they turned and marched after the cortege.

When they all discussed it later, no one could say just how many people had turned out to pay their last respects to a woman who had touched the lives of so many of them. Others had also come just to pay their respects to John, and offer him their support.

All the men were bare headed, or else they removed their hats as the cortege approached. There was no shortage of tears from the women, and from some of the men. The policemen recognised several men, whom they had sent to prison. But none of them smiled or smirked at John's misery. Many acknowledged John as he passed, but he did not see them.

Among them were Pa Morgan and his sons. Ma Morgan, his very formidable wife, had died some years ago. Both John and Harriet, along with several other policemen, including Sam, had attended her funeral. Tears ran unashamedly down Pa's face.

When the cortege turned into Church Street, it nearly stopped because of the huge crowds thronging the roadway. It took all of Mathew and Sam's patience to force a way through the crowds. They had expected a great number of people to witness the procession, but never this many.

At last they drew to a halt under the great tower of St Mary's church. The Reverend George Lamborne watched the pallbearers slide Harriet's coffin out of the hearse. As they did so, they were replaced by John's officers, each wearing his best uniform and white gloves.

Once Harriet's coffin was on their shoulders, he went across to John, and shook his hand. Both John and Harriet had been regular members of his congregation.

'A sad day, John. A sad day.' He paused for a moment, as he struggled to regain his composure. There were tears in his eyes. 'But she had a good life, and improved the lot of many people. Let's remember her with gladness, not sadness. We'll make this a celebration of her life.'

John nodded absently. He felt so numb inside, and still unable to accept what had happened. Surely this was a bad dream and he would wake up soon.

'I am the resurrection and the life, and he that believeth in me, although he be dead, shall live. And everyone that liveth and believeth in me...'

intoned George Lamborne, as he led the way into church, immediately followed by the pallbearers and Harriet's coffin.

Silas nudged John, and they followed the cortege into church.

Thomas and Silas gasped in surprise.

St Mary's was packed to overflowing with people. All the pews in the main body of the church were full, and so were those in the balcony. Other people stood in the side aisles. John noticed many uniforms amongst the mourners.

There were police officers from Leamington and the County Force, including Mathew's two sons. Amongst the prison staff were Governor Stephen Mitchell, and Charles Johnson. The latter had been allowed a seat, as he still needed to use a crutch. Several officers from the Warwickshire Regiment and the Yeomanry were also there.

At one stage, John passed Daniel Roberts, his old friend, who had been invalided out of the Birmingham Police, after being shot in the knee. He walked with difficulty, which was why he had not joined the mourners at John's house. Daniel was now a very successful local businessman.

His wife, Emma, turned her tear stained face to John. Much as she had wanted to join John at his house with the others, it had been agreed for her to go to church directly, with her husband.

Also with them was a smart, sturdy, well-dressed young man who was their son Benjamin. As a child he had been sickly and not expected to live. But he had confounded everyone, and survived.

John and Daniel had been policemen together, in London. Daniel had moved to Birmingham on promotion to inspector. Soon afterwards, John had moved to Warwick. It was Daniel, and his superintendent, who had helped John during his first hectic days at Warwick. There was a strong bond between them, which made them more like brothers than friends.

The funeral service passed in a haze. John had no memory of it, although he knew they would sing *How Sweet the Name of Jesus Sounds* and *Amazing Grace*, which were two of Harriet's favourite hymns. She had been a great admirer of John Newton, their composer. Finally, the service had ended by singing *Abide With Me.*

Along with the principal mourners, John filed out of church, to the newly dug grave. It was very close to his back garden gate. As the coffin was being lowered into it, the vicar intoned the words of the committal, and he looked at John. Silas nudged his father, and led him forward.

John threw a single red rose onto Harriet's coffin. He followed this with a handful of earth.

'Goodbye my darling: until we meet again.'

Thomas and Silas led him away from the grave, through the garden gate, and back into his house.

After the last of the mourners had left, John sat quietly with Silas. Neither man spoke, but just sat in companionable silence. At last Silas stood up. He had been staying with John since Harriet's death.

'I think I'll go to bed now, father. Will you be all right?'

John nodded. 'Thank you for all your help in the past few days, and for looking after Harriet.' He shook his head. 'I don't know what I would have done without you.'

Silas said nothing as he went to leave, not trusting himself to speak. He just nodded to his father. How he wished John would give way to his emotions and weep. It would have helped his father's grieving process. But he knew John well enough, by now, to realise it would never happen.

John watched Silas leave, then poured himself another brandy and gazed longingly at Harriet's portrait. How well Lucy had captured her. He still found it hard to believe he would never ever see her again: certainly not in this life. But he knew, no matter what happened to him from now on, he could never forget her, and the immensely happy years that they had enjoyed together.

In all his years as a policeman, he had often dealt with misery and grief being suffered by other people. It had all been part of a day's work. But now, he was the one who was grieving, and he had no answer for it. Somehow you were always detached, when it was another person's problem. But now it was different.

It was his problem.

His thoughts were interrupted by the ringing of the front door bell. Idly, he wondered who could be calling at this time of night, and on this particular day of all days.

Perhaps he was wanted on duty? But he knew Mathew would never call him tonight. Moments later there came a gentle tap on the drawing room door, and Seth Walters came in, carrying a silver salver, on which John saw there was a visiting card.

'Excuse me sir,' he said. 'But there's a lady asking to see you. This is her card. Shall I tell her to go away?'

'Yes. No. Wait a minute.' John took up the card, and held it towards the light. It read *Mrs Madeleine Pascoe.* The name meant nothing to him.

'On second thoughts, Seth, it would be churlish not to see her. Please show her in, but give me a few moments first.'

Soon, Seth returned and showed a well-dressed woman into the room. 'Mr Mayfield,' she announced. 'I'm Madeleine Pascoe, and I just want to apologise most profusely for what happened this morning.' Her voice was rich, and she had an accent which he could not immediately place.

John had already stood up, and he looked quizzically at her. She was not much younger than he was, but had worn well, although her face showed some lines, especially around her dark blue eyes. They toned well with her blonde hair.

Seeing his look, she explained. 'I've just taken over the rent of the house next door, and I arranged to move in today. You can imagine my horror and distress when just as I arrived, I found you were just leaving, especially as you are the local chief of police.'

Somewhere, John seemed to recall something like that happening, but it had all seemed to have been in a dream. 'Forgive me,' he said. 'I'm not very good company tonight.'

'I had no idea you were just about to bury someone. I felt I just had to come and apologise. It was just so unforgivable. Was it somebody very close?'

'My wife.' John looked fleetingly at Harriet's portrait.

Madeleine gasped and reached out and touched his arm. 'I know how you were feeling.'

John raised his eyebrows. 'Do you?' he asked harshly.

'Yes. I've lost my husband as well.'

'It's my turn to apologise,' replied John. 'I am forgetting my manners. Please take a seat. And can I get you something to drink?'

She smiled, sat down, and looked at the half-filled brandy glass, on the table by his chair. 'One of those brandies would do me very nicely, please.'

As he poured the drink, it gave him more time to study her. She was about five feet eight inches tall, with a rounded figure, making her neither fat nor thin. Her lips covered strong white teeth. He noticed she was wearing a dark blue velvet skirt and matching jacket over a white blouse. There was still a wedding ring, and a mourning ring, on the third finger of her left hand.

John liked what he saw. I think I could like this woman, he thought, as he handed her the glass.

She took it, raised it to her lips in a silent toast, then looked up at Harriet's portrait. 'Is that your wife?' she asked gently.

John nodded. 'It's a superb likeness. A friend of ours did it for us. She captured Harriet magnificently.'

'She looks a very beautiful woman. You must have loved her a lot.'

'Yes. We loved each other greatly.'

They sat in silence for a while.

'Were you...?' He asked.

'Were you...?' She asked at the same time.

They both laughed. Oh yes, thought John. I could like this woman. But what am I thinking of? Harriet's hardly cold in her grave, and I'm here on my own speaking and laughing with a widow.

Madeleine finished her drink.

'Would you like another?' he queried.

'Thank you, no. I don't want to outstay my welcome, on my very first visit.'

He smiled. Given time, he thought, I would like the chance to know this woman more. After having escorted her to the front door, he watched as she went down his front steps into Jury Street. Seconds later, she was at her own front door.

She briefly waved to him and he waved back. Opening her front door, she went inside. Moments later he heard her front door close. Turning, John returned once more to his drawing-room, where he poured himself another drink. Considering the amount he had drunk that day, he still felt completely sober.

He knew drinking would not cure his heartache.

Turning to Harriet's portrait, he raised his drink to her. 'God bless you and keep you my darling,' he said, and drained his glass. He stood for a while gazing at her portrait.

For a moment, he thought he saw her smile.

Next morning, John was back in his office by 8 a.m. Harry Barlow looked at him, and privately thought he should still be at home, and taking some compassionate leave. But that was not how John worked. He had plenty of catching up to do, and in his book, work was the best cure for grief. In particular, he wanted to discover who had murdered poor Lottie.

'Any chance of some tea?' he asked Harry.

Whilst having felt he was still sober last night when he went to bed, his head, tongue and stomach were all telling him a different story this morning. He was looking at the pile of papers in his in-tray when Robert Andrew arrived, bringing John's tea with him.

'Morning guv'nor.' Robert spoke softly, recognising the symptoms of John having a hangover. He had experienced them before. 'Have you seen this?' He handed over the advertisement he had seen in the *Chronicle*, to do with the White House.

John read it, and immediately recognised Madeleine's name as being part of the *Society For the Proper Education of Fallen Women*. He remembered their meeting last night, and recalled they had not discussed what she was doing in Warwick. Secretly he was pleased as it would give him an opportunity to call, but not just yet.

They were joined by Sam and Mathew, who had just come on duty. Firstly, John thanked them properly for arranging Harriet's funeral. He was aware all three of them seemed a little embarrassed, and he knew why.

'Guv'nor,' started Mathew. Although they were all friends, they rarely used Christian names in the office, or whenever they were on duty. 'Guv'nor,' he continued awkwardly, not really knowing how to broach the subject. 'Do you know about Harriet's will?'

John smiled. 'Of course I do. I know how much she left you. But you all deserved it, and she had very special reasons for the legacies. There's something for Caleb as well.'

Harriet had left them all very generous bequests in her will.

Mathew for helping her save John's life at the White House, many years ago. Sam for saving Laura's life before she married John. Robert who had lost the use of his left hand, whilst helping to save her uncle. And Caleb, in particular, for his quick actions which had saved John's life after he had been poisoned.

'Now,' John continued, changing the subject. 'How is the murder enquiry progressing?'

It was the question they all been dreading.

'It isn't,' Mathew confirmed John's worst fears.

'We know her name is Charlotte Goodwin, but she preferred to be called Lottie, and was not unattractive as whores go. She lived in Monk Street, and tended to ply her trade in the town centre, often going into St Mary's churchyard,' Mathew continued.

'The word out on the streets,' Sam took up the report, 'Is that she was getting, not exactly past it, but wanted to pack it all up, and get herself a proper job. If only these people at the White House had come earlier, she might still be with us.'

'I've also only just heard,' Mathew added, 'It seems she had a gentleman friend, somewhere up in town. She tended to see him at least two or three times a week. It's possible that's where she had been before she was murdered.'

'Dr Waldren seemed to think she could have been murdered by someone with medical knowledge,' commented John, recalling what Thomas had said at the scene. He turned to Robert. 'Have there been any similar cases reported anywhere else?'

Robert shook his head. 'No reports as yet. I've written to all other forces, but I've had nothing back. I know it's early days, but if there had been anything similar, then I'm sure we would have heard about them by now. Also, there's nothing in my records.' He paused.

'As you can imagine, it has caused quite a stir in the newspapers, and we have been inundated with reporters from all over the country, who have reported it nationwide. But to date, we have not heard of anything similar, which makes me think this is a first. I just hope it's not going to be the first of many.'

The others nodded in agreement.

'I've had the body photographed, and the scene,' announced Sam. He held his hand up. 'No, not by Lucy. Lawrence did it.'

'Is your son all right?' checked John.

'Oh yes. He's done some bad ones before. Remember the train crash?'

They all nodded.

'And there's this,' Mathew held up a bloodstained scalpel, by the label that had been tied to it. 'Thomas is convinced this is the murder weapon, which strengthens his opinion about our murderer having some medical knowledge.'

Lastly, Mathew held up the scrap of red and yellow checked woollen material which had been found clutched in Lottie's hand.

'I know Thomas spoke to you about this. And he's still of the same opinion. He feels it could have been torn from something, almost certainly a scarf,' he paused. 'But he doesn't think Lottie could have done it. She just didn't have the time to do it, before she died.'

'Does he think it's been planted? To make us start looking in the wrong direction?' John asked. He looked at the material. It seemed slightly familiar to him, but he couldn't think from where. No doubt he would remember in due course.

'He won't completely commit himself,' chuckled Mathew. 'You know what these doctors are like. But he's almost certain that is the case. It's too coincidental otherwise.'

'And we don't believe in coincidences,' they all said in unison, in their time honoured way.

John smiled at their age old custom. He had introduced his disbelief in coincidences when he first came to Warwick. It had stuck in all their minds and had always been a correct way of thinking. Now, whenever any person mentioned the word *coincidence*, the others always replied accordingly.

They discussed the case for a while, and agreed their most important task, at present, was to discover who Lottie had been seeing; even if it was only to eliminate him from their enquiries.

John worked until late, and his thoughts kept coming back to the scrap of material in Lottie's hand. If, as seemed likely, she had not torn it from her attacker, then it had been placed there deliberately. True, it might have been a ruse to put the police onto the wrong scent, but he did not go along with that theory.

From his own experience, if evidence was deliberately planted, either at the scene of a crime or on a body, it usually meant someone was being set up as being responsible. If this was the case here, then whoever owned that scarf, or whatever it was, stood a good chance of being in some danger.

Even more worrying was the thought that, if the first attempt failed, there might well be more similar crimes ahead.

At last, when he could put it off no longer, John went home.

His house, no longer their house, seemed so empty, although he could still feel Harriet's presence there. Any moment now, he thought, and she'll come into the room. But he knew it was only in his imagination.

Yet somehow, it comforted him.

CHAPTER SEVEN

Developments

During the next few weeks, in spite of all their efforts, the murder enquiry struggled, and no new evidence came to light. Try as they might, none of John's men could even get as much as a whisper as to the identity of Lottie's unknown male friend. If anybody knew, and undoubtedly someone did, they were not prepared to tell.

Robert had not received any information regarding similar attacks, from anywhere else. Consequently John had to accept Lottie's murder was not related to any others in the country. They all hoped there were not going to be any more. The *Chronicle* was not very complimentary about their lack of progress.

John and his immediate squad of investigators met regularly to discuss the case. At one such meeting, he suggested advertising through the *Chronicle*, for Lottie's mystery man to come forward.

'I don't know, guv'nor.' Mathew was not in favour of the idea. 'If he's innocent, all well and good. But, if he's not, we could lose him altogether. And what if he's married?'

'And wouldn't the *Chronicle* love that!' commented Sam drily.

'You've always encouraged us to keep one or two clues to ourselves,' reminded Caleb. 'God knows there's little enough to help us as it is. At the moment, he's about the only lead we've got.'

'Which is now at a dead end,' replied John. 'So I take it you're not in favour of advertising for him, eh?'

The others nodded.

'Right. It stays with us for the time being. Does anybody have any other suggestions?' John looked at his men. 'Yes Robert?'

'I hate to make this suggestion, as it will cause me a lot of extra work, and us some expense. But having drawn a blank with circulating all the English forces, I feel we should try further afield, say to Wales, Scotland and Ireland.'

'And after that? Where do we stop?' asked John, not exactly in favour of the idea.

'Europe and possibly America.'

'Any particular reason?' asked Mathew.

'Yes. I've got a bad feeling about this one. I just don't believe it's the first. I'm certain there have been others. As I don't have any details in my records, I can only assume they have not happened in England. And before you ask, I don't have any hard evidence to support my belief.'

'I'm inclined to agree with you,' added Sam. 'Call it policeman's intuition.'

'There's one thing we've forgotten.' Caleb brought the meeting to order. 'Don't forget this murder happened when the races were on. The town was full of strangers, and we've no record as to who they were. There could have been, and probably were foreigners amongst them. I think Robert has got some work to do.'

The meeting broke up, and Robert started on his latest task of circulating details to many more police forces. As the details had already been printed, it was just a case of circulating them as necessary. No covering letter was necessary. Those going to Europe would not be so easy, especially with the language problem. His best way forward was to approach their embassies, in London, first.

Then he thought about how to deal with America. Although there was no language problem, he had no idea of how many police forces there were. He assumed hundreds, but he knew of a short cut. The Pinkerton Detective Agency would be his first call.

Founded by Allan Pinkerton in 1850 as a private detective force, it had been active during the Civil War in counter-espionage activities on behalf of the Federal Government, with varying degrees of success. After the war,

Pinkerton extended his business into chasing and arresting felons. Robert knew here would be a good place to start.

Three nights later, John took an early night. It was a late mid-summer evening, and having dined, he sat out in his garden for a while, replying to some of the many letters he had received after Harriet had died. Pausing for a moment, he heard a gentle tapping on the door leading into his walled garden, from, St Mary's churchyard.

He crossed the lawn and opened the door, and found a smiling Madeleine Pascoe standing on the other side.

She carried a small basket, which was covered by a freshly laundered white linen cloth. He invited her into the garden, and offered her his chair at his writing table. It took him only a few seconds to tidy up the letters, and find himself another chair.

Madeleine sat down, removed the cloth from her basket and took out two glasses, which she set up on the table. Next she produced a small bottle of port, and a corkscrew from the basket, which she gave to John.

'Will you open the bottle please, Mr Mayfield?' she asked in a gently teasing manner.

'Only if you call me John, Mrs Pascoe,' He replied in a similar manner.

How well he remembered the time he had met Sarah Waldren, when he first arrived in Warwick, all those years ago in 1840. It was almost a repeat of their very first conversation. That meeting had led to his knowing, and ultimately marrying Harriet. He had also had a similar one with Laura.

'Certainly John. But only if you will call me Madeleine.'

They both laughed. John opened the bottle and left it for a while to breathe.

'I saw you from my bedroom window,' she explained. 'I know how lonely it can get. As you know, my back garden opens onto the churchyard, just like yours, so I thought I'd come and see you. I hope you don't mind?'

'Not at all,' John smiled. 'I'm glad of the company.'

For a while they just made simple conversation. Then John asked her about the work she, and Mordeccai Carew, were doing at the White House.

'Mordeccai is my brother,' she explained. 'He is also a churchman who has very strong feelings for improving the lot of the working class, and especially of those women who are even less fortunate.'

'I don't expect those views endear him to his mother church,' commented John wrily.

'You're quite right. No church funds us. We have to raise all the money we need ourselves. Some people appreciate what we do, but as for the greater majority…' her voice tailed off.

'I know. I regularly come up against similar prejudices, especially in this job. Just get on with it, but it's not a job for a gentleman. And don't involve us!'

Madeleine laughed. 'I can see I'm preaching to the converted.'

'Why the White House?'

'It has plenty of rooms and grounds. This gives us scope for dormitories, staff rooms, class rooms and so on.'

'Obviously you don't sleep there yourself.'

'Any more than you sleep over your office,' she smiled.

'Touche,' chuckled John good-humouredly. 'Although I was supposed to, both Laura, my first wife and Harriet, made it quite clear they would not sleep over the office. If I was wanted, then I could be fetched.'

'Laura? I didn't know you'd been married before.' She saw an angry, hurt look come into John's eyes. 'I'm sorry. I really shouldn't have asked.'

'It's all right. It was a long time ago. Laura was murdered and we've never found her killer.'

'I'm so sorry.' Madeleine reached out and touched John's arm. He found it to be a pleasant experience. 'As you know, I live here. Quite often Mordeccai stays as well. It's nice to get away from the White House. I find it has got a strange atmosphere. That's probably why it has been empty for such a long time and the rent is very cheap.'

Her last remarks were almost phrased as a question, but John chose not to enlighten her.

Madeleine went on to explain how she, and her brother, had formed their *Society* with the express aim of getting prostitutes off the streets, and into regular honest employment. The *Society* had branches in America and

Canada, although they had originally started up in Ireland, which, she added, was where she had been born.

'I suppose I'm something of a gypsy,' she laughed. 'It probably explains my strange accent.'

'It's a pity you hadn't started up here just a bit earlier,' said John. 'Then you might have been in time to have saved young Lottie Goodwin. She was a local whore, who was murdered a few days before you moved here.'

'That was awful. I take it you still don't know who did it?'

'Sadly no.'

'It's rumoured it could have been a doctor. Is that right?'

John hesitated for a moment, but he knew the rumours were already flying around. 'Possibly,' he replied at length. 'But we're keeping an open mind.'

'You must come up to the White House, sometime, and see what we're doing. I know Mordeccai would love to meet you.'

'I'd like that, but can we leave it for a while?'

'Of course.' She stood up. 'I really ought to go now, or else the neighbours will start talking,' Madeleine smiled.

John stood up. 'Goodnight Madeleine. Thank you for coming round. Next time, it'll be my turn.'

He escorted her to the door, then into the churchyard, and to her own back garden.

'I'll leave you here John. Good night.'

'Good night.'

After she had gone, John moved back into the churchyard, and stopped at Harriet's grave. He stood there for a few moments and wondered if she would approve of his growing friendship with Madeleine.

Before going to bed, as he did every night, John went into the drawing room, where he gazed for a few moments at Harriet's portrait, and told her what he had been doing.

He was certain she was smiling at him.

The following night, Jessie Brampton was quite happy. Ever since Lottie's murder, and the arrival of the *church people* in the White House, as she called them, there had been a noted reduction in the amount of whores available in Warwick. Hers was a job which greatly involved supply and demand. She quickly discovered whilst there was much demand at the moment, there was a limited number of suppliers. It was a busy time for her, and she was making the most of it.

If the truth were known, whilst she enjoyed her work, she had no intention of staying a street walker for all of her life. She wanted to graduate into having her own house, decent clothes and a higher class of clientele, who would pay much, much more for her services.

For the few whores such as Jessie, who were prepared to work, it was a licence to mint money. After a few hard weeks, the other girls would start drifting back on to the streets. But with luck, by the time they did so, hopefully, Jessie would be in a better position to go up market.

It was a warm summer's evening, and almost dark, as she strolled through St Mary's churchyard.

'Psst! Psst!'

Jessie turned towards the sound, and saw a dark figure beckoning her. At first she was delighted, thinking of even more money. But then she was not quite so sure. The figure beckoned her towards a clump of trees and bushes, which she knew was where Lottie's body had been found.

'No,' she said. 'Not there.'

Suddenly, and for no immediate apparent reason she was worried. Something did not feel right. Jessie hesitated again, and debated with herself whether or not she wanted the money so much as to put her life at risk

Having decided she did, Jessie followed the figure into another small clump of bushes. As she did so, she thought what a lovely night it was.

By rights it should have been her very last thought.

Before she knew what was happening, her hair was violently pulled back. Possibly she might have been expecting such an attack, because the moment she felt her hair being pulled, Jessie let out a piercing scream. Her attacker immediately let go, and ran off into the churchyard, but Jessie continued screaming.

John was sat in his study, writing, when he heard Jessie scream. Without any hesitation, he leapt up, ran down the back stairs, through the kitchen, across his garden and into the churchyard.

He was followed by several of his servants. They followed the sound of the screaming, and quickly found a frightened, but otherwise unharmed Jessie on her knees, in the churchyard. Minutes later, they were joined by Silas and Caleb Young.

Silas put down the bag he was carrying, and quickly examined the very frightened Jessie. 'I was just on my way back from a call,' he explained.

Once Jessie had recovered from her fright, she explained what had happened and began to realise just how lucky she had been. She could only say her attacker was dressed in black, carrying a case, and might have been wearing a mask.

Jessie also found she was enjoying all the attention she was getting, especially from the new American doctor. All the women were talking about him, but now she had met him for the first time, and liked what she saw. Silas escorted her to the police station, where he bade her goodnight.

'Is there anything I can do to thank you?' she offered, fluttering her eyelashes at him and holding his arm. 'It would be on the house.' She added.

Gently he removed her fingers and shook his head. 'Not tonight, but I thank you for the offer. Another night perhaps?'

Meanwhile, Caleb, John and his servants had made a quick search of the churchyard, but as they expected, nobody was to be found.

Just as John was about to leave, Madeleine suddenly appeared. 'I've just come back from a meeting, and heard. Is the girl all right?'

'Luckily yes. Her screams frightened off the attacker.'

'Do you think it's the same man?' Madeleine looked anxiously about her.

'Possibly. But he's long since gone.'

'I don't suppose she got a look at him, did she?'

'No such luck. All she could say was he was carrying a case, just like the ones doctors do, and she thought he wore a mask.'

'Could it be a doctor, do you think?'

'I just don't know, but I can't rule it out. Now, let me escort you home.'

'Thank you, kind sir.'

When they arrived at Madeleine's back garden door, both of them seemed reluctant to say good night. Finally Madeline broke the silence.

'Can I invite you in for a drink?' she asked.

'Regrettably, I must go. I need to be at the police station to find out more about this attack.'

'I understand.' She touched him on his arm. 'Will you come out to the White House, tomorrow? I really would love to show you around.'

'It's a date.'

She touched him gently, on his cheek, and she was gone.

CHAPTER EIGHT

The White House

By the time John had arrived at the police station, Jessie had told Caleb everything that had happened to her that evening. She repeated her story in front of John, but was unable to add anything further.

John waited whilst Caleb wrote her story down. When Jessie had finished, she stood up to go. 'Just a minute,' he said. 'Two questions. Firstly, have you ever thought about taking advantage of this special help being offered by the Reverend Carew and the *Society for the Proper Education of Fallen Women?*'

She laughed harshly. 'I shall need much more convincing than that. I've never yet met a canting priest who had the welfare of us whores at his heart. There's only one thing they want from us, unless it's boys they prefer. Why should this one be any different?'

Unable to help himself, John smiled.

'And you crushers ain't any different,' Jessie continued. 'You wouldn't be the first crusher I've had, nor the last.' She grinned good naturedly at them. 'So who's going to be first?'

'That'll do, Jessie,' John instructed, but not unkindly. 'Now for the second question. Who was Lottie Goodwin seeing? Who was her special man? The one she had probably been with just before she was murdered?'

'I ain't got no idea,' Jessie replied, but at the same time began to pick an imaginary piece of fluff from her dress.

'Come on Jessie,' Caleb took over the questioning. 'We know none of you are telling us the truth. Why are you all protecting this man?'

'Because he's a good man,' Jessie snapped. 'And he didn't kill her.'

'If that's so, please tell us,' pleaded John. 'He might be able to help us.'

'I ain't saying nothing. Can I go now?'

John waited until Caleb returned from showing Jessie out. 'She knows who this mystery man is, doesn't she?'

Caleb nodded. 'It's the same with all of them. They know, but they just won't tell.'

'I don't doubt some of the men have sex with the likes of Jessie. I can't condone it, and I definitely don't want to encourage it. But if it will identify this mystery man, then I'll say nothing for the moment. However when we have his identity, I want all staff to clearly understand, such liaisons will not be tolerated.'

'Understood, guv'nor. Now I'll make arrangements for the churchyard to be searched when it gets light, but I doubt we'll find anything.'

'Unfortunately, I tend to agree with you. And you realise this little episode tonight, means our killer is still with us. He hasn't gone away.'

Next day, in the early afternoon, John and Mathew made their way to the White House, to see Madeleine and her brother. Neither man had been there since the end of the James Cooper affair in late 1840. John was amazed to realise that had been twenty-seven years ago! Like Mathew, he had his own memories of those long gone days.

'I see they've rebuilt the coach house,' observed John drily.

Mathew nodded. It was where they had very nearly died, when the building had been deliberately set alight, with both of them trapped inside. They would have died if Harriet had not suddenly appeared, and rescued them. Even then, it had been a hard struggle to get away.

John smiled when he saw Madeleine waiting for them. She introduced him to a brooding man, who was a similar height and build to herself. He was dressed in black and wore a clerical collar. His dark face was surrounded by dark brown hair, well flecked with grey. Like John, Mathew found the man's hard, staring dark brown eyes, were his most unsettling feature. The man oozed aggression, which was in complete contrast to what one would expect from a churchman.

'This is my brother, Mordeccai Carew,' introduced Madeleine. They all shook hands.

Neither visitor found any warmth in Mordeccai's handshake.

'I don't like policemen,' announced Mordeccai, without any preamble. 'It's nothing personal against you, but I feel you should be doing much more for these street women, and not leaving them to us.'

Like Madeline, he had a strange accent, which John noticed contained more than a little Irish in it. An Irish background, thought John, could explain the man's hostility. Without consciously realising it, John found himself looking at Mordeccai's hands. He had noticed how rough and gnarled they were, when they had shaken hands. They seemed more appropriate for a labourer, than a cleric.

'I can see what you're looking at,' continued Mordeccai, pointedly looking at his hands. 'Where I came from, everybody had to work, not wander around wearing fancy uniforms.'

'Mordeccai,' interrupted Madeleine. 'Enough. John and Mathew are here as our guests. Hopefully if we can convert them to our cause, we will be able to get more women off the streets.'

Her brother shrugged, and walked away.

'I'm so sorry, John. Mordeccai takes his work very seriously. And, as children back in Ireland, the police were our enemies, not our friends.' As she spoke the last words, Madeleine squeezed John's hand. Mathew noticed and he smiled to himself.

For the next hour or so, Madeleine took them round the White House. In some of the rooms they saw women being taught to read and write. Elsewhere, cookery and sewing lessons were taking place. They were introduced to the matron, a formidable looking woman called Jane Howatt.

She had a hard lined face, and looked to be in her mid-fifties. Grey hair, swept back in a bun and fixed under a mob cap, all added to her severe looks. Jane Howatt was thin, and she spoke with a slight Scottish accent. When John tried asking her questions regarding the welfare of the women, and details about the course work, she only answered in monosyllables, and would not enlarge on any topic.

Yet, both policemen thought she seemed almost too keen to say the right things whenever Mordeccai was around. John had a strange feeling she was following orders, and only explaining what she was allowed to tell them. He also noticed, in spite of her being the matron, she was never on her own. There was always another member of the staff with her.

One of her main functions, she explained, was to act as chaperone, whenever Dr Whiting or another doctor came to medically examine the women. John had not been aware his son was a regular visitor here. Madeleine had not said anything. But then, she did not know his real identity. For some reason, John had not told her, and he had no immediate intention of doing so. He would do so, when the time was right, but not before.

At the end of their tour, John and Mathew joined Madeleine for tea. Although invited, both Mordeccai and Jane Howatt made their excuses, and declined. It was a pleasant enough tea, served by two of the women. However, when Madeleine was called away, John and Mathew were not sorry to depart. They had left the drive, and turned into the Birmingham Road, before Mathew spoke.

'I don't know about you, but I was glad to get out of there. And it wasn't just because of the old memories.'

John was thoughtful for a moment, playing for time before replying. 'I'm inclined to agree with you. However can someone like Madeleine, have such an obnoxious brother? Apart from being one of the rudest people I've met in a long time, there's something about him that worries me. Something's not quite right, although I can't exactly say what. Or are we being influenced by our memories of this particular building?'

'I agree about Mordeccai's rudeness, but that wasn't what I meant,' Mathew shook his head. 'The whole place was far too quiet. These women were supposed to be embarking on an educational programme, but there was no sense of enjoyment amongst them. And there seemed to be an awful lot of padlocked doors.'

'I know. The whole place reminded me of being in the workhouse or a prison, complete with a rule of silence. And as for that Jane Howatt woman...brr! She bothered me. In one breath she was distant and hardly deigned to answer any questions. And then, in the next moment, I felt she wanted to say something, but would not or could not do so, because she wasn't on her own.'

'There's something else. Did you recognise any of the women we saw?'

'No. Yet I would have expected to. Some of our whores have certainly vanished. So, if they're not there, then where are they? Have they been moved on already to new employment? And who were the women we saw?'

'I'll have Robert make some discreet enquiries. There's something not right here.' Mathew hesitated. 'John, old friend, we've known one another a long time, so can I speak freely?'

'Go ahead.'

'We all know you are smitten with Madeleine. Servants gossip and many people know you visit one another's houses regularly.' Mathew held his hands up. 'Nobody is criticising you. Harriet would never have wanted you to remain celibate, but be careful. I cannot see any problem with Madeleine, but how much do you really know about her? And I am concerned about her brother. He strikes me as being a very violent man. Not what one would expect from a clergyman.'

John said nothing; but nodded his head, without looking at Mathew. What the other man had just said made a lot of sense. He knew he was vulnerable at the moment, but Madeleine was really making a difference to him. Like Mathew, he could not see any problem there, but her brother was a different matter.

Mathew did not pursue the matter, but he had already made up his mind to have enquiries made into Mordeccai Carew's family background. He would have Robert do it, whilst he was looking into the *Society for the Proper Education of Fallen Women.*

Perhaps it was just the old memories of the White House, which had flooded back and raised his suspicions. But Mathew would need more convincing than that.

He had been a policeman far too long.

Later that evening, as John sat in his garden waiting for Madeleine to appear, he mulled over what Mathew had said. Was he making a fool of himself with her? After all, Harriet had only been dead a few months, and he really ought to still be in mourning for her.

Yet, it was a discussion they had often had. They had both been adamant they wanted no long periods of mourning. The only reservation John had expressed was that she should be careful, so no man came along solely to get his hands on her money. It never occurred to John that similar advice might be applicable to him. Yet, Madeleine did not give the impression of being poor.

As John had said, Harriet would not have wanted him to remain celibate. But he had to agree with Mathew on one point. What did he really know about Madeleine?

He knew she was a widow, but so far he had been unable to establish just when, and how, her husband had died. John did not even know his name. Madeleine maintained she would tell him one day, but insisted the time was not right, and he had respected her privacy. After all, he had been widowed twice, and still found it difficult to talk about Laura's death, even after all these years.

His thoughts were interrupted by Madeleine's arrival.

They sat for a while in his study, as the evening had become chilly, with a distinct touch of autumn in the air. He poured them both a cognac, and waited for her to talk about their visit that afternoon.

'I really must apologise for Mordeccai this afternoon,' she said. 'His behaviour was unforgivable. As he says, it wasn't directed at you or Mathew personally, but it was against your uniform. Please don't think too badly of him.'

'I won't, for your sake. I hope we will become friends in due course.'

'What did you think of our work?' Her eyes sparkled.

'It was interesting. We were both impressed by how clean everywhere was. But, if I'm honest, it seemed to be unnaturally quiet.'

'Everybody says that. I suppose it's Mordeccai. He is such a very serious person, and believes you have to concentrate on what you're learning. I suppose he's a bit on the harsh side, but it's only when there are classes taking place or at church. Mrs Howatt has similar views, but you should hear the noise at other times.'

'Where had you found the women we saw? There weren't any of our locals amongst them. And where were our locals?'

'You're quite right. I told Mordeccai you'd see that. In fact, we did it as a little test for you. To see if you really know who your whores are.'

John stiffened. 'You do us an injustice there,' he bridled. 'I've policed this town for some twenty-seven years, and to hint that neither I nor my men do not know our local whores, is rather unkind.'

'Oh John! It wasn't me. I told you it was Mordeccai's idea.' She put her glass down and took his hands in hers. 'I have now been proved right. Am I forgiven?' Madeleine smiled wistfully at him.

'Of course,' he smiled. 'So where were they from?'

'Mainly Leamington and Kenilworth, and also some have come from Solihull and Stratford. We are a wide ranging organisation. As for your local girls, some were resting. You remember we did not visit the sleeping quarters. Some were out being taken for a walk. And others have already had jobs found for them.'

'One last question. Why did so many doors have padlocks on them?'

'As a policeman, you ask me that? Why do you think?' Madeleine howled with laughter. 'Because some of these girls are thieves.'

He joined in her laughter, much relieved by her answers.

In the following days, they continued to meet on a regular basis. He started to walk with her in town, and began introducing her to some of the more influential people, with a view to helping her raise funds. When an invitation to a civic ball at the Court House arrived, it was addressed to *Mr J Mayfield & Mrs M Pascoe*. Their names were now being linked together.

John had never been much of a dancing man, and so he was quite happy to let Madeleine dance with all the other men whom she wanted to dance. When everybody broke off dancing at around midnight, they all adjourned for supper at the *Warwick Arms*, where she had no shortage of admirers.

Madeleine used many of her feminine charms to extract numerous promises of funding for the *Society*. It was John's first attendance at such a function since Harriet had died, and he was able to renew old friendships. He was delighted to find Daniel and Emma Roberts were also there.

Like John, Daniel did not dance, because of his previous injury. John introduced Madeleine to them.

Whilst Daniel was friendly towards Madeleine, John was surprised to see Emma holding back. For a moment he thought she resented Madeleine's new familiarity with Daniel, who escorted her into the buffet. Emma hung back, and John stayed with her. Clearly she wanted to talk. He hoped there was nothing wrong between them, as they were his oldest friends.

'John,' Emma said without any preamble. 'How well do you know Madeleine?'

He explained how they had met, and their subsequent meetings.

Emma bit her bottom lip. 'I've got a feeling I've met her before. But for the moment, I cannot just remember where it was. I'm sure it will come to me in time.'

'Is that why you don't like her? Or is it because of the way she's flirting with Daniel?' He teased, suspecting, rightly, that she knew full well where they had previously met.

'No. It's not that. We've had dealings with her before, but not in this area. It must be through our business connections.' Clearly something had happened between them, but Madeleine had shown no signs of recognition, and Emma was not going to explain.

Daniel was now a partner in a very successful transport carrying business, which had many international connections. Emma and Benjamin, their son, helped to run it.

'And as I recall, it was not a happy connection. I wish I could remember when and where it was.' Apart from dropping hints, Emma was not going to elaborate any further. John knew she would tell him all, but at another time.

They talked about other matters for a few minutes, before Emma agreed to let John take her into the buffet. 'Be careful, John,' she cautioned. 'Be very careful.'

At about the same time as John was talking to Emma, Sean Collins arrived for work at Pinkerton's Detective Agency, in Chicago. He was officially employed as a clerk, but, unbeknown to his employers, Sean also had another job. To be fair, he did not know the identity of his other employer, as they only communicated by letters, left in strange places. However, his second job paid well, and it appealed to Sean's Irish background.

He knew only too well there was a very strong Irish community in America, including Chicago. There had already been an attempted invasion of Canada by the Fenians in support of their *Free Ireland from the British* campaigns. The invasion had been a failure, but attempts for Ireland to gain her independence would continue for many years.

Sean was well aware of the attempts being made by certain of the victorious Union generals, to persuade the government to declare war on England. The excuse was in retaliation for their support of the Confederacy, during the war. Saner advice won, but there was still a network of operatives, doing all they could to cause problems for the British Government and its agencies.

It was one of Sean's duties to open the post every morning, and distribute it accordingly. One of the letters he opened this morning, had come from Robert Andrew. For a moment he considered just scrapping it, which would cause yet another minor cause for discontent between their two countries. But then he decided to pass it on to his other employer.

In fact the letter was in no way political, and was of little interest to him. But it had come from England, which was why he thought it might be of interest to his other employer.

CHAPTER NINE

More Attacks

In the next few weeks, John and his men still came no nearer to discovering who had murdered Lottie. Likewise, they could not discover the identity of the man she had been seeing on the night of her death.

As the summer had given way to autumn and early winter, John saw more and more of Madeleine. His friends began to speculate on the possibility of another wedding, probably sometime in 1868. The couple regularly visited one another in the evening. It had become something of a competition to see who could provide the most interesting bottle of wine, or other liquor.

On this particular night, in mid-November, John was entertaining Madeleine in his study. He preferred to be in here with her instead of being in the drawing room, where Harriet's portrait hung. The chillier nights had put an end to their sitting outside.

They were sat close to each other and laughing at a small joke. Suddenly they stopped talking, and just looked at each other.

'Oh John,' she said huskily.

He made no reply, but put his arms round her. Tentatively they kissed, and then became more passionate. She closed her eyes, lay back on the sofa, and pulled him down on top of her. His fingers began to undo the buttons on her dress. Madeleine did not object.

Meanwhile, a figure, dressed all in black, hovered around St Nicholas churchyard. A bully by nature, he enjoyed preying on women, because he found them to be easy targets. A patient man, he waited until he saw his next victim. She was middle-aged and was walking along St Nicholas Church Street, in the direction of Castle Hill.

Peering along the street, he saw there was nobody else to be seen. Quickly tying his scarf around the bottom part of his face, he took out a wicked looking knife, and waited. As the woman passed him, he crept out, and quickly made his way behind her.

Some sixth sense warned Sarah Waldren that all was not well. Although she had not seen the man creep up behind her, she was not surprised to feel his hand on her shoulder.

As he started to turn her round, she ducked and lashed out with her bag. He grunted with pain, and released his hold on her shoulder, as the bag hit him. But for Sarah it was only momentary relief. Recovering quickly from his surprise, the man lunged at her with the knife.

Sarah screamed at the top of her voice, as she saw the knife, and hurled herself backwards. At the same time, she threw her bag at him. He caught it with his free hand, but still kept coming towards her.

By now she had turned round, and was running back toward the *New Bowling Green*, screaming loudly as she did so. Suddenly men were pouring out of the inn and Sarah's attacker ran off into the churchyard, and into the darkness.

'Damn you bitch!' he snarled. Sarah had hurt him, and he would have liked to make her suffer. But he had her bag and perhaps there was something worth having in there.

The men from the inn made a half-hearted effort to find Sarah's attacker, but none of them relished going into the unlit churchyard. Some of them, sensing a possible financial benefit, escorted her home, where they were suitably rewarded.

Back in John's house in Jury Street, he had just begun to undo the buttons on Madeleine's dress, when there came an urgent knocking at his study door. He had not heard the doorbell ring.

'Yes!' he called impatiently, but did not invite his caller to enter.

'I'm sorry, guv'nor,' answered Harry Barlow's urgent voice. 'But there's been another woman attacked.'

John felt Madeleine stiffen.

'Do we know who?' queried John, as he pulled himself off Madeline and began to tuck his shirt back into his breeches.

'Yes. It's Dr Waldren's wife.'

John went cold.

'But she's all right.' Harry continued. 'She's at home, and Sergeant Perkins has gone to see her.'

'I'm on my way. Don't wait for me.'

John finished dressing and smiled ruefully at Madeleine. 'I'm sorry my love. But duty calls.'

'Shall I wait up for you?' she smiled back at him.

'I don't think so. I've no idea how long this will take.'

He kissed her gently on the lips and was gone. On his way out, John left instructions for one of his servants to escort Madeleine home. He did not bother to change into uniform, but went straight to the Waldren's house, where Redman let him in.

Thomas came out to meet him.

'How's Sarah?' asked John.

'Remarkably well,' chuckled Thomas. 'I rather gather our attacker got more then he bargained for.'

Later, John sat with Sam at the police station and discussed the case.

'Is it the same attacker?' queried John.

'I'm not sure, but I'm inclined to think not. Sarah Waldren's not exactly a street walker. And this attack took place in the open street, which is hardly the place to commit a murder.'

'Was murder in his mind or was it something else?'

'I just don't know John. I only hope we haven't got somebody else trying their hand. The last thing we need now is an imitator. God knows, we're having enough trouble trying to find one killer, without having to look for another.'

'Have the churchyard searched in daylight, but I doubt we'll find anything.'

★ ★ ★

Three nights later, there was another attack. This time it was a barmaid as she left the *Red Lion* in Swan Street. She also managed to escape from her attacker. Like Sarah, she had seen the knife which was wielded by her attacker, and wisely decided not to fight him. Dropping her bundle, she fled.

John arranged for extra patrols at night time, some of whom were not in uniform. As is the way with preventative measures, there was no way of proving if they had been successful: only unsuccessful if another attack happened. To make matters worse, the *Warwick Chronicle* was not very friendly towards him.

He read their latest report with an ever increasing anger.

MORE ATTACKS

IT IS OUR UNPLEASANT duty to report how two more women have been attacked in Warwick. Even more unpleasant to report is the fact their attacker still remains at large.

Whilst we have always had implicit faith in our Superintendent of Police, it now seems he is quite unable to solve these particular crimes, which are quite clearly connected with the vicious murder that happened several months ago, in St Mary's churchyard. To date her murderer, who is obviously one and the same man as in these latest attacks, remains at large.

We are aware of Superintendent Mayfield's personal loss, earlier this year, and it may be this has affected his ability. But the fact remains, Warwick is a frightened town. Our women are afraid to go out alone at night. This is a state of affairs which cannot be tolerated and must not be allowed to continue. The women of Warwick deserve better from their police.

If Superintendent Mayfield cannot find the person responsible for these heinous crimes, then perhaps he should consider taking retirement and encouraging a younger and more energetic officer to take his place.

John threw the newspaper down in disgust. He was only too well aware of his failures in these cases and he did not need any such reminders in the press. Why was it, everybody else knew how to do his job better than he did?

Whilst it was true there were some similarities in the attacks, it was by no means certain they had been committed by the same person.

Miles Grafton was becoming bored with Warwick. Disappointed with the results he was getting, he wanted to move on somewhere else. It was only when he read the *Chronicle*, a few days after it had been published, that he realised his mistake. Now he knew why there were no unescorted women around. Tonight would be his last chance to make some money. Then he would leave on the train tomorrow morning.

At last, after patient watching, he chose his victim. To be fair, she did not look like a prostitute, but if not, he reasoned, why was she going through St Mary's churchyard, so late at night? He quickly looked around to make sure there was no one in sight. Seeing everywhere was deserted, he ran silently after her.

Taking out his knife, he crept quietly towards her. He had already pulled his scarf up to disguise his features. Gripping her by the shoulder, he swung the woman round, expecting to see the look of terror on her face.

That was the part he enjoyed most. All he wanted was some token of resistance or better still some evidence of fear from her, and he would use the knife. Instead, he saw a furious look on Madeleine Pascoe's face, which was accompanied by her kicking him hard in the testicles. As he sank to the ground, a heavy blow hit him across the back of the neck, and everything went black.

When he next opened his eyes, Miles blinked against the unexpected light. Opening his eyes again, he saw two stern looking men, in uniform, standing before him. At the same time, he realised his hands were secured behind him, and his feet were in leg-irons. He recognised the uniformed men as belonging to a police constable and his sergeant.

'Welcome back,' greeted Harry Barlow.

Miles noticed there was no warmth in the man's greeting. Struggling to sit up, he remembered what had happened, and his very alert brain quickly began working.

'Can you release me, please?' he asked in a mild, yet aggrieved tone. 'Why am I manacled?'

'Perhaps you'd like to tell us?' The question came from Caleb this time.

'I...I...don't know what was going on. I was just walking down by the churchyard, and the next thing I remember is waking up in here.'

'Nice try,' said Harry in an expressionless voice. 'Now can we have the real story please?'

'I've just told you, I was...'

'Be quiet! And listen,' instructed Caleb. 'Very soon our guv'nor is going to get here. He will not be in a good temper having been got out of bed. The other night, you attacked the wife of one of our highly respected doctors, and a good friend of all of us. Tonight you attacked our guv'nor's lady friend. So I suggest you stop wasting our time, and start answering our questions.'

Whilst Caleb was speaking, Miles was carefully thinking about what to say next. He suspected his pockets had been emptied, and this gave him an idea.

'Look! I've been attacked and robbed. And you're treating me like a felon.'

'You have not been robbed,' Harry took up the questioning. 'The contents from your pockets are here on the desk. So, I suggest you think again, before our guv'nor gets here.'

'I've told you what happened. Now please let me go so I can make an official complaint of robbery. I can see my watch and money are missing from that pile.'

'You did not have any money or a watch on you, when you were detained,' answered Caleb.

'Then one of you must have taken them, when I was unconscious. I've read about you in the newspapers. You've got problems and need to solve them quickly, so you've picked on me.'

'No,' Caleb spoke in a friendly fashion. 'You were kicked in the balls by the lady you attacked. Then her brother hit you on the back of the neck and out you went.'

'What rubbish. They must be the ones who attacked me.'

Caleb and Harry burst out laughing.

'This will really look good in Court, won't it,' said Caleb still laughing. 'You were floored by a lady, who you had lined up to be your victim. Instead she kicked you in the balls.'

'And her brother, who just happens to be a reverend gentleman, finished off the good work. It was he who brought you in here. Guess who the jury will believe? You or a vicar?' added Harry.

When John arrived, he was relieved to learn Madeleine was safe, and overjoyed that they might have found their murderer. He spent a few minutes looking at the prisoner's property. Caleb picked up the key that lay there, with the other items.

'Unless I'm much mistaken, I think this belongs to the *Green Dragon*. Shall we go and check and search our friend's room?'

'Yes. Do that, and we'll take him with us,' instructed John.

Several minutes later they all stood in the room Miles Grafton had rented in the *Green Dragon*. One of the staff had identified him and taken them up to his room. Among the items they found were a pair of pince-nez spectacles, which John recognised as being Sarah's, and other items taken from the barmaid.

All the while Miles denied knowing anything about the stolen items. They returned to the police station, where Harry began completing the necessary paperwork.

'How many times do I have to keep telling you!' protested Miles. 'I'm totally innocent of these crimes. Those items were planted in my room: probably by one of you.'

'Let me get this right,' said John, in a reasonable and puzzled voice. 'You are saying you are totally innocent of attacking three women here in Warwick during the past few days.'

'Yes that's what I keep trying to tell you.'

'Fine,' said John. 'Is that your last word?'

'Yes,' Miles replied feeling his luck was changing. If this was the man they had warned him about, then what was the problem? It seemed the *Chronicle* had been right. This man was too old and should be retired.

'Then we'll say nothing more about it.' John looked at Caleb and smiled. But it was a mirthless smile. 'Lock him up on suspicion of having murdered Lottie Goodwin. Then he can tell his lies to the judge and hangman.'

Miles gulped. Murder! The hangman! 'Just a minute. There's been a dreadful mistake. I...'

'Another mistake, Mr Grafton?' John continued, but his friendly manner had gone. In its place was the icy cold tone he used, and which had caused so many felons to tremble. Miles Grafton became another such felon.

'We'll talk again in the morning; good night! I hope you sleep well. The Assizes will be with us soon, so you can start counting the days till you climb the scaffold for your execution.'

Several minutes later, John left the police station and went home. Although he knew Madeleine was safe, he wanted an excuse to make sure. However, he was to be disappointed. Her house was in darkness. He would have to wait until tomorrow.

Going into his drawing-room, he poured himself a cognac. He was certain Harriet's portrait showed her with a smug smile, but he wondered if it was only in his imagination.

John took a while to go back to sleep, as he pondered over what had happened. She had reacted very quickly, and luckily Mordeccai had been with her. However, he wondered why they had used the back entrance into her house, when the front door was the expected way in. It seemed a little strange, but perhaps they had not wanted to disturb the servants.

Then there was the very vexing question about Miles Grafton. There could be little doubt he had attacked Sarah, Madeleine and the other woman. The evidence was overwhelming. His arrest alone should serve to get the *Chronicle* off his back.

But was he Lottie's killer? It would be nice and very convenient if he was.

Yet, deep down, he had reservations. He was not convinced, and nor were his men. What would the day bring? Consequently, sleep continued to evade him. After lying in bed, tossing and turning for over two hours, he got up. After washing, shaving and dressing, John went on duty. If anything, his doubts had increased.

On his way to the station, he was congratulated by several early morning traders for arresting Miles Grafton. Clearly word had already spread. Joining his men for their early morning briefing, he congratulated them on arresting Grafton, but warned against being over-confident that he was Lottie's killer.

It was about 9.30am, when there came a knock at his office door, and a worried looking Constable Eddie Chadwick came in.

'I think you'd better hear this, guv'nor. There's a man at the counter who thinks Grafton is not our killer.'

John went out to the front office where a middle-aged man with grey hair and a checked suit stood.

'Hi, Mr Mayfield?' The man had a pronounced American accent. He held out his right hand.

'I'm Cornelius Lake, one of Allan Pinkerton's agents. I think you've got the wrong man locked up for the murder of Miss Goodwin. You see, you and me have a common purpose in life. To rid the world of a certain evil bastard killer.'

CHAPTER TEN

Cornelius Lake

John invited Cornelius into his office, asked for Robert, Mathew, Caleb and Sam to join them, and ordered some tea. He decided interviewing Miles Grafton could wait. Perhaps this stranger might be able to convince them, one way or the other, as to the man being guilty of murder, or just robbery. After the introductions had been made, Cornelius began his story.

'You'll have to bear with me, gents,' he said. 'But I have to go back a few years, to when this sorry tale started, way back home, during our civil war. When the war started, I was really impressed by Abe Lincoln and what he stood for, so I enlisted into his Union army. By the early part of '62 I found myself sergeant in the Provost-Marshal's Department. I don't know why that was, as I'd never had any police background.'

Cornelius went on to explain how he had been tasked with investigating the first of a series of murders, which happened during the Battle of 2nd Bull Run. He continued with outlining the others. All but one of the victims had been whores. But all of them had been killed the same way, by having their throats cut, and their bodies cut open.

The fourth victim, Martha Maudsley, was murdered at Gettysburg in 1863. This one had particularly affected him, as she had been a decent young woman.

There were two others some months later. Whilst Cornelius did not have any photographs of the victims, from his description of the bodies, there was no doubt they had shared the same fate as Lottie Goodwin. Now it seemed the same killer had come to Warwick.

'Although, as I said, I didn't have a police background, I found I was quite suited to that type of work,' Cornelius continued. 'So, when the war ended, it seemed a logical move for me to make. However, I was considered to be too old for the police, but Pinkerton's welcomed me with open arms.'

'I take it you are here as a result of my letter?' asked Robert.

'Letter? What letter?' Cornelius looked genuinely puzzled. 'I haven't seen any letter from you.'

'Then why are you here?' asked John.

Cornelius explained.

Seven weeks earlier, Cornelius had been working in the Chicago office of the Pinkerton Detective Agency, when Sean Collins told him he was wanted, immediately, by his supervisor. Collins did not like Cornelius and he was only too happy to give him such instructions. They usually meant trouble.

Knocking on the door, Cornelius was summoned in by Theodore Dexter, his supervisor, who was always known as Theo. As he entered the office, Cornelius saw a late middle-aged couple sitting there. Theo introduced them as Mr and Mrs Maudsley.

Cornelius frowned slightly at the mention of their name. Any lingering doubts he may have had, were quickly dispelled.

'I see our names mean something to you,' said Herbert Maudsley in a tight voice.

He was a thin man, with grey hair and a world-weary look about him. It was a common enough look on most people's faces, during the immediate post-war years in America. The man, in fact both he and his wife, were old before their time. She sat still, and said nothing.

'Are you Martha's parents?' asked Cornelius, quietly. In his mind he could still see the poor girl's torn body at Gettysburg.

'We are sir. I believe you found her?'

'Not exactly Mr Maudsley. But I was one of the first to see her. I was a provost-sergeant at the time.'

'And you never found her killer?' Herbert Maudsley continued accusingly.

'You are quite correct, Mr Maudsley. I have not found him yet. But I intend to.'

'Detective Lake has worked on nothing else, since he joined the Agency several months ago.' interrupted Theo Dexter.

Herbert Maudsley looked sceptical.

'Martha was the fourth of six such similar victims,' continued Cornelius. 'I saw them all.'

Edwina Maudsley gave a small gasp and clutched her husband's arm.

'Detective Lake,' instructed Theo Dexter. 'Go and get your file.'

Cornelius returned a few minutes later, with a file of papers several inches thick.

Herbert Maudsley now looked less sceptical. Cornelius looked at Theo, who nodded back.

'These papers represent all my enquiries into those murders, since the first one at 2nd Bull Run in August 1862. I have collated several lists of all the medical personnel who were at each of the locations.' Cornelius stressed the words *medical personnel.*

'Whilst the war was still on, all I could do was to collect as much information as I could. In each case, I was allowed just forty-eight hours to make my investigations,' he paused. 'And that included taking written statements from as many witnesses as I could find, and who were able to be interviewed. As you can probably imagine, during and immediately after such battles, it was a very hectic and chaotic time. And I was not allowed any help whatsoever.' He paused.

'Since I started with Mr Pinkerton, I've carried on with my enquiries. I cannot remember just how many people I've interviewed, but they're all in there. Take a look.' Cornelius pointed at the file.

He waited whilst Herbert Maudsley stared at the papers in the file. His face now showed uncertainty. Edwina had not moved, and she made no attempt to look at the papers.

Whilst he felt extremely sorry for the couple who had lost their daughter in such a terrible way, Cornelius was also offended by the implications he had not taken their daughter's murder seriously.

'That won't be necessary, Mr Lake. I can see I've misjudged you. Please accept my apologies.'

Cornelius nodded.

'Now for the reason we are here.' Herbert Maudsley continued.

He opened the document case he held on his lap, and took out a newspaper. Cornelius saw it was a copy of the *Warwick Chronicle*, which Herbert explained, had been sent to him from England. Herbert handed the newspaper to Theo, and pointed to an article which had been heavily ringed in ink.

Theo took it, quickly glanced over the article and passed it to Cornelius. The article referred to Lottie Goodwin's murder, and went into some detail of her injuries.

'So, the bastard's struck again,' Cornelius commented, not caring if his language upset any of the other people in the office. 'He wasn't killed in the war, like we had all hoped. But why has he suddenly started killing again? And what is he doing in England? Can I keep this?' he asked Herbert Maudsley, and pointed to the newspaper.

The man nodded. 'A friend of ours was travelling round Europe, and quite by chance saw this article. He posted it back for me.'

'Thank you,' replied Cornelius. 'I'll study the paper carefully. There may be other clues in it.'

They discussed the case for a while and the Maudsleys left.

Theo leaned forwards on his desk, smiling with his chin resting on his interlaced fingers. 'You're off to England my friend, and the Maudsleys have offered to pay your costs. I think we're both convinced it's the same one. It seems the local limey cops haven't made much progress. Perhaps you could show them how it's done, eh?'

Suddenly he became very serious. 'But be careful Cornelius. This man is very dangerous.'

John broke the silence as Cornelius finished. 'Do you think, like we do, that a medical man is involved?'

'It almost certainly has to be someone with some medical knowledge, for the way he cut the girls up.'

'That raises another question,' John continued. 'Why cut them up like that? All of us here have dealt with various murders, but never anything like these ones.'

'I don't know. It seems to me he's trying to make sure he's noticed.'

'Why?' asked Mathew. 'Surely with all the battlefield deaths, why does he need to go out of his way to draw attention to himself?'

They had no answer to that.

'Now, what about your murder?' Cornelius asked, and gasped, feeling a sudden twinge of pain in his chest. It was not the first one he had experienced. Cornelius rubbed his chest and the pain eased.

'Is there something wrong?' asked John, concerned for his visitor. 'Would you like to see a doctor? We can soon have Dr Whiting here, if you want?'

'It's probably something I've eaten,' replied Cornelius. 'There's no need to bother the doc.' Just at that particular moment, Silas Whiting was the very last person he wanted to see.

'Would you like to go and look at the scene of our murder, before we go through the file?' asked John.

Cornelius agreed, and he left with Sam and Mathew.

'What do you think?' John asked Robert.

'I don't know. I wonder what happened to the letter I sent to America? But at least we know there have been some other murders, albeit on the other side of the Atlantic. So why choose Warwick for another one? And the attempt on Jessie's life.'

'They'll be back soon. Get our file, but remove the piece of cloth found in Lottie's hand. I think I'm starting to get an idea about this one, but it's early days yet. So we'll keep that bit of evidence to ourselves.'

When the others returned, John produced the murder file, and they discussed it in some detail. If Mathew, Caleb and Sam noticed the piece of cloth was missing, they made no comment about it. They knew their guv'nor well enough by now to know he would have removed it for a very good reason.

After further discussion, John had some refreshments brought in, and they ate as they talked about the case.

'You say you never received my letter. Is that normal?' Robert queried in between a mouthful of bread and cold meat.

'I must admit it's not normally the case. Possibly the mail packet sank or the letter got lost somewhere.' Cornelius sounded calm enough, but inside he was worried, and he had hesitated slightly before answering Robert's question. Hopefully, the others would not have noticed.

He knew important papers had gone missing from the office before, but it was the first time it had happened to him. For a moment he thought about mentioning his suspicions, but decided not to. It was something he would attend to, when he went back home.

Sam had noticed his hesitation, and he made a mental note to mention it to the others.

'You said the Maudsleys gave you a copy of the *Warwick Chronicle* for you to look through?' asked Mathew.

'No, just the actual article about the murder,' he lied, regretting ever having mentioned that incident in his earlier narrative. Perhaps these limeys were not so stupid as he had thought. He would need to be careful.

'Apart from telling us about the other similar murders, for which we are truly thankful,' began John. 'When you arrived, you said we had the wrong man locked up. Would you care to explain?'

'I only arrived at the *Warwick Arms* yesterday, and found the town was concerned about these other attacks on women. I found an old copy of the *Warwick Chronicle* and read about them. Then I heard about your arrest last night, and it set me thinking.' He paused. 'You see, our murderer never bothered with robbery. All he did was kill his victims, and always in a quiet place. Although it was not so far away from the hospitals that his disappearance would be noticed. Do you agree?'

The others nodded, as they had already begun to have some reservations about Grafton's guilt, certainly as far as Lottie was concerned.

'We actually agree,' confirmed John. 'The methods are different. Whilst I have no doubt Grafton is behind the recent attacks on the women, I cannot accept he is our murderer.'

'You could always say he was. Nobody would really mind if you had the wrong man. And it would get you off the hook.'

Cornelius realised he had said the wrong thing, by the sudden and very hostile silence which greeted his suggestion.

'Sam! Show this…person out, and if he refuses to go, lock him up!' instructed John, in a disgusted tone. 'How dare you make such a suggestion?'

John's voice had become very quiet, and his eyes glittered dangerously. It was a sign his officers had come to know well, and one which struck terror in the hearts of felons.

'I don't care what you might do on your side of the Atlantic. But in my town, a life is a life, regardless of what you might think,' John continued relentlessly.

'Forgive me, Mr Mayfield,' apologised Cornelius, holding his hands up in submission. 'It was a test question. I needed to know just how keen you were to bring the right person to justice, and not just to find a scapegoat.'

In truth, it had been a test question, and he had been both frightened and impressed by John's sincerity. This man was nobody's fool, and Cornelius knew he would have to be very careful in how he dealt with him.

'What are your plans, here in Warwick?' John asked, slightly appeased by Cornelius's explanation.

'I have one or two people to see,' was his guarded reply.

'May I ask who?'

'You may Mr Mayfield, but I have no intention of telling you. Should you wish to follow me around, then that is your affair. But it won't get you anywhere.' Cornelius held up his hand to stem John's protests. 'Look, you are a professional investigator, like me. I may come from another continent, but I still have certain standards. I have to, otherwise Pinkerton's would not employ me. Would you divulge all your lines of enquiry to me, if you came to America?'

'Of course not,' snorted Mathew.

'Exactly.'

An uncomfortable silence followed.

'Look Mr Mayfield,' Cornelius continued in a gentler tone. 'We're all working to achieve the same result. We want to catch this bastard, and put him before the hangman. If he's here in Warwick, and I think he is, then you can have him. I don't want to take him back to Chicago with me. And I don't think my supervisor would thank me for the extra costs. You can have him, and you can hang him. All I want is for him to be brought to justice.'

His offer appeased John and his colleagues. But at the same time, it strengthened their suspicions that Cornelius Lake was not telling them everything. It seemed Cornelius had a suspect, whose identity he would not reveal.

'It's a deal. But we need to be there to make an arrest and secure any evidence. If not, then we won't have a case against him, and he will be acquitted. Don't forget you have no power of arrest in England.'

'I understand. Now Mr Mayfield, I wonder, could I have a word with you alone please? No disrespect intended gentlemen.'

John nodded, and the others left his office. Cornelius waited until they had closed the door. Then he picked up his document case, opened it and took out a large pile of papers, which he handed to John.

'Don't get me wrong. It's not that I distrust your fellow policemen, but here is my file, or rather a copy of it, which I did on the crossing. Everything is in here. Feel free to read it and let the others do so. Hopefully it will explain much. But I want you to read it first. The answer is in there somewhere. It has to be.'

He paused. 'I think I'm right in thinking, just as you are, our killer is the same for all these crimes. And that he is a doctor or at least, has had some sort of medical training or knowledge?'

'Yes. That was the opinion of the doctor who examined the body.'

'That has always been my view as well. And it's why I concentrated all my enquiries in and around the field-hospitals. It was no easy task, believe me.'

Cornelius stood up, collected his case and hat. 'Mr Mayfield,' he said solemnly. 'Between us, we're going to get this bastard. But be careful. He's dangerous: very dangerous.'

'You be careful, too.'

After Cornelius had gone, the others filed back into John's office, and he told them what had happened.

'I don't think Detective Cornelius Lake is telling us the whole truth,' said John. 'He knows more than he's letting on. But, I suppose we'd do the same if we were over there. I'm convinced he knows, or at least suspects who our killer is.'

The others agreed with him.

'I'll read the report tomorrow. Meanwhile, I'm taking Madeleine to the theatre tonight, and I do not intend to be late.'

'And a romantic supper afterwards?' teased Mathew.

They all laughed. It was good to see John getting his spirit back at last.

When John and Madeleine left the theatre, along with the rest of the audience, they were still laughing. The play had been called the *Black Dog,* and was a comic ghost story.

Over a late supper, at the *Warwick Arms*, she asked him, as always, how his day had been. John was about to answer, when he felt a hand on his shoulder.

'Hi there, Mr Mayfield!' came Cornelius Lake's booming voice. 'Won't you introduce me to the young lady? Would I be right in thinking, from her accent, she has spent some time in my part of the world?'

John did so, but he noticed how Madeleine was not over enthusiastic in her responses to him. After a while Cornelius left them.

'Are you all right?' asked a worried John. 'You seem a bit bothered?'

'Who was that dreadful man? Clearly he was an American, but one of the more objectionable ones.'

'He's a Pinkerton agent, who spent most of the day with me. He's staying here in the *Warwick Arms*. Hopefully he can offer us some help with the murder of that poor girl in the churchyard. Apparently he has investigated some similar murders, back in America, during the war. He thinks they have all been committed by the same man.'

'But I thought you already had him? Surely he's the man who attacked me, last night?'

'It would be nice to think so, but we're fairly convinced he's not our murderer.' John explained why.

But Lake's appearance had spoiled the evening, and Madeleine began to complain about having a headache. When they arrived back at John's house, she declined an offer for a late night drink.

John escorted her to the door, where she kissed him briefly, before going inside.

John went indoors and had a solitary late night drink.

'Damn you, Cornelius Lake, and your aggressive attitude,' he said aloud.

On looking at Harriet's portrait, as he did every night, he was certain she was smiling, but there was another look on her face: one he had not noticed before. It was almost a look of triumph.

Was she jealous of Madeleine finding her way into his life?

'Don't be so silly,' he said aloud. 'She would never begrudge me any happiness.'

His mind went back to the time he had taken Harriet to the theatre, many years ago. And that visit had been the disaster which caused her to go back to Australia, getting shipwrecked on the way. He felt a cold shiver of apprehension run across his back. Hopefully it was not going to be a case of history repeating itself.

But if she had not been shipwrecked and believed dead, then he would not have married Laura. He would have married Harriet earlier, and she might have been poisoned, instead.

It was a sobering, and worrying thought.

CHAPTER ELEVEN

Cornelius Lake's Report

After he had attended to the routine matters of the following morning, John settled down to take a quick look at Cornelius Lake's report. In addition to numerous written statements, it consisted of various lists of names, with his personal remarks alongside most of them. These were *killed in battle, died, eliminated from enquiries* or *a question mark*.

One list, in particular recorded all the names of his prime suspects.

All the names had at least one number against them.

By checking on a master index, he saw each number referred to a specific battle, which was where one of the murders had taken place.

1 ...... August 1862 ......2nd Bull Run.
2 ......September 1862 ......Antietam.
3 ......December 1862 ......Fredericksburg
4 ......July 1863 ......Gettysburg
5 ......June 1864 – April 1865 ......Siege of Petersburg
6 ......April 1865 ......Appamattox

Many names had more than one number against them. There were several who had all six against their names. John sat up with a jolt when he recognised one of them.

It was Lieutenant Silas Whiting: his son.

Dear God, he prayed, please don't let it be Silas. Then a horrible thought came into his mind. Lottie's murder happened after Silas had arrived in Warwick. Damn Cornelius Lake! Not only had the man spoilt his night out with Madeleine, he now threatened to cause a rift between himself and his son.

To make matters worse, whilst Silas had been mentioned by name, he had not been cleared or accused. And, if that was not enough, there were some pages of the report missing, which no doubt referred to Silas. John did not know whether to be thankful or even more agitated that they were not there. Some more disturbing thoughts occurred to him.

When they were speaking to Cornelius the day before, he had mentioned the *Warwick Chronicle* which Herbert Maudsley had given him. Then he had denied saying that, explaining it was just the article he had been given. What else had he found to be so interesting in that paper? Why had he denied it?

Clearly there had to have been something in the paper which interested him, and also had a bearing on his enquiries. They had all agreed Cornelius was holding some information back. He had been sufficiently secretive about it, for a reason. But what was the reason?

Standing up, John crossed to his door, opened it and called for Robert. When he arrived, John asked him for his press file relating to events, advertisements etc, that involved Warwick, for the period of Lottie's murder.

One of the many records Robert kept was a press cuttings file, which he culled each week from the *Warwick Chronicle*. It contained everything which involved the town: not only police reports, but also all the advertisements with a Warwick connection. Robert's files had proved their worth on many occasions.

'Are you looking for anything in particular?' queried Robert, trying to be helpful.

'Not really. It's just something Lake said yesterday.'

John took the file away and thumbed through it, until he found the date he wanted. Somehow he was not surprised to find a small article, which gave an update on a Dr Silas Whiting, who had arrived from America a few weeks earlier. There could be no doubt Lake had also seen it.

He closed Robert's file and sat still for a long time. Finally he realised he had to get the broader view of the whole affair, and began to read Lake's file in earnest.

Given the circumstances in which the man had to work, John felt Cornelius had done the best he could. His report was well put together, and cross-referenced to various documents, as and when they were mentioned.

He quickly discovered how there was an unpleasant regularity about the manner in which the murders had been committed. They were almost identical to the one in Warwick, except for two differences.

Firstly, there had been a war in progress. Secondly, if the killer had medical knowledge, as seemed to be the case, then it was not surprising the scenes of crime had all been near to field-hospitals.

Whilst it could be argued that Lottie had not been very far from Harriet's hospital, she had been killed in the nearby churchyard, which was a regular haunt of many of the town's whores.

There was another difference.

Why was Martha Maudsley the only victim not to have been a whore? Could it have been a case of mistaken identity, or was there some other dark reason? Try as he might, John could not come up with a satisfactory answer.

As he read on, John discovered Silas had been talking to Martha shortly before her death. He had been taking a break from tending the wounded soldiers. Having overstayed his time, he had to be fetched back into the hospital. Moments later, Martha had been seen going into the bushes, after Silas was back in the hospital. They were the same bushes where her body was found.

Cornelius added it was well-known the nurses had to use the bushes instead of the latrines. Had her murderer known that?

The report raised John's spirits. Cornelius's general feeling was that, although Silas had been seen with Martha, he had gone straight back to work. Several witnesses testified to his having stayed there for several hours, before having another break.

Whilst it certainly cleared Silas of Martha's murder, there were still the others to consider. As they had discussed, it was very unlikely there were two such murderers. He needed to speak to Cornelius again, and the sooner the better.

John had come across a reference to the *Voluntary League of Medical Helpers*. That was it. Like the reports referring to Silas, there was nothing else. Perhaps it was because V and W were close together in the alphabet, and for no other reason. But John disliked such unexplained mysteries. He decided to try and see Cornelius again that evening.

The rest of the day dragged by, but John had difficulty in concentrating on anything. His thoughts kept coming back to Silas. Just how involved was his son in all this? He took comfort from the fact Silas was almost certainly in the clear, regarding the murder of Martha Maudsley. But John was tormented by the fact that her murder was different to the rest. And was it just coincidence the Warwick murder had occurred so soon after Silas had arrived?

As John always insisted, he did not believe in coincidences. And so the roundabout of thoughts began again. Oh how he missed Harriet. She would have examined the evidence in a detached way, as she had done many times for him in the past. Then she would analyse what she saw. Over the years, she had rarely been wrong.

For a moment he thought about discussing it with Madeline, but then decided he did not yet know her well enough. And he had not told her about Silas, although he knew they had met several times. Clearly the beard was working and she had not seen the family likeness. Silas was a regular visitor at the White House, where he carried out medical examinations on all the women, when they arrived for the beginning of each new course.

John, like many people in the town, was impressed by what she and Mordeccai were doing. The numbers of whores and other unfortunate women had decreased since the project started. Ironically her success worried him. What would happen when they had cleaned up Warwick and the surrounding district? Would she move on or, if he asked her, stay with him in Warwick?

He had no easy answer.

In another part of the police station, Robert Andrew was carrying out his own enquiries. He too had picked up on Cornelius Lake's comments about the *Warwick Chronicle*. After John had returned the press cuttings, he checked it out. Like John he found Silas Whiting's name, and immediately made the American connection.

However, Robert guessed, rightly, that John had been looking for his son's name. But Robert remembered seeing another name at the same time. He quickly checked it, and knew his memory had not let him down. It was time to start making some other enquiries.

He had already started them in connection with Mordeccai Carew, whom he had never met, but had seen. Lawrence Perkins had been happy to assist in making a sketch of Carew. Whilst Lawrence was not as good an artist as his mother, he still had remarkable talent. He made several copies of the sketch for Robert to keep, and use as he saw fit.

Robert had already sent one to Gordon Mayne, an inspector in the Detective Branch of the Metropolitan police. Gordon had married Robert's younger sister, and the two men were firm friends. It would not be the first time he had used that friendship to good effect. To be fair, Gordon was a dedicated police officer, who was more than willing to share information whenever he could.

Gordon's reply had been what Robert hoped for and expected.

Dear Mr Andrew
I regret I am unable to help you in this matter.
Gordon Mayne

Robert knew his brother-in-law had information for him. Whenever he had sought confidential information, he had always written to him at home. If there was no problem with being given the information, Gordon would do so. Should the subject be of interest to the police, then he would send a coldly formal reply, which was a code.

It was then a simple matter for Robert to travel to London and meet up with his brother-in-law. That time was rapidly approaching. But now, he had another name to give Joseph.

And, for good measure, he added that of Silas Whiting to his list.

The remainder of the day dragged slowly for John. At last he was able to go off duty. Having returned Lake's file to his safe and locked it up, John went home and changed, prior to going to the *Warwick Arms* to seek out Cornelius Lake.

On arriving home, he was relieved to find a note from Madeleine, cancelling their date for that evening. She explained how *something had cropped up.* It saved him from having to cancel, and use the same excuse.

Thirty minutes later, now out of uniform, he made his way to the *Warwick Arms*. It did not take John long to discover which room Cornelius had booked into, although the landlord advised him that the American had not been seen all day. Nevertheless, John made to go upstairs and check for himself.

'Mayfield! A moment please!'

John stopped and saw Mordeccai Carew standing in the hallway.

'Reverend?' he replied, and slowly went and joined the other man.

'Look,' began Carew. 'I'm sorry about the last time we met. I know it was a while ago, and I should have apologised before, but I've been rather busy. I want to apologise. Madeleine was furious with me.' He dropped his eyes as the ghost of a smile played around his mouth. 'Am I forgiven?' He held out his right hand.

'Of course,' smiled John, as he took the proffered hand.

'Come. Let me buy you a drink, just to celebrate our new friendship. Eh?'

John could but agree, and he followed the big man into the tap room. Carew purchased two glasses of wine, and brought them over to John. Together they selected a small settle in the far end of the room. They sat down and each raised his glass to the other.

'Look, I'm sorry about what happened. It's just me, I'm afraid. You see I've had problems with the poliss in America, and generally speaking don't trust 'em.' Carew used the term *poliss,* instead of *police.* 'Whilst some of us were out trying to help in the war, too many of them stayed behind, and made a lot of money.'

'I thought it would have been against your religion to take a life, or fight in a war?' John was not completely sure if his thinking was correct, but Carew's sudden appearance and friendlier attitude had caught him unprepared. He was just making general conversation.

'A good question. No, I didn't fight. With Maddy, I started various voluntary groups who provided medicine and nursing services, not only for the troops but also for the civilian population who were affected. The military took care of its own soldiers, but left the non-combatants to fare for themselves. The poliss didn't like it, as they wanted to see all of our resources going to the army. That way, the war continued and they got richer.'

John could only nod. There was no answer to that. 'Tell me. Did you ever come across or hear about an organisation called the *Voluntary League of Medical Helpers*?' he asked.

Mordeccai was pensive for a few moments. 'The *Voluntary League of Medical Helpers*, you say?' He shook his head. 'No, I can't say I have. Why do you ask?'

'It's a name I seem to have heard of a while ago. But everyone I ask doesn't know anything about them. I get the impression they provided nurses or something. But it doesn't really matter.'

'Ah, wait a minute. That now rings a bell. But I cannot be exactly sure. You see there were so many voluntary groups, such as the one I was in, who were dedicated to trying to relieve suffering. We don't believe in having fancy names, but just got on with it.'

'Were you at many of the big battles?'

'I was at enough. But can we leave it now? It was a part of my life which I want to forget, and hope I never have to experience again.'

'I'm sorry.' John fully understood.

He rarely spoke about his own military experiences, which he realised were very tame when compared with what this man must have seen. His father had the same attitude towards the time he spent in Spain, and France, with the Duke of Wellington. It was the same, to a degree, with policemen. Amongst their colleagues and former colleagues, it was different. They had shared similar experiences. But they were not for sharing with outsiders.

'Enough of my sounding off. I've heard how well you run this town, and are considered incorruptible. I am afraid I misjudged you.'

'Think nothing of it.'

'I appreciate we are probably too different to become real friends. But, at least, for Maddy's sake, we'll try and not be enemies. What do you say?'

'I'll drink to that,' answered John, and he raised his glass.

They talked for a while about various matters, but avoided the war, and Carew's difficulties with the police. John bought them both another drink. When they had finished it, Carew made his apologies and left.

John was not exactly sorry to see him go. Yet again he wondered how Madeleine and her brother could be from the same family.

As he had discussed with Mathew after their visit to the White House, there was something about Carew which bothered him. He could not say what it was, but he had been a policeman for too long now, not to heed such feelings. Mathew agreed with him.

And he was fairly certain Mordeccai was not telling the truth.

He had denied knowing about the *Voluntary League of Medical Helpers* just a little too quickly. When John had suggested about the *League* providing nurses, which is what he had thought they did, Mordeccai had been very quick to agree. By now, John was even more intrigued about what this *Voluntary League of Medical Helpers* really did. It would be another little task for Robert.

Mordeccai had said how he did not believe in using fancy names for what he did. But, if that was so why did he now operate the *Society for the Proper Education of Fallen Women*? The man was inconsistent, and that worried John.

After Mordeccai had left, John finished his drink and went upstairs and tried Lake's door. Although he knocked on it several times, there was no reply.

After a restless night, in which he kept thinking about Silas and his possible involvement in the murders, John arose early. He was now becoming more than a little concerned about Cornelius Lake's whereabouts. A little voice was whispering to him that all was not well where the American was concerned. Before going to the police station, he called back at the *Warwick Arms*, where his fears began to grow.

'If you've come to see Mr Lake,' called the porter, as he saw John going upstairs, 'you're wasting your time, as he still hasn't come back.'

John cursed and went on duty.

What was the man playing at? Clearly he knew much more than he had let on, and had been carrying out some of his own investigations. Damn the man. Just when had he arrived in England? And what had he been doing since he arrived in Warwick?

As John thought about it, he put himself in Cornelius's shoes. He maintained he had only just arrived at the *Warwick Arms,* which had quickly been verified. But all that did was to confirm his arrival there. Before then, he could easily have been staying elsewhere, possibly in Leamington. He made himself a mental note to pursue that idea further.

Once he arrived on duty, he made sure all his officers had a description of Cornelius Lake. John instructed them to bring him into the station, wherever he was found. They were to arrest him if necessary. He needed to know what Lake had been doing, and, just as importantly, what he was doing.

He had already decided to speak to Silas sometime that evening about how he figured in the report, regardless of whether or not he had found Cornelius Lake. His thoughts and plans were interrupted by a knock on his door.

'Come in,' he called and looked up to see Harry Barlow with a worried look on his face.

'I think you'd better come, guv'nor. They've found a body in the canal. It looks like a murder.'

CHAPTER TWELVE

Cornelius Lake's Enquiries

When he left the police station, Cornelius Lake had taken great care to make sure he was not being followed. Only when he was completely satisfied did he make his way back to the *Warwick Arms.*

By and large, he thought, it had not been a bad day. Fairly soon into his meeting with the local police, Cornelius had revised his opinion about them. They were not fools. Possibly, had they been in possession of all the facts, they might be much closer to solving their murder.

He was also impressed by their honesty, especially when he made his suggestion about letting Grafton take the blame. Cornelius knew of places where that course of action would have happened. He was glad Mayfield had reacted as he had. In the short time he had known John, Cornelius had taken a liking to him.

As they all suspected, Cornelius had told them the truth, but not all of it. Whilst he was quite happy to let Mayfield have a copy of the file, he had first made sure certain important papers had been removed from it. In spite of what he had told Mayfield, Cornelius wanted to be the one who unmasked the killer.

After all, he had lived with very little else since 1862, and 1868 was fast approaching. He wanted these crimes cleared, and he wanted to see the bastard hanged. It was true he did not care whether it was in America or England. In fact, it would be simpler in England.

There would be too many boundary problems to overcome in America. And the pains in his chest were starting to cause him some concern. So the last thing he wanted was to have to take a prisoner back across the Atlantic to America.

He had little doubt the pains were indicators of heart problems. Over the years he had seen enough dead bodies, not all of whom had met violent ends. Several had succumbed to heart attacks, and Cornelius was fairly certain he recognised the symptoms. Perhaps it would give him an excuse to visit Dr Whiting. That would be interesting.

His thoughts were interrupted by another onset of pains in his chest. This time they lasted a little bit longer. But he was too close to his quarry now to worry about them.

It had been a long trail, and he was certain the key was Dr Silas Whiting. He was one of the few suspects who had been at the location of all the crimes, including the one in Warwick. To be fair, he did not really consider him to be responsible for Martha's death. Also, he was fairly certain he was not involved in the others, but he could not be entirely sure. It was just possible there were two different killers, but like most policemen, he did not believe in coincidences.

No doubt Mayfield suspected he had not just arrived in Warwick the previous night. And he would have been right. Cornelius had been in the area for more than two weeks. He had spent his time well, although it had cost him a lot of money. Or to be correct, it had cost Herbert Maudsley.

For instance, Cornelius had discovered Lottie Goodwin had been with Silas shortly before her death, where it seemed she was a regular visitor. For what reason, Cornelius could only guess, given her chosen way of life. Although some of the girls had remarked on how she was now speaking differently. They described her as getting above her station, and telling them how she was going up in the world.

Obtaining that knowledge had cost him a considerable amount of money, but Jessie Brampton had finally given him the information.

He had also spent time in the *Warwick Chronicle* office looking at back issues of the newspaper. It did not help him a lot, but he discovered where Silas lived and worked. Apart from building up his own, albeit temporary practice with Dr Waldren, he discovered Silas was a regular visitor to the

White House. Here he examined all the women brought in, under Mordeccai Carew and Madeleine Pascoe's educational programme.

Once more, after spreading his money around, Cornelius discovered how the women who went to the White House, were quickly moved on. This was something which both intrigued and worried him.

He became even more intrigued when he discovered John Mayfield's current liaison with Madeleine Pascoe. Cornelius had already discovered John was a widower. And there were enough people to tell him about Madeleine's unfortunate arrival, just as Harriet Mayfield's funeral cortege was leaving her house.

Going back to the *Chronicle* office, he read the report of Harriet's funeral, and was not surprised to see no mention of the incident. He was just on the point of closing the newspaper, when a paragraph caught his eye in the report.

The hearse was escorted on foot, by Superintendent John Mayfield, who was flanked by Dr Thomas Waldren and Dr Silas Whiting.

This report was intriguing.

Why should anyone, regardless of whether he was a doctor or not, who had only been in town a few weeks, be a principal mourner at such a prominent funeral? Even if he had been treating the deceased, why was he in such an important position?

Cornelius had learnt Dr Waldren was a long term friend of John Mayfield, and also was the deceased's uncle. That gave him sufficient reason to be there with the mourners. But that was not the case with Silas Whiting.

Why was he there?

Possibly it was not important, but on the other hand, if he was close to Mayfield, for whatever reason, might that cloud the policeman's judgement? It was one of the reasons he had kept part of the file back. He needed to test him first. If he got the right response, and if his final enquiries were successful, then Mayfield would get the rest of the file.

Cornelius was not stupid.

On arriving in England, he realised he was on his own, in a foreign country, with a possibly corrupt police force.   There was always the possibility of his room being searched, so he hid the last few pages in his hotel room in Leamington, where he had been staying.

Although he kept that room hired, Cornelius now moved to the *Warwick Arms*, and made it appear he had only just arrived. The news about Grafton's arrest was just the excuse he needed for an interview with Mayfield. It gave him the perfect opportunity to find out just what the local police had by way of evidence. And they had shown him the lot, which actually was not very much.

He had been relieved to find Mayfield and his immediate subordinates were honest. For a moment, Cornelius thought Mayfield was going to hit him for his suggestion about Grafton.

There was only the question of the activities in the White House to resolve, which he felt were somehow connected, before he would be in a position to solve the case. He would go home to a rapturous welcome, and hopefully promotion.

The name Mordeccai Carew meant nothing to him, but, somewhere back in the mists of time, he could recall hearing about a similar sort of organisation to the *Society for the Proper Education of Fallen Women*, operating in America before the war. Although he had glanced through the files, there was nothing immediately obvious to suggest any connection with his current case, so he had not really studied it.

Whilst the name Mordeccai Carew meant nothing, he was beginning to suspect it was not his real name. The more he thought about it, he began to suspect the man might not be all he was supposed to be.

As far as he could recall, the organisation had not lasted long once the war started. With the sudden flux of thousands of soldiers, there was just too much trade for the whores to even think about giving it all up.

Also, as he recalled, there had been concerns for what had happened to the women taken in on the scheme. None of them had ever been seen or heard of again. But, with the outbreak of war in 1861, the enquiry had been dropped for more important matters. Very few people had given the case of the missing whores a second thought.

He would have to see Mordeccai for himself. All he needed was an excuse to go to the White House. Having already been out there, he knew trying to keep observations outside was not a viable option.

When he had seen Mayfield having supper in the *Warwick Arms* with Madeleine Pascoe, it was just too good an opportunity to miss. Putting on his most obnoxious attitude, he had barged in on them, forcing an introduction.

No-one could deny Madeleine was an attractive woman, and Cornelius felt a touch of envy when he saw her. His love life had never been that brilliant, and he used the services of quality whores when necessary. But she was a good looking woman. After being a nuisance for a short while, he made his way back upstairs as if going to bed, with his brain in a whirl.

The moment Cornelius saw her face, he realised he knew her from somewhere, back in America. So, if he knew her, the chances were he knew her brother, and that just might give him a clue. Going to the White House was becoming a pressing necessity.

As far as he could remember, there was nothing to suggest she had been involved in anything criminal. But he had seen something in her eyes, which suggested she recognised him as well.

Having left them, Cornelius went into the tap room and took a seat where he could watch the dining-room. His patience was rewarded when he saw then leave soon afterwards.

Madeleine Pascoe had looked decidedly unhappy.

Cornelius waited for nearly two hours, before making his way to keep an appointment with Jessie Brampton. She was waiting for him, by the stables, at the rear of the *Warwick Arms*. He beckoned to her, and she ran lightly towards him at the back door of the inn. He had already bribed the porter to look in the other direction, as he guided her upstairs to his room.

Once she was inside, he closed and locked the door.

'Now,' he said, without any preamble. 'Have you thought about what I said?'

'Yes…' Jessie hesitated.

'But what?'

'The price has gone up. It could be dangerous, couldn't it?'

Cornelius did not reply, but stood up, and went across to the door, and unlocked it.

'No, wait, please,' she called. 'You've offered me five guineas. Will you make it ten?'

'Good night,' Cornelius replied, and began to open the door. He knew he was taking a chance on losing her

'I'll do it.'

He closed the door and spent the next fifteen minutes explaining what he wanted her do. Having paid her half the money, she left. Several minutes later, he climbed into bed. He gasped as more sharp pains, longer and harder than before, surged through his chest. Finally he fell asleep.

Cornelius was a light sleeper, so he woke quickly on hearing a gentle knocking at his door some time later. Grasping his revolver from under his pillow, he quickly turned up the lamp, which he had left burning, and crossed to the door.

'Who is it?' he asked.

'It's me, Mr Lake,' came a trembling voice. 'Tom Benson, the night porter. I've got a very urgent message for you, from Superintendent Mayfield.'

'Can't it wait?'

'No sir. He says there's been another murder, and can you come?'

'Just a minute.'

Cornelius laid his revolver down on his bed, and quickly put on some trousers, unlocked the door, and began to open it. Before he could react, Cornelius was gripped by a pair of powerful arms, and a sweet smelling cloth was pushed into his face. Seconds later, he was unconscious as the chloroform took effect.

Nobody saw him being taken down the stairs, and out through the back door, where he was bundled into a carriage. The driver softly flicked the reins, and the horse moved quietly away, out of the yard, into Back Lane, and then into High Street.

Back in the *Warwick Arms*, the real Tom Benson emerged from the cellar, and cursed gently when he saw the back door was open. He closed it, then settled back in his porter's chair, and went to sleep. It had been an easy way to earn a few guineas.

'Just be out of the way, for about fifteen minutes, when I bring a lady in,' said one of the guests, who Tom knew had only just booked into the hotel.

He did not ask for the man's name, as he was far too discreet to do that. It was the second time that night he had been paid, to keep out of the way, for just such a request. Little perks like this made his job well worthwhile. Tom hoped they would continue.

The smell of burning feathers being wafted under his nose, slowly brought Cornelius back to consciousness. He struggled to sit up, but found he was unable to do so. Slowly, as his vision cleared, he could see by the light of an oil lamp, that he was tied down to a bed. There were three other people in the room.

'Good of you to join us,' announced one of them.

Cornelius squinted, and gasped in surprise when he recognised the speaker. 'You!'

'Absolutely. Now that you've woken up, we can get down to business.'

"You are making a big mistake in abducting me. The police know where I'll be, and they'll soon come looking.'

'Don't be stupid,' continued the speaker. 'They haven't seen you since last night, and probably won't even miss you. Now let me make myself completely clear. Your chances of leaving here alive are very slender. You will have to convince me you are more use to us alive than dead. And, just at this moment, I cannot think of any use you are to me alive, but I can find a very good use for you dead.'

Cornelius felt cold inside. To have got this far and failed through his own stupidity! Why had he tried to do it all himself? Just for the glory of being the one who solved the case. But now it seemed as if the case would never be solved.

'As I was saying,' continued the speaker. 'Let's not waste any more time. You are almost certainly going to die in this cellar. And you won't be the first one to do so in here. However, it is up to you whether you die quickly, or slowly. Do you understand?'

'Go to hell!'

'Undoubtedly I will. But you will be there before me.'

The speaker paused, and studied Cornelius in a cold detached silence. So far the other men had said nothing, but watched the speaker intently. When the speaker nodded, they moved to another part of the cellar.

Cornelius watched fearfully. For the first time he saw there was a fire burning in the hearth. The two men made a great show of selecting several long metal rods, of varying thicknesses, which they placed in the fire to heat up.

'I'm sure you don't need me to explain just what they are going to do to you,' said the speaker. 'We can avoid all this pain and discomfort by you just answering my questions. Who are you working for?'

'Pinkerton's,' Cornelius replied, fairly certain his captors knew that already.

'Good. Now, what are you doing here in England?'

Cornelius explained how he had come to help clear up the murders.

'And to spy on us?'

'Why should I want to spy on you?'

'Because that's what Pinkerton does. He's hand-in-glove with the Brits, and is anti-Fenian.'

'You're Fenians?' Cornelius was incredulous. 'Seeing you now, I recall you being part of the *Voluntary League of Medical Helpers,* but not Fenians.'

The speaker looked at him quizzically. 'I could almost believe you. But you know, it's shame, a crying shame, that someone like you, clearly with Irish ancestors should side himself with the Brits. You should have helped us instead, but it's too late for that now.'

For several hours the speaker continued with the interrogation. Throughout, the other two men said nothing. From time to time, one of them would cross to the fire, and select one of the rods. Cornelius broke out in a cold sweat whenever this happened, especially when the man brought it closer to the bed, and let him feel its heat.

But Cornelius was unable to answer any questions about the Pinkerton counter-espionage measures, because he was not involved in that work. After a while, the questions returned to his evidence about the murders.

'Just what have you got in your report?'

Cornelius told them.

'Where is it?'

'In my room at the *Warwick Arms.*'

'No Cornelius. You've got to do better than that. I suspect it's probably with Mayfield. Would I be correct?'

'No. It's in the *Warwick Arms.* I swear it. Take me there and I'll get it for you.'

'Nice try! We'll go, but you stay here. And heaven help you if it's not there. We'll be back.'

The three went to leave the cellar. 'By the way,' said the speaker. 'Feel free to scream and shout as much as you like, but I can assure you no-one will pay any heed to you, if they even hear you.'

They left.

The moment they had gone, Cornelius began to work on his bonds. During the course of the interrogation, he had been allowed to sit up, and drink some water. In order for this to happen, the bonds on his right wrist had been untied. When they were re-tied, they had not been quite so tight. All during the next session, he had been moving his wrists, ostensibly to encourage the circulation of his blood. In reality he had loosened the right hand rope.

Soon after his captors had left, Cornelius managed to slide his right hand out of the bond. Next he began to worry at the knot on the rope on his other hand. In a few minutes he had it free. Now able to use both hands, he set to work releasing his ankles.

Having been abducted in the night meant he had no boots to wear, which would slow down his progress, plus the fact he did not know where he was, or where he was going. He had long since realised his chances of completely escaping were fairly remote.

But at the same time he was determined not to go meekly to his death. If he could only take his interrogator with him, Cornelius would be happy.

Selecting one of the rods, he took up a position behind the door, and waited.

After what seemed an eternity, he heard footsteps in the passageway outside, and a key being inserted into the lock. The door opened and a large man he had never seen before, entered. As the man hesitated on seeing the empty bed, Cornelius swung the heaviest of the metal rods, which he had taken from the fire.

The rod hit the man hard above his left ear, and he fell to the ground, and lay still. Seeing he had a bunch of keys in his hand, Cornelius reached down and took them. For a few seconds he wondered whether or not to tie the man up, but decided against doing so. Moments later, he was in the passageway. But should he go to the left or the right?

He chose the right. But it was another wrong decision.

Cornelius soon found the door at the end of the passageway was firmly locked, and none of the keys he had would open it. After wasting several precious minutes in the process, he turned to retrace his steps.

As he did so, his legs were kicked from under him, and he fell heavily. Before he could regain his breath, his assailant, the man he had earlier hit with the rod, knelt on him and quickly had his wrists retied. Minutes later, he was part dragged and part pushed back into his cellar, and locked in.

After what seemed an eternity, his interrogator and some other men arrived. It did not take them long to force him back on to the bed, and tie him down again.

'Very stupid, Mr Lake,' said the speaker, waving the report. 'And I don't mean your attempt at escaping. No, we searched your room and found your report.' The speaker's voice hardened. 'But where is the rest of it?'

'I don't know. It was all there when I saw it last.'

'Very well.' The speaker looked at the man Cornelius had attacked and nodded.

'Thank you!' The man rubbed his head, and grinned evilly at Cornelius. 'I shall enjoy this.'

Cornelius heard the rattle of a metal rod being thrust into the fire, which he noticed had been banked up. From time to time the man extracted the rod, and examined it. Finally he took it out and brought it over to Cornelius, who tried to recoil from its heat, but his bonds would not let him.

'Where is the rest of the report?' asked the speaker once again.

'Go to hell!'

The speaker nodded to the man with the heated rod. He spat on its heated end. They all watched his spit evaporate.

Grinning sadistically, he applied the heated rod first to one of the prisoner's bare feet, and then to the other. Soon Cornelius's screams and the smell of burning flesh filled the cellar.

As he strained against his bonds, Cornelius felt the onset, once more, of the pains in his chest. They took over from the pain on his bare feet and grew in intensity. He realised they were not going to stop this time.

'Where is the rest of the report?' The question came again, although the voice seemed to be coming from far away.

Cornelius was aware of an approaching darkness and roaring in his ears. 'Mayfield,' he cried.

His head fell forwards and he was still.

His interrogators stood undecided for a moment. Then one of them threw a basin of cold water over him. But Cornelius did not move.

Another one felt for a pulse, then put his ear to Cornelius's chest. There was no pulse, nor any heartbeat.

'He's dead.'

'Damn! Damn! Damn!' snarled the speaker. 'Getting it from Mayfield won't be that easy. And I'm not so sure he has it.'

The others nodded. They had all seen the ghost of a smile on Cornelius's face as he died. No, it was fairly certain Mayfield did not have the missing parts of the report. Surely if he had, he would have acted on them before now.

'Get rid of Mr Lake here. I think he can go into the canal. But first, tie this scarf tightly round his neck and make it look as if he's been strangled. It'll help shift suspicion away from us.'

The speaker produced a scarf, which had a piece, approximately hand sized, already missing from it.

CHAPTER THIRTEEN

Revelations

John sat upright. 'Not another whore?' he asked, silently praying that would not be the case.

'No guv'nor,' replied Harry Barlow. 'It's a man, and it looks like he's been strangled. He's down the Saltisford.'

Several minutes later John arrived at the canal basin. Caleb had already arrived there, and he had taken charge. John pushed his way through the gathering crowd, to the canal bank, where the victim had already been pulled from the water.

He saw it was the body of a partially dressed male lying on his chest. A scarf had been tied tightly around the man's neck. Even without seeing the face, John had a fairly good idea who it was.

The check trousers were a give away, and the scarf also looked very familiar. Then he remembered where he had seen it before.

Sarah had given it to Silas as a present.

He took a closer look, and was not surprised to find a piece had been torn out of it. That piece was even now in his office.

'What have we got?' asked Silas, as he too pushed his way to the front of the crowd. He nodded, smiled at John and Caleb then he knelt beside the body.

'Help me turn him over,' he asked.

Caleb obliged, whilst John watched his son's face intently.

They turned the body over onto its back, and John saw he was right. It was Cornelius Lake. He watched as Silas turned white, clearly recognising the body.

'Good God!' he said quietly.

'But of course,' said John, also quietly, so no one else could hear. 'I forgot you have already met Cornelius Lake.'

Silas nodded. 'Yes. It was during the war.'

'I know. Soon after the murder of Martha Maudsley, wasn't it? I think you and I have got to have a talk.'

'What are these marks on his feet?' asked Caleb, unaware of the quiet conversation between father and son.

Silas and John took a look.

'They are almost certainly burns, and fresh ones,' said Silas as he looked at Lake's feet. 'And look.'

He pointed to Lake's wrists and ankles, where the rope burns could clearly be seen. 'He was tied up, and it looks like he has been systematically tortured, poor bastard.'

'How long do you think he has been dead?' asked Caleb.

'Difficult to say.'

Silas rolled Cornelius's body onto its left side, and lifted up the shirt. 'Look!' he instructed, pointing to the post-mortem staining. 'As you know, that means he's been dead at least four hours.'

Silas now began to manipulate the body's arms, and, as he had expected, encountered some stiffness. 'I would say *rigor mortis* is well under way. But, if he's been in the canal, and it's cold, then that process would have been delayed considerably. I would say he's been dead about ten hours. Possibly a little less, and certainly not much more.'

'That would make it some time around ten and midnight last night?' suggested Caleb.

Silas nodded, and seemed a little pre-occupied as he studied the body. Pulling a slight face, and biting his bottom lip, he knelt closer to the body and pulled gently at the scarf. 'I'm not taking it off,' he reassured the policemen, and continued with his examinations.

'I can't be certain until I've carried out an autopsy,' he said at last. 'But I have a feeling our Mr Lake was dead before this scarf was tied round his neck. I'll get Thomas to confirm my suspicions.'

John took Caleb on one side. 'Go to the *Warwick Arms* and search Lake's room. I don't think for a minute you'll find anything, but a part of his report is missing, and there's just a chance it might still be in his room. I'll join you there.'

As Caleb left, Lawrence Perkins arrived with his camera and began to take photographs of the body. Two other policemen arrived, and they set about interviewing the men who had found Cornelius. Meanwhile, Silas arranged for the dead man to be removed to the hospital.

As Silas went to follow the body, which was already being escorted to the hospital, John caught his sleeve. 'In view of your knowing Cornelius Lake, it would be better if you did not carry out the autopsy,' he said quietly.

'Don't you trust me?' flared Silas.

'I must look at this from a prosecution point of view, and I have to present unbiased evidence. The fact that you knew him and were interviewed by him during a murder enquiry, could cast doubt on your evidence. And that, coupled with the fact his death is linked to Lottie Goodwin's murder, and I suspect your scarf, and it is your scarf, was used in both, would give the defence unlimited ammunition.' John paused.

'As for trusting you, God knows I want to. After all you are my son: my only son. But there's a lot we have to talk about, and the sooner the better.'

They arranged to meet at the police station later that day. Silas left to attend to his surgery and John went to the *Warwick Arms*. He went straight up to Lake's room, where Caleb waited for him.

The room was a mess, and had clearly been ransacked.

'It's just as you thought, Guv'nor,' said Caleb.

'We're missing something obvious here,' muttered John. He went on to explain about Cornelius's report, and the missing pages. However, he made no mention of how Silas figured in the report.

'And to think, I was only here last night, on my way to see him.' John paused as he remembered being intercepted by Mordeccai, whom he had never ever seen in the *Warwick Arms*, or any other hostelry in the town. Had Mordeccai deliberately stopped him from going up to Lake's room, because he knew it was being searched? Or had he genuinely just happened to have been there?

It was just too coincidental. And he did not believe in coincidences. He had to admit, however, there was just a slight chance he had misjudged the man, and was letting his personal feelings affect his judgement. Just for the moment he decided to keep those suspicions to himself. But the more he thought about them, the more convinced he became that Mordeccai had to be involved somehow or another.

'Guv'nor,' asked Caleb, interrupting his thoughts. 'If you were making enquiries in another place, say another country even, would you go straight to the local law when you arrived?'

'Possibly. But then again, probably not, especially if I thought there was the slightest chance they were not to...be...trusted.' John spoke the last few words slowly, as he remembered how Cornelius had tested him.

'No, I probably wouldn't,' he replied more forcefully. 'I would want to make many of my own enquiries first, and only go to the local law when I had to, or when I was fairly certain they were honest. It's a good point. But where does it get us? We know he only booked in here the night before he came to see me. Oh!' John slapped his head.

'I'm not thinking. He would have stayed elsewhere, probably in Leamington. Get over there and check out all the hotels and inns. Lawrence will give you his picture, when it has been developed. I don't know for sure what you are looking for, but I suspect it could be the missing pages of the report.'

Caleb saluted and went to leave the room. Then he stopped. 'I'm the one forgetting now. The proprietor here knows about Lake's death, and he wants to speak to you about a guest who went off without paying.'

John raised his eyes. 'Can't you get one of the duty constables to see him?'

'Sorry, guv'nor: I'm not making myself clear. His guest vanished the same night the late Mr Lake seems to have disappeared.' Caleb grinned.

'Thanks Caleb,' John grinned back.

Thirty minutes later, John had spoken to the hotel's proprietor, shared a pot of tea with him, and was now sat opposite a clearly nervous Tom Benson, the night porter.

'Tell me, Tom,' he said quietly. 'How much did this missing guest, what was his name? Oh yes, a Mr Davis, how much did he pay you?'

Tom Benson looked around nervously, licking his lips. Already a sheen of sweat had broken out on his forehead. 'I don't know what you're talking about,' he muttered.

'That's a pity,' replied John as he leaned forward. His steel blue eyes bored straight into Benson's face. 'That's a pity,' he repeated icily. 'Because that means I will have to arrest you for being an accessory to murder. Come on, let's go!' He stood up and reached across to Benson.

'Oh no!' wailed the other man. 'If I tell you, will you promise not to tell him?' He indicated the hotel owner's office with his thumb.

'I make no promises. You answer my questions then I will decide, and not before. Alternatively you can take your chances with a jury at the Assizes. It's your choice.'

Reluctantly, Benson told him about how he had been paid to keep out of the way, by the missing guest. 'He told me it was so he could take a woman upstairs. It was the second time that night I'd been asked to do it.'

'You were asked to keep out of the way by somebody else?'

'Yes, by that American man. I actually saw him take the first woman upstairs, but she didn't stay too long.'

'Who was she?'

'I don't know, as I didn't see her face. But she's a regular round the town, one of the ladies of the night, if you know what I mean.'

John quickly took a statement from him, which included a fairly full description of the back view of the woman who had been visiting Lake. It also included a description of *Mr Davis,* which was not very helpful. He would have to see if Lucy Perkins could come up with some sort of picture, based on the description.

On his way back to the police station, John called on Thomas. As he had expected, Thomas was preparing to go and visit some patients, having just finished his surgery. He would start Lake's autopsy on his return, although he was a little concerned as to why John did not want Silas to do it.

Thomas had been the very first person to befriend John, when he had first arrived in Warwick, in late 1840. Consequently John had no secrets from him, and told him about Lake's connections with Silas.

'If you want my opinion,' said Thomas thoughtfully, after John had finished. 'Whilst I can understand the difficult position you are in, I really do believe you have nothing to worry about. Silas is an excellent doctor and he is totally dedicated to the relief of suffering. I just cannot see him inflicting such horrific injuries on anyone.'

'Speaking as a doctor, is it possible his war experiences might have affected him?'

'It has to be a possibility.' Thomas pulled at his chin. 'But, speaking as a doctor, in his case, I think it's highly unlikely.'

John felt relieved. 'One last question, if I may? Do you know where Silas was last night?'

'I'm afraid not,' Thomas shook his head. 'I believe he is seeing a young lady. Possibly Sarah knows who she is, but I don't. You'll have to ask her when she comes back from London at the end of the week.'

It was not the answer he had wanted to hear.

Not for the first time, he began to feel old, and he missed Harriet dreadfully. Perhaps it was time for him to consider retiring. It might be a good time to think about marrying Madeleine. She seemed keen enough, and then he could devote the rest of his life working with her. The problem was her brother came too.

That was not something he fancied.

And, he argued to himself, how could he possibly go and leave these murders unsolved, to say nothing of Laura's killing, which still haunted him? He owed her that at the very least. Also he argued, could he really go, without discovering just how involved Silas was in this affair? John just hoped and prayed that he was wrong about Silas, and that the boy was innocent. With luck, he thought, that side of the problem should soon be resolved.

It was just after 2.30 p.m. when Silas arrived at the police station.

Unbeknown to him, there was a speaking tube in John's office, which connected it to where Robert worked. Robert was now sat with numerous pens, pencils and paper. His job was to record the main points of the coming interview. He had already placed a large **DO NOT DISTURB** notice on the other side of his office door.

Over the years he had developed his own form of shorthand, which was unintelligible to anyone else. However, it ensured he did not lose too much of any interview he was recording.

Meanwhile, in Leamington, Caleb was having more success than he had anticipated. The proprietor at the second hotel he visited, Mrs Lydia Janaway, thought she recognised Lake's description. Caleb had not waited for Lawrence to develop his photographs.

'Is he an American?' she asked.

Caleb confirmed he was.

'He's definitely staying here. He came about ten days ago, and paid for the full month. I haven't seen him for a few days, but he did say he would be out a lot and I wasn't to worry if he didn't come back for a few days. He seemed such a nice man. What's he done?'

'Can I see his room please?' he asked, ignoring her question.

'Oh, I don't know about that. What's he done?'

'I'm sorry, Mrs Janaway, but he has been murdered.'

'My poor, poor Cornelius,' she muttered and began to cry.

A few minutes later, Caleb was in Lake's bedroom. It was very clean, complete with some fresh flowers in a vase, on the washstand. The room was a complete contrast to the ransacked one he had recently left in the *Warwick Arms*. He had rightly guessed Lydia Janaway was more than Lake's landlady.

Caleb started his search on the right-hand side of the door, and worked his way around the room. When he reached the wardrobe, he went through all the clothes hanging in it, paying particular attention to their pockets.

When they revealed nothing, Caleb felt all round the linings and collars, but still he found nothing. He treated the clothes in the chest of drawers to a similar search, but still he found nothing. Next he took out each of the drawers, and looked underneath them, but there was nothing attached anywhere.

Pulling back the carpet, he checked for loose or recently moved floorboards, but they also revealed nothing. Finally, he pulled back the bedclothes and felt all round, and under the pillows and mattress, but still found nothing. He had paid particular attention to the mattress, but there were no signs of it having been recently repaired.

The guv'nor had given him a good idea of what to look for, mainly some papers missing from a report. Perhaps they had been found back at the *Warwick Arms*, by whoever had ransacked the room, but he did not really think so. They had to be here in this room: but where were they? Caleb tried to put himself in Lake's shoes and think where he would hide such papers.

He stood holding on to the iron rails at the foot of the bed. All the places where he had just searched, were obvious. They would be where an experienced searcher would look first. So, Cornelius must have found somewhere less obvious. That could mean him having to break up the furniture and, if necessary, having the floorboards lifted. If that had to be done, then it had to be done.

As Caleb was thinking, and planning what to do next, his right hand idly strayed to the brass bed knob near where he was standing.

It was loose.

On looking closer, he quickly discovered it had not been threaded, but loosely soldered on to the upright. Over time, the solder had broken, and the knob was loose. Trying not to become too excited, he removed the knob and looked into the upright.

It was hollow.

And just inside it, he saw the ends of some rolled up pieces of paper. With trembling fingers, he pulled them out, and saw at a glance how they were all fairly new. Caleb sat on the bed, spread them out beside him, and began to read.

Dr Whiting had been seen talking to Martha Maudsley, shortly before her murder. However, he has a very good and unshakeable alibi and is, therefore, eliminated from her murder. But I cannot be quite so positive about the others. My feeling is he is not involved, as such, but he was there at the times. So if it was not him, then who was it? He was last heard of, after the war, going to Europe, possibly England.

However, I have grave concerns about the organisation known as The Voluntary League of Medical Helpers, or the VLMH as they are usually called today. This was a large organisation which prided itself on helping both sides, from a medical perspective during the war. As such, they were present at most of the major battles, and many of the lesser known ones. They were certainly present at the main battles I have outlined above.

Caleb stopped reading and went back to the beginning of the paperwork, but he could not see any mention of specific battles. Obviously they must have been outlined in the earlier parts of the report, which he had not yet seen.

Like most people in England, he had been aware of the war in America, but names and dates of the battles etc, had not meant much to him. Now he regretted not having shown more interest. He read on:

The VLMH consisted of nurses and orderlies, for the most part untrained, who gave assistance to the medical services of the day. By the very nature of their work, these people would have acquired some considerable medical knowledge. With the peace, most of these groups disbanded very quickly. The VLMH was one of them.

However, I can find no trace of what happened to its members. I should also add that despite official edicts, the VLMH, headed by a Michael Concannon, steadfastly refused to record the names and details of its members.

Concannon is a man of unconfirmed origins, but with a name like that, he almost certainly had some Irish ancestors. There is no real description available of him. However, it is known he was very anti-authority and utterly ruthless. He seems to have kept very much in the shadows. Although he supplied all the nurses and orderlies, he rarely got his own hands dirty.

It has to be said the professional medical services, certainly as far as the Union Army were concerned, did not appreciate the VLMH appearing, and then vanishing just as quickly. Several instances were referred to us at the Provost's department, but as they were all volunteers, and not enlisted people, they were not subject to military discipline, and could not be considered as deserters. Even if they had been, any attempts at prosecution without their personal details, would have been doomed to failure.

Since 1865, I have been in communication with members of the former Confederate States medical services. It would appear they had similar problems with the VLMH. After some battles, there was evidence, on both sides, of a well organised plan whereby many of the wounded were systematically robbed. The VLMH was strongly suspected of being behind it.

In more recent months, I have discovered how certain members of the Union Government, in Washington, actively encouraged the smuggling of medical supplies to the enemy, who had very little. This was in return for other much needed goods being brought back into the Union. Thus the war was prolonged, so people could make more money.

Consequently the war went on for far longer than was necessary and it cost many more lives.

Concannon and the VLMH have been identified as playing a leading role in these smuggling activities. In addition, he is thought to be responsible for the wholesale theft of medical supplies, arms, ammunition etc, which he sold to the Confederacy, and made vast profits.

Caleb stopped again, unable to believe what he was reading. How could one side in a war, supply the other with medicines etc just to keep the conflict going, all for the sake of making money? Disgusted, he read on:

As I stated before, Concannon and his gang are utterly ruthless. They are clearly a well organised crime syndicate, who will stop at nothing to get what they want. I also believe there is no crime that they will not undertake in order to make money.

It is my belief these murders were not random killings, but were committed with a specific purpose, possibly for intimidation purposes. However, I do not know how the victims were chosen. It might have been, as almost certainly in Martha's case, their being in the wrong place at the wrong time. But I cannot be sure. But with five of them being whores, plus the one now in Warwick, I feel poor Martha was not the intended victim.

I am almost certain that the murders have been committed by a member of the VLMH, probably Concannon, who has the reputation of enjoying hurting people, and that particular group has moved its operations to England, where I am now headed.

There still remains the mystery of Dr Silas Whiting. Just where does he fit into all this? It could be a coincidence he has always been not very far from the scenes of the crimes, but I do not believe in coincidences. There has to be more to it than that. Perhaps I have misjudged him, and he is the brains behind it all? But, I don't really think so.

It would have been extremely difficult for him to be absent from his duties for any length of time. No. I'm certain it is not him. But somewhere he figures in it. Meanwhile, I have separated this part of my report, from the rest, just in case something goes wrong.

Hopefully I will find the answers in Warwick.

Caleb could not resist a smile when he read about Lake's views on not believing in coincidences. How many times had they all heard John, and other policemen say something similar to them?

He finished reading the pieces of the missing report, and carefully placed them inside his tunic. Caleb made arrangements for Lake's property to be bagged up and sent across to Warwick police station. He thanked Mrs Janaway, shared a pot of tea with her, and returned to Warwick.

CHAPTER FOURTEEN

Later

When Silas had settled himself down, he looked at John. 'I don't really know where to start. But it would help me if you could explain what Cornelius Lake was doing here in Warwick, and how he came to be murdered?'

'Why he was here, is one thing, and I don't know why he was murdered. However, I suspect it has a lot to do with the reason he was here. And somehow, you fit into this story. But I don't know where. Perhaps you could start with how you knew Cornelius Lake?'

'It was after Gettysburg when he came to see me. Apparently a young woman had been brutally murdered. He came to me because she had been seen talking to me shortly before she was murdered.' He shrugged. 'That's all I know.'

'Did he tell you how she'd been murdered?'

'No. And, to be honest, I wasn't particularly interested.'

'You sound rather nonchalant about it. A young woman, who you had been talking to, was murdered and you weren't even curious as to how she had died?' John sounded incredulous.

Silas gave a big sigh. 'You were once in the army. Did you ever fight?'

'Sometimes: mainly against local tribesmen.'

'And what sort of casualties did you receive? Thousands? Hundreds? How many?'

'I suppose a few dozen throughout the years I was in India. We lost many more through disease.'

'Have you any idea just how many casualties there were at Gettysburg?'

John thought about making a guess, realising just how little he knew about his son's war. 'I've really no idea. Several hundred I would expect.'

'Let me tell you. If you include the several thousands who were never seen again, then there were over fifty thousand casualties in that battle alone. Over fifty thousand! Many of them died in the field hospital where I was operating.'

John was lost for words.

'And that was during a period of three days. Nearly half of them were from the Union Army, in which I served. Not that we treated just our own soldiers. We treated them all.'

'I really had no idea.' John was appalled at such casualty rates.

'So if you think I was particularly, or even remotely interested in another death…' Silas's voice tailed off.

'I …I…don't know what to say. We knew there was a war going on over there, but somehow the casualty figures meant very little.'

But Silas continued remorselessly. 'During those three days, none of us in the field hospitals slept. If we were lucky, and whilst waiting for the next ambulance, there might be a chance of a quick coffee. If you had to piss, there was a bucket in the tent. If you needed something else, you went to the latrines, where the stench was indescribably vile, and you did not hang about. Do you seriously think any of us had the energy to go off on our own killing spree?'

'Forgive me, Silas. I had no idea of the conditions you had to work in. I don't think any of us here in England had. We read the reports, but they didn't mean very much to us.'

Father and son sat in silence for a moment. John waited until Silas had regained his composure, before he continued. 'Did Lake mention any other murders?'

'Oh yes. There was one at Antietam: another at Second Bull Run: and, I remember correctly, another at Fredericksburg. But he didn't go into too much detail.'

'Why did he ask about those other battles?' John asked, although he knew the answer.

'Because I was also there.'

'What about Petersburg?'

'Ha! Yes, I was there for a few minutes, until I became one of the first casualties. A shell exploded outside our hospital tent, and I was hit by shrapnel.'

John was even more aghast. He had not even known his son had been wounded. What sort of father was he? Even as he absorbed that news, Silas stood up, and took off his coat, waistcoat and shirt. Turning away from John, he displayed a long series of jagged scars which ran diagonally up his back from his right hip to left shoulder.

'Luckily I was bending over a patient. Only seconds earlier, when I had been standing, it would have killed me. As it was, I was hospitalised for nearly six months. I should have gone on to Appomattox, but I was still in hospital then, or on light medical duties. In fact, I never returned to active service again. By the time I was classed as being completely fit, it was all over, thank God.'

'According to Lake's notes, you were shown as being at Petersburg and Appomattox, when the other murders were committed?'

'Quite possibly. Commanders often employed useless and totally ineffectual clerks. Many of them were crooked. By falsifying the actual muster of personnel, they made money.'

John waited whilst Silas put his clothes back on, before resuming.

'Did you ever come across the *Voluntary League of Medical Helpers*?'

'Those bastards!' spat Silas, his face going white with genuine fury. 'Those evil parasitic bastards! Whoever let them loose in the Medical Corps, should be put up against a wall and shot. And, I'll gladly be the first one to volunteer to pull the trigger.'

John had never seen Silas look so angry.

'Do you know what they did? They terrorised young nurses and even doctors, like me, into stealing medicines for them. Then they smuggled them into the South, in return for cotton and other commodities such as tobacco. And it was all done with Government approval. It prolonged the war and the suffering.' Silas paused.

'You say they terrorised their victims?'

'If they had families, then *'accidents'* would happen to them. Or, they were attacked. So most of them gave in, and did as they were told. Some of us, me included, banded together and we resisted them. It was quite successful, and we had mama's full support.'

'What about Katherine?' John asked, with a cold knot of fear forming in his stomach.

'Oh they tried, but she was too powerful for them. She had too many friends in high places, and her own bodyguards.' He smiled. 'As you should know, mama is a strong minded woman, and a very formidable enemy, as they soon discovered.'

John felt a wave of relief flow over him. Yet he was not surprised, knowing Katherine as he did.

Silas opened the case he had brought in with him, and pulled out some papers, which he handed to John.

'This is my service record, including the dates of my wounding and discharge. I can assure you they're genuine.' John was relieved to see his son's eyes twinkle. 'Am I still a suspect?'

'I think probably not as far as those murders are concerned. But we need to talk about your scarf and Lottie Goodwin.'

There was a pause as Silas gathered his thoughts, and he stopped thinking about his military days. 'I met her soon after I first came to Warwick. Shall we say she attended to certain of my sexual needs.' Silas held his hands up, before his father could protest. 'Of course I made sure she was clean. I'm not that stupid, and after all I am a doctor!'

'Were you the man she was seeing regularly in town?'

'I suppose I was. But it wasn't all sexual. I was finding that elsewhere, and not having to pay for it.' His face had such a mischievous grin, that John could not help but smile. 'However, I quite liked Lottie and knew she wanted to better herself. So I was teaching her to read and write.'

'Was she with you the night she died?'

'Yes. She can't have long been gone. There was a chill in the air and so I lent her my scarf. I never saw it again until this morning tied round Cornelius Lake's throat.'

'Did you know a piece of the scarf had been found in Lottie's hand?'

'Not really. I was spending a lot of time with Harriet, and was concerned for you. Thomas mentioned something about some material, but that was it. I didn't even see poor Lottie's body.'

'Oh Silas! Why didn't you tell me this before?'

'I don't really know. I suppose part of me was worried about what you would think. I was going with a whore. Mama always said you were a very thorough policeman, and I suppose I was worried you'd think I was responsible for Lottie's death. The longer I left it, the harder it became to talk about, until now. I'm sorry.'

'Just one last question. Where were you last night?'

Silas hesitated. 'With Caroline Moore, in Church Street. She'll vouch for me not having left her side all night.'

Both men laughed. The tension between them had gone.

After Silas had left the police station, Robert came in to see John, and handed him the notes he had made of the interview.

'What do you think?'

'I know he's your son, but I believed every word he said.'

'Thank you. So did I,' John shook his head. 'I never realised what a hard time he'd had in the war, and that he had been wounded.'

Robert left him with a mug of tea to think over the interview. But he was not to be left alone for very long.

His first interruption came from Thomas.

'I was just passing and thought I'd tell you myself. I've just done the autopsy on Lake, and guess what killed him?'

'He was strangled? He was drowned? I don't know. You're the doctor, so you tell me,' John bantered.

'Neither. He had a massive heart attack, probably whilst being tortured. His heart was not very good, and it could have happened anytime.'

John recalled how Lake had complained of pains in his chest. 'That being the case, then why did his torturers tie the scarf round his neck?'

'I don't know. You're the policeman, so you tell me.'

They both laughed, and John told Thomas about the interview he had just had with Silas.

'I'm delighted, for both your sakes.'

His second interruption was the arrival of Caleb, who had a large grin on his face as he handed over the missing parts of the report. John read them, and he was relieved to find how they agreed with his own feelings.

'I think we'll call it a day,' he said looking out of the window. It was dark, and the sky had looked full of rain or even snow, for most of the day. 'We'll have a conference at 9.0 o'clock tomorrow morning. Can you let the others know, please?'

Caleb left, and John went across to his safe and opened it. He put the missing parts of the report in it, and closed the door. As he was just about to lock it, John had second thoughts. Cornelius had seen fit to keep them apart, so perhaps he should do the same.

Quickly he re-opened the safe, and removed the missing parts of the report, which he put into his case. Then he closed the door and re-locked it. The main body of the report was important, but the missing pieces were more so. As an afterthought, he put Robert's shorthand notes into the case as well. After turning off the gaslight, he locked his office and went off duty.

There was a decided spring in his step as he walked home. So far the day had ended much better than it had started. Silas had been effectively cleared. And he felt they were making progress, although he couldn't say how.

They now knew who Lottie's mystery man was. The piece of cloth in her hand had come from the same scarf tied around Lake's throat. It had belonged to Silas.

Yet, Lake had already been dead when the scarf had been tied. Surely the killer must have known that? And, if so, why did he do it? By doing so, the killer had linked Lottie's and Lake's murders together, and now the American ones were firmly linked to Warwick.

The obvious interpretation was that the same person had committed all the murders. The fact Lottie had been wearing the scarf, and not her killer, meant one thing. Her killer had wanted to put the blame onto Silas. Likewise, the same killer had wanted to blame Silas for murdering Cornelius.

But why blame Silas?

Obviously he was the common thread throughout. But why him? Was it because he was too honest, and would not agree to supply the *VLMH* with stolen drugs? He had the feeling the murderer had just made a very big mistake, by planting Silas's scarf on Cornelius's body.

It was clumsy and almost smacked of desperation. Surely the killer must have realised it would not take long for the real cause of Cornelius's death to be discovered.

The answer had to lie somewhere with Silas. And why did this all happen soon after Silas had arrived in Warwick?

The more he thought about it, the more he knew this would be one of the topics to be discussed on the morrow. He was convinced that somehow, Mordeccai was involved. Yet, even if he was right, he had no evidence to substantiate his suspicions: just a feeling he was on the right track. He had experienced similar feelings before in his career, and he had never been wrong.

John had another reason for feeling good. He was going to enjoy a quiet and intimate supper with Madeleine, in her garden summerhouse. There would just be the two of them.

But first he had to hide the pages from Cornelius's report. There was only one place, and that was in his study. The room was lined with oak panels, one of which opened, when a secret switch was operated. Only he and Harriet had known about it. None of the servants knew there was a safe hidden in the wall, let alone how to open the panel.

After having hidden the papers in the safe, alongside Katherine's letter, John bathed and dressed for his forthcoming date. An hour later, he had crossed his back garden, gone into the churchyard, and then into Madeleine's back garden. By now it was snowing heavily, and he was grateful when she opened the summerhouse door, and ushered him inside.

Not having bothered with a coat for the short distance, he was glad to move straight across to the blazing log fire, and warm himself. For a while they talked about how his day had been. She had heard about Lake's murder and wanted to know how his enquiries were going. He told her about Lake's room being ransacked, but said nothing about the Leamington connection. John always believed in not giving too much information away to another person, although he had always made an exception where Harriet was concerned.

It was not that he did not trust Madeleine, because he did. But, as yet, they did not have the same relationship he had enjoyed with Harriet. He was confident it would come, and hopefully sooner rather than later. For the same reason, he did not tell her about Silas. And there was the problem of Mordeccai, which would have to be resolved first.

Although the man had gone through the motions of wanting to make friends, John's policeman's instincts were telling him differently. There was something about the man he found hard to believe, or even like.

After they had eaten, John and Madeleine sat together on the floor, on cushions, in front of the fire. 'I hear you met Mordeccai last night,' she said after a while.

'Yes. We had a drink together.'

'I'm so glad, my love,' Madeleine put her hand on John's arm. 'He's my only brother, and it's important to me that you two get on well together. You both mean a lot to me.'

'You mean a lot to me, as well,' John's reply was husky.

'Oh John!' She flung her arms around his neck and pulled him close to her.

They kissed, each tasting the wine still lingering on each other's lips. Then his hands were on her breasts. At the same time she began to pull his shirt out of his trousers. His fingers began to undo the buttons on her blouse. Soon they were both naked, studying each other's bodies, and liking what they saw.

'Make love to me, dearest John,' she breathed, almost inaudibly.

He moved towards her.

But, at the same time he suddenly thought of Harriet, and it was as if she was in the room watching them, and disapproving of what was happening. Immediately, his sexual urge subsided.

'I'm so, so, sorry,' he said weakly. 'It's not that I don't want to make love to you. I really do. It's just...' His voice tailed away.

'It's all right, my love. I fully understand. It will come back, I promise you. Don't forget, I've been there too.'

For a while she held him, but she was unable to rouse him again. Finally as the fire began to die down, they dressed. After drinking a glass of port together, John made his farewells and left.

He was so pre-occupied in his own thoughts about what had happened, that he failed to notice another set of footprints, which the now lightly falling snow had failed to cover.   These footprints led from her house to the summerhouse, and then back again.

Neither he nor Madeleine had seen Mordeccai's hate filled face looking at them through the window.

Constable Edward Chadwick, usually known as Eddy, was grateful for having been given station duty that evening.   There were two drunken prisoners snoring in the cells, and he had won gaoler duty for the rest of the night.   Normally he would have objected, but when it was snowy and cold, like tonight, he was happy to be inside.

Believing in the principle that a good policeman never got wet, he had been looking forward to spending time and drinking tea with Lily, a maid in a nearby house.   He had just sat down in the kitchen, by the fire, waiting for the kettle to boil, when there had been a gentle knocking at the kitchen window.

Lily had drawn back the curtain, and Eddy was horrified to see Sam Perkins standing outside in the snow.   The sergeant beckoned him with his right forefinger, and Eddy had no option but to obey.

On the way back to the station, Sam had given him his instructions about looking after the prisoners.   He made no mention of Lily.   But that was typical of him.   As long as you did your duty, were honest and worked hard, he would turn a blind eye to tea stops.   But it was a different matter if you were lazy or dishonest.   Then he would make your life such a misery, it was easier to leave the force.

St Mary's struck 2 a.m. as the sergeant left, and Eddy went to heat up the kettle.   Moments later, he heard the station door open, and thinking Sam had forgotten something, went to greet him, with a smile on his face.

The smile faded, as he found himself in the presence of three men, each dressed in dark clothing, and with scarves pulled over the bottom parts of their faces.   One of them pointed a revolver at him.

'The keys!' he ordered.

'Now look…' Eddy started to object, but he broke off as the man pushed the revolver closer into his face.

'The keys!' He repeated, and cocked the revolver.

Eddy gulped, and reached for the bunch of keys hanging at his waist, and laid them on the desk.

'Mayfield's?' The man said very few words. With the revolver, he did not need to.

Eddy licked his now very dry lips, and pointed to John's office key.

'Cells?'

Eddy showed him.

One of the other men took the cell key, and motioned Eddy to follow him. He did so reluctantly. The man opened the cell door, and indicated Eddy to enter, which he did. Suddenly Eddy felt a hard knock on the back of his head, and he collapsed unconscious onto the floor.

The man quickly locked the cell door and rejoined the other two. Swiftly they opened John's office door, and lit the gas light. A few seconds later, one of them opened up his bag and removed a tube measuring about eight inches long, and one inch in diameter. He tied it to the safe door handle.

It was a stick of the new substance known as dynamite, which had only been invented the previous year. To this he attached a length of fuse, which he fed out into the passageway.

Whilst he was doing this, the other two men forced open and emptied the drawers from John's desk, and his filing cabinet. They quickly sorted through the papers. As they finished looking through the papers, they brushed them onto the floor.

'Not here,' said one of them, when they failed to find Lake's report.

'Out!' instructed the man with the fuse, which he now lit.

They left the office quickly, as the spluttering fuse hissed towards the safe. Several seconds later, the dynamite blew open the front of John's safe, which they quickly ransacked. Finding Cornelius Lake's report, one of them bundled it into a bag. Other documents, both in the safe and around the office were left smouldering where they lay.

They left the police station without any further delay.

John was dreaming. Or, to be more accurate, he was having a nightmare.

He had gone to bed thinking of so many things, which all stemmed from Cornelius Lake's murder, and his interview with Silas. Surprisingly, his failure with Madeleine did not appear in it. Yet, he was sure Harriet did not approve of their liaison, which was why he had failed. He hoped her memory would not get in the way of his growing fondness for Madeleine.

In his nightmare, John was fighting in the Union Army, when he had been wounded, and taken back to Gettysburg. Here he was being treated by a grinning Cornelius Lake who wanted to cut both his legs off, without any anaesthetic. Silas stood alongside him, grinning evilly and holding a rusty saw.

All around him, he could hear the sounds of battle in the background. Suddenly there came the sound of a large explosion.

Soon afterwards, John heard a bell ringing furiously. But at the same time, Cornelius Lake was having him tied down on the operating table, whilst Silas put the saw to his legs.

'Mr Mayfield! Mr Mayfield!' a voice was calling urgently.

John slowly woke up as his bedroom door opened as his duty footman, and Sam Perkins came in. He could tell by the look on Sam's face that there was a big problem.

Whilst John dressed, Sam told him about the police station being attacked. He noticed the footman was in no hurry to get back to bed. The news would soon be all round the house.

Several minutes later, John arrived at the police station with Sam. Even at this early hour, he was not surprised to see a small crowd of people gathered around the town's fire engine, watching. The firemen let him into the station. On the way he passed Silas who was attending to Eddy Chadwick, who was not too badly hurt. The two drunks had slept through the explosion, without waking.

John's office was a mess, and there would be no more sleep for him that night.

CHAPTER FIFTEEN

Later

By the time the early morning constables came on duty, John had managed to sort through most of the papers lying around his office. Some were partially burned, and others had been damaged by the water thrown or pumped onto the fire, by the firemen. By the time he had finished, John was not all surprised to discover Cornelius Lake's report was missing, although he could not say whether it had been stolen or destroyed.

Whilst the missing pages were safe, on reflection, he thought, perhaps it would have been better if he had put the whole report in with them. On the other hand, the fact the missing pages were not with the report, might just put the murderers off their guard. After interviewing Eddy Chadwick, he now knew they were up against more than one person.

The fire brigade lieutenant had recently seen a demonstration of the new dynamite, and he clearly recognised its effects in John's office. Being such a new commodity, it was not yet generally available, so whoever had used it on John's safe had influential contacts.

This meant it was unlikely to have been used by any run-of-the-mill felons, and would have been used by people who already had it in their possession. There had not been enough time from Lake's disappearance and death for any outside gang to have been brought in. They had to be in the area already.

John's first visitor was Madeleine.

'I've only just heard? Are you all right?'

'I am, but not my office.'

He took her to see it, and her eyes widened in shock as she saw the damage, especially what was left of his safe.

'What was in there that was so important?' she asked.

'Only some papers, and a large file which the unfortunate Mr Lake gave me. And that's gone'

'Did you have a copy?'

'No,' John shook his head. 'But whoever took it will be disappointed. It's not complete. There are some pages missing. I had been going to ask him where they were, but he was killed before I could speak to him.'

Further conversation was prevented by the arrival of Thomas Waldren, Lawrence Perkins with his camera and other members of the Watch Committee, who had come to inspect the damage. Madeleine made her excuses and left. Although it was Sunday morning, they were soon joined by three builders, and a reporter from the *Warwick Chronicle*.

The builders started taking measurements, and generally got in each other's way. But the Watch Committee had insisted on having three different quotations, both for the cost of the repairs, and who could carry them out the quickest. After a while John left them to it, and moved into the charge office.

Although he still wanted to have his meeting, it had been impossible during the day, with so many people wandering around. It was late afternoon before they all left, and the police station was back in some semblance of order. Taking out his watch, John studied it for a moment.

'Right!' he announced. 'We'll meet at my house in thirty minutes time, and you'll all stay for supper. It's high time I started entertaining again.'

Jessie Brampton was unsure of what to do.

Earlier that day, she had met up with Edith Dennison, who was another whore. Edith was unhappy, and she sat holding a leaflet from the *Society for the Proper Education of Fallen Women,* which she had been given by Jane Howatt. Although it was a condition not unknown amongst people in her walk of life, Edith was reluctant to admit she could not read or write.

She had heard about the *Society* and how it offered to educate fallen women, like her. The straight-faced woman, Jane Howatt, who worked for the *Society*, maintained she was too busy to read it for her. She just gave Edith a leaflet. Edith knew Jessie could read and so they sat together in the *King's Head*, in the Saltisford.

Edith gave Jessie the leaflet and asked to read it to her. Jessie did so. The leaflet gave details of the courses being run at the White House, coupled with the types of employment being offered.

'What do you think?' she asked Jessie. 'Is it worth going on one of these courses? The woman said one starts today?'

'It sounds good, almost too good,' Jessie answered cautiously.

But, if the truth were known, Jessie felt she could be tempted herself, to enrol on one of these courses. There would be no more money from Cornelius Lake, and what she had taken off him the other night, would not last long. Also, the snow had reduced her trade considerably. To be honest, she thought having sex, whilst lying in a snow drift, was not exactly ideal or remotely pleasant.

'Let's say we go together. At least we'll be out of the cold for a while, and be properly fed. Then, if we don't like it, we can always leave.'

For a while they discussed what to do, but finally agreed to join the current course being offered at the White House.

Although they knew where the house was, neither of them had been there before. Having gone through the gates, they were overawed by the front of the White House. When it had been built, its then owner, James Cooper, had ideas of becoming a Knight of the Realm, and he had the house built accordingly. Inside and out, it had been decorated and furnished to resemble a castle.

'Are you sure this is for us?' queried Edith.

'I don't know,' answered Jessie. 'Let's go back?'

Before Edith could reply, the front door was opened and Mordeccai Carew stood in the threshold.

'Don't be shy, girls,' boomed his deep voice. As he spoke, Mordeccai studied them intently, with his deep set intense eyes. 'Come on in. A new life awaits you here. Forget your old whoring days. They're over.'

Neither Jessie nor Edith could turn away from his eyes. There was something hypnotic about them. They seemed to resemble dark limpid pools, into which the two women felt they were falling.

Mordeccai beckoned them, and they walked into the White House. Jessie was the first to recover.

'I think this is a mistake,' she said.

'It's your choice entirely,' smiled Mordeccai, yet she saw there was no warmth in his smile, and his eyes did not change. 'But it would be a mistake to leave without having seen what we have to offer first.' He indicated the interior of the house, with his right hand. 'Then if you don't like what you see, you can go. Is that fair?'

They agreed, and followed him towards the rear of the house.

For the next hour, they were given a conducted tour of the house by Jane Howatt. She was a taciturn woman who said very little.

'Our lessons are taken very seriously,' she explained. 'So if you have the slightest doubts, then I urge you to go. Once you agree to start, it will be too late for you to leave. I urge you to think very carefully about staying.'

'What do you mean, it will be too late?' queried Jessie. 'Are you trying to get us to go now?'

'Of course not!' boomed Mordeccai who had suddenly reappeared. 'Mrs Howatt is merely trying to help you make up your minds. You see, it costs money to run these courses, and we only want people who are keen to stay. We are not in the market of providing free board and lodging.' He glowered at Mrs Howatt. 'I'll complete the tour. You can go.'

He showed them the kitchens and the classrooms, where there seemed to be a hive of activity going on. Yet Jessie noticed how lifeless some of the women looked. Whenever she tried to ask Mordeccai about them, he changed the subject. As the visit progressed, Jessie found herself becoming more uneasy. But Edith seemed to be enthralled by the whole venture.

'Well now,' said Mordeccai, at the end of the tour. 'Do you have any questions?'

'Yes,' replied Jessie. 'Why are there so many men in and around the house?' She had noticed there was a man in each of the classrooms and the kitchens. Also, she had seen several wandering around outside.

'That is a fair question. Just think about it. They're here for your protection. There are quite a few women in this house, many of whom have the reputation of being whores, or others of easy virtue. Do you think the local men don't know about you all being here? My men are here for your protection. They patrol the grounds, day and night. As you know, we are quite isolated here.'

Jessie had to accept that answer, although she was not entirely convinced. She had seen the eager way some of the men had looked at her.

Mordeccai then left them on their own for a few minutes.

'What do you think?' asked Edith.

'I think we should go. That man gives me the creeps. And I didn't like the way his guards were looking at us.'

'But that's what we do. We get men to look at us. It's our job.'

Jessie could not fault her argument. Further conversation was stopped as Madeleine Pascoe came into the room, with Mordeccai. He introduced her as his sister.

Madeleine outlined the course programme for them. The course would last for four weeks, during which time they would receive intensive lessons, in their chosen subject. Those who could read and write already had an advantage. Otherwise it meant extra lessons for those who could not.

Once the basics of reading and writing had been mastered, there was a choice of learning cookery, needlework or housework.

'The idea,' explained Madeleine, 'is for you all to leave here with enough skills to get a proper job.' She paused. 'And with our contacts, we can put you straight in touch with employment agencies. You are guaranteed a job.'

Jessie began to relax. She had seen Madeleine in Warwick, and quite often in the company of Superintendent Mayfield. And she was much friendlier than her brother. Perhaps this course would be a good thing. She glanced at Edith, and saw her friend was convinced.

'What do you think?' asked Madeleine. 'Are you going to come and join us?'

Back at John's house, his long delayed meeting got underway. With him were Mathew, Sam, Caleb and Robert. Firstly he assured them the missing pages from the report were safe, but would not say where they had been hidden. He produced them for the others to read.

When they had read the papers, John asked for their views.

'I hate to say it,' said Mathew. 'But how does Silas fit into all this?'

'Let me answer that one,' replied Robert. 'Yesterday afternoon, John interviewed him at length, whilst I sat the other side of the tube, and recorded everything that was said. To be honest with you all, I totally believed Silas. Whilst Lake suspected him initially, he more or less changed his mind.'

'It seems some of the information he was given about my son's whereabouts were false. I did not even know he had been wounded in May 1864, at a place called Petersburg, I think they called it. He was hospitalised, and never saw any more active service. I saw his scars. He's lucky to be alive.'

'And,' continued Robert. 'That being the case, he could not have been at the other murders. It appears some clerk had added his name to the muster roll, to claim his wages. Lake suspected him, initially, because he believed Silas was at all the murder scenes, when in fact, he wasn't.'

John was relieved to see the others relax.

'I think we can eliminate Silas from those enquiries. But, he has caused us another problem. He was the man who Lottie was seeing. Not for sex: he was teaching her to read and write. And it was his scarf from which the piece of material came, that we found in his hand,' said John.

There was a sharp intake of breath from Mathew, Sam and Caleb. There was no reaction from Robert.

'And,' John continued. 'It was the rest of his scarf which had been tied round Lake's throat, to make it look like he had been strangled.' He paused. 'Let me return to that in a moment. Robert.'

The other man took up the story. 'Silas has a watertight alibi for the night of Lake's murder. He spent it with a lady. And I've checked it out.'

They chuckled, glad Silas was no longer considered to be a suspect. Regardless of him being John's son, he was universally liked, and well respected as a doctor.

'To return to Lake's death,' John said. 'He was not strangled. There was no doubt he had been tied up and tortured, but he actually died of a heart attack, albeit probably brought on by what was happening to him.'

'But surely his…his interrogators would have realised that?' Mathew was the first to recover.

'Exactly. Which begs the question, why did they use Silas's scarf to make it seem like he had been strangled? They must have known we would soon see through the deception?'

'It seems to me,' said Sam. 'They wanted to link the two deaths, but why?'

'John,' Caleb spoke for the first time. 'Whether we like it or not, Silas is the common factor throughout all these deaths, both here and in America. I wonder why they, whoever they are, want him to take the blame.'

'Could it be because of his stance against the *VLMH*?' asked Robert.

He explained about the *Voluntary League of Medical Helpers*: how Silas had stood up to them, and how Katherine had been involved. They all knew of John's relationship with her, and had not been at all surprised to discover she was Silas's mother.

'What better way to take revenge than by having her son executed for murder?' Robert continued.

Silence greeted his observations, but they all nodded their heads in agreement.

'Take Lake's report,' Caleb resumed. 'Why were they so desperate to get it, that they blew up part of the station?'

'But it's not that report they wanted,' said Mathew. 'They wanted the missing pages.'

'Let's assume they ransacked Lake's room at the *Warwick Arms*, and found the other copy,' Sam mused. 'Only it wasn't complete, was it? So they tortured him to discover where the remaining pages were hidden.'

'And let's just say he named you as having the report. After all he was being tortured,' stressed Caleb. 'Hence why they blew up your office, and took the copy report.'

'Now, the question is whether or not they believe you never had the other pages,' added Sam.

'I think that it would be a good idea if I copied these missing pages, and we each have a copy,' said Robert.

'A good idea. Do it, Robert, please,' said John. 'Then, I'll get you to write to the American Embassy, in London, and tell them about Lake's death. No, wait a minute. Go to London yourself and see them. And whilst you're at it, ask them about the *VLMH*. I asked Mordeccai about them the other night, but he maintained he had only heard of them, and knew nothing else. But I find that hard to believe, in view of his comments about supplying medical aid during the war.'

'I know how you're getting on very well with Madeleine, but there's just something about her brother, that's not right,' said Mathew.

The others agreed.

'I know,' replied John, thoughtfully. 'Have you had any luck checking on his background, Robert?'

'No, and that's odd. I can discover absolutely nothing about him. Can't you persuade Madeleine to tell you?'

'I've tried, but she always changes the subject. I get the impression he is an embarrassment to her, and she's not a little scared of him. But keep trying whilst in London. The Embassy might know something.'

'I've already tried, without any luck. If they do know anything, then they're certainly not telling me.'

Robert did not tell them about his forthcoming meeting with Gordon Mayne. It was not because he distrusted them, but he could see no point in doing so, until he had something to report.

Back at the White House, the new course began with an introductory talk from Mordeccai.

'As you have been told already,' he began. 'It's a very intensive course, which lasts for about four weeks, depending on your individual abilities. As long as you work hard, you'll reap the rewards. But be warned. I will not tolerate any slackness on your part. People have parted with good money for you to receive this education, and the chance of a new start in life. And I will not let them down.' He paused. 'And neither will you.'

An almost frightened silence greeted his words. They all saw he had a wild look about his eyes. Many of them began to wonder if being here was such a good idea.

'Let me explain something else,' he continued. 'You leave this building, at night, at your own risk. Dogs will be roaming around, loose, and there are man-traps set all over the grounds. They are for your safety and security, and to keep out unwanted visitors. Yes?' he asked.

One of the women had stood up. 'I don't wanna stay.'

'Feel free to go.' Mordeccai crossed the room and opened the door. They all felt the sudden draught, and saw the swirling snowflakes. 'Go now!' There was a silky menacing tone in his voice.

'But what about the dogs? It's dark. I'll go in the morning?'

'You'll go now or not at all.'

She sat down and stayed. Mordeccai closed the door.

'Now, if all the interruptions have finished,' he continued. 'All those of you who are whores, go over there to Mrs Smith.' He pointed to one side of the room where a hard faced woman stood.

Mordeccai waited until she had led them all away, and locked the door behind her. 'The rest of you go to Mrs Brown.' He indicated a woman stood in another part of the room.

The other women left with her. After they had all gone, he moved to another wing of the house, where Madeleine waited.

'They're all sorted now. One tried to leave, but I put the fear of God into her. I have no doubt they will all respond well. The doc can examine them in the morning.'

Back downstairs, Edith and Jessie and the rest of their party were taken to a dining area, and given some food. Neither thought the food was very exciting. It was just bread, cheese and a single mug of tea.

Jessie did not feel particularly hungry, and she accidentally spilt her tea. She looked around for another, but could not find any. It was then she noticed something which gave her cause for concern.

All the other women were yawning, and starting to fall asleep. It seemed to her the food, or more likely the tea, had been drugged. Unsure of what to do, she feigned to be asleep with the others.

Several minutes later, some of the men arrived and they picked up the women, including Jessie. Through her semi-closed eyelids, she saw they were being carried along a passageway, and taken up three flights of stairs, to the top of the house. Here they were taken into a large room, which housed several beds. Every woman was laid on a bed, and left. As the last man left, Jessie heard the key turn in the lock.

She lay still for several minutes, until she was certain there were no men left in the room. Cautiously she opened her eyes and sat up.

The room was dark, with the exception of three lit oil lamps, which were set at regular intervals in the room, going away from the door, which she thought was a dangerous practice. Quietly she swung her legs over the side of the bed, tiptoed over to the door, and tried the handle. As she had expected, it was definitely locked.

Looking at the door, she saw it had a small hinged hatch cut into it. It was not really big enough to pass food through, but it served as a spy hole. Now she knew why the oil lamps were lit. Anyone outside could easily check up on the women, without having to go into the room.

Reaching up to her head, Jessie removed one of her hairpins, and inserted it into the lock. After several attempts, she managed to unlock the door. She had not lost her skills at picking locks. Keeping an ear open for the sound of any of the men returning, she went over to Edith's bed, and tried to wake her. But her friend was too heavily drugged.

Jessie knew she could, and in fact, she should now escape, but she was unwilling to leave Edith behind. She would have to wait. However, she decided to use her time profitably, and explore, which would help her plan their escape.

She slowly opened the door, and peered round it, but there was no one about. Just before leaving, she closed the door, and went back into the dormitory. Returning to her bed, Jessie moved the pillow into it, and roughed the bedclothes around it. With any luck, a casual observer would think she was still in there.

Going back to the door, she went out onto the landing. Then she closed and locked the door once more.

She tiptoed along the landing, counting off the doors she passed, and saw they all had spy holes in them. Suddenly she heard footsteps on the stairs, but knowing there was no time to get back to her room, Jessie shrank back into the shadows and waited.

Several men appeared, each one carrying a large wicker work hamper, similar to a laundry basket, complete with leather fastening straps. They opened one of the doors, and took them inside. Jessie did not dare to move, as everywhere was so quiet. The only sounds came from inside the room as the men put down their hampers.

As they came out of the room, another person arrived. She had difficulty in not gasping as she recognised the new arrival.

'Right, men,' the figure said. 'You know the system. Tomorrow is Monday; which unlike today, will not be a day of rest.'

The other men dutifully laughed.

'But instead, these ladies are going to be put through their paces, as they're going out on Friday night.'

This time there was a ripple of mutterings.

'Yes, I realise it's very soon after the last ones, who won't get to London until tomorrow night. But the arrival of this Pinkerton man is something we did not need, nor want. We don't know what he's told Mayfield, and we can't find out. It may not have been anything, but we can't afford to take any chances. So, this will be the last consignment from here, before we move on.'

'Does this mean we've got just five days to break them in?' asked one of the men.

'Yes. You'd better prepare to shag yourselves stupid, but not until tomorrow, after the doctor has been. You don't know what you might catch,' the figure warned. 'I'm hoping we'll get a very good price for them, so don't give them any permanent marks. I've got an oriental gentleman interested in increasing his harem with some white women.'

The men chuckled.

'You can bribe them if you like. The ones who obey can travel in the top baskets, and piss on those underneath them!'

They all laughed and returned downstairs.

Jessie stayed in the shadows for a long time after they had gone, petrified by what she had just heard. She and the other women were not going to receive an education. They were all going to be sold into forced prostitution, or taken abroad as white slaves.

She and Edith had to get out of here, but how could she do it? Certainly she could not go whilst Edith was still under control of the drugs. Although, she reasoned, if they were being seen tomorrow by the doctor, then the drugs would have to have worn off by then.

Knowing there was nothing else she could do until then, Jessie returned to the dormitory and tried to sleep for a while.

But sleep deserted her that night.

CHAPTER SIXTEEN

Monday

R obert had made an early start, and thanks to the improved train service, was in London by midday. His first visit was to Scotland Yard, to see his brother-in-law. However, he was informed Detective Inspector Gordon Mayne was in court, and likely to be there for most of the day.

Declining to leave either his name, or details of his business, Robert went to the American Embassy. Here it seemed that anyone of any importance was either out at lunch, or else could not be found. And anyone who was available, was far too busy to spare the time to speak to a mere clerk from some unknown provincial police force.

But Robert would not go away. He sat down and stated he would wait until someone could see him. Finally a young man appeared. He made no secret of how important and busy he was, and really resented having to come and speak to Robert.

'Well, what do ya want?' he drawled, making no secret of his resentment at having to speak to Robert. 'Are ya looking for a job back home or something?'

'No. I've come here to report the death of an American citizen in Warwick.'

'Oh yeah? He just died did he? I suppose ya gotta name for him?'

'His name was Cornelius Lake, a detective in Pinkerton's Agency. And he was tortured to death.'

All of a sudden, the clerk was no longer quite so bored, and he asked Robert to explain what had happened. He now listened and made several notes.

'Do you know who killed him?'

'No, but we suspect his death may have had something to do with the *Voluntary League of Medical Helpers,* and a series of murders you have had back home, and may be connected to one we've had in Warwick, in addition to the unfortunate Cornelius Lake.'

'Who did you say?' The clerk's voice was very low and quiet.

'*The Voluntary League of Medical Helpers.* I believe you may have heard of them.'

'Would you mind waiting here a few minutes, sir, please?'

Robert chuckled to himself as the clerk vanished, rather quickly. This interview reminded him of one he had undertaken many years ago, when the Warwick force had first started. It had been the same, bored and barely tolerant attitude towards him, until a certain name was mentioned.

Several minutes later, the clerk returned and led Robert into a small office. A well-dressed man, with a distinct military appearance, rose to greet him. Robert saw he had short grey hair and intense steel blue eyes, which totally belied his soft drawl, and reminded him of John Mayfield. The clerk left the office.

'Mr Andrew,' he began, but made no attempt to tell Robert his name. 'Would you please tell me what you just told my clerk?' Although phrased as a request, Robert recognised it as an order.

For the next few minutes, he told the unknown man about the murder of Lottie Goodwin and the subsequent arrival of Cornelius Lake, who had linked all the American murders with Lottie's death. He included the attack on the police station. The other man listened politely, until Robert had finished.

'Why do you think Mr Lake met his death in such a manner?' he asked.

'In his report, he mentions two main suspects. A Dr Silas Whiting, who coincidentally was in Warwick at the time of both Lottie's and Lake's deaths. But we are convinced of his innocence.'

'And the second suspect?'

'Lake believed he may be connected with or even part of the *Voluntary League of Medical Helpers*, who is possibly in Warwick at the moment.'

'What do you know of the *VLMH* as we call them?'

'A bit, thanks to Dr Silas Whiting and Cornelius Lake, who wrote about them in the part of his report, which we were able to save. He was very interested in a Michael Concannon, whom he believed to have been very important in the *VLMH*. They both said how dangerous and ruthless members of the *VLMH* are.'

His listener sat still and quiet for a while. At last he spoke.

'Mr Andrew, I am going to tell you something, but it comes at a price. You may not make any notes and I will not sign anything. And, if necessary, I will deny this conversation ever took place. Understood?'

Robert nodded his acceptance of the conditions. It was not an ideal arrangement and not what John wanted, but it would be better than nothing. He knew something was better than nothing, and he had a good memory.

Back at the White House, as it grew light, the women in Jessie's dormitory began to stir. None of them could remember anything of what happened the night before. As soon as she could, Jessie took Edith to one side and told her what she had discovered.

Initially Edith totally disbelieved what she was being told, but Jessie persevered.

'What do you remember about last night?'

'We had tea…and then nothing more.'

'How did you get to bed?'

'I don't…I don't remember.'

'You cannot remember being carried upstairs?'

'No.'

Slowly Edith began to realise her friend was probably telling the truth. 'What are we going to do, Jess?'

'I don't know. But there's a doctor coming some time today to examine us. I know it's usually Dr Whiting. If we tell him then I'm sure he'll find some excuse to get us away.'

'I hope you're right.'

During the course of the morning, Silas arrived and began to check the women. At last it was Jessie's turn.

'Hello Jessie,' he said with a smile. 'Fancy seeing you here? I never thought I should, but I'm sure you are doing the right thing.'

Jessie's heart sank. She had hoped to have seen the doctor on his own, but he was always accompanied by the hard faced woman known as Mrs Smith, who watched every move she made, and listened to every word she said.

Silas examined her carefully, but with Mrs Smith always hovering at his side. Jessie cursed herself for not having foreseen this possibility. Try as she might, she was unable to block Mrs Smith's view even for a few seconds. Clearly she was there, not as a chaperone, but as a wardress. Their only chance was for her to write a short note and hope Edith could give it to him.

But her hopes came to nothing as Edith was called in next to be examined.

Silas dined with Madeleine and several members of her staff, in the same dining area as the women. It was a far more cheerful meal than their tea had been the previous evening; undoubtedly because Silas was present.

After Silas had left, with Madeleine, Mrs Smith gathered the men together.

'You know what to do, lads. So get on with it!'

They all grinned lecherously and moved towards the women.

At the American Embassy, Robert waited for the man to start.

'Basically, what Lake wrote about the *VLMH*, and what Whiting told you is true. They were heavily involved with smuggling drugs through the lines to the Confederates. In return they brought back cotton and other commodities. Apparently it was all done with the blessings of the respective governments. However, Michael Concannon the leader of the *VLMH* was far too clever to do the actual work himself. He coerced others to do it for him.'

The man went on to explain how the *VLMH* existed solely for the purposes of making money. Since the war, the *VLMH* had been disbanded and was now known as the *Green Diamond Society*. The *Society* consisted of Concannon and many other extremely vicious individuals. In common with their days in the *VLMH,* there was no crime they would not commit, in order to make money.

In an attempt to be regarded as a legitimate organisation, they openly supported the Fenians in their attempts to gain independence for Ireland. Many Americans supported the Fenians, especially as a considerable number of them had emigrated there in the 1840s.

Only the previous year, the Fenians had attempted an invasion of Canada. Concannon, trading on his Irish heritage, had agreed to supply them with arms and ammunition, for a big fee. Only he never provided the goods, and went on to betray them, for another big fee. Since then, he and the *Green Diamond Society* had vanished.

It was common knowledge that the Fenians had put a very large price on his head and, it was believed, Concannon had probably gone to ground in England.

Pinkerton agents were actively involved in counter-espionage activities, and they had discovered Concannon was in communication with certain former Union high ranking officers. These men favoured a war with England, in revenge for the support they had initially given to the Confederates.

Other members of the former *VLMH* had stayed in America, where they were heavily involved in post-war speculation, particularly in land, in the former Confederate States. Some had joined the Ku Klux Klan, which had quickly become involved in promoting racial hatred and violence.

'In short,' continued the Embassy official. 'There is nothing this man Concannon and his gang, will not do to make money. They are totally ruthless. We believe he has a wife somewhere, but we know nothing else about her. She seems to have just been on the very fringes, and not too actively involved. We would love to know where he is, and so would the Fenians.'

He paused, then opened a drawer in his desk and took out a piece of paper, which he kept face down.

'What you would like to know is whether or not Concannon is the same man as your Mordeccai Carew? And if so, is he involved in all these murders? Am I correct?'

'Yes sir.'

The other man turned over the piece of paper, which was a photograph.

'If you have anyone who looks like this in your list of suspects, than I would say Warwick is where Michael Concannon is now operating.'

He handed over the photograph.

Robert turned it over, and nodded triumphantly. His suspicions had been correct. Delving into his case, he took out the picture of Mordeccai, which Lawrence Perkins had drawn for him. He placed it alongside the photograph of Michael Concannon.

There was no doubt. Michael Concannon and Mordeccai Carew were one and the same person.

'You don't need me to tell you, Mr Andrew, that you are dealing with an exceptionally dangerous man.'

Back in the White House, the screaming started.

'What shall we do?' Edith sobbed, as she clung to Jessie.

'Don't argue or fight with them. Do what they say. After all it's how we earn a living. But whatever you do, don't drink any of the tea next time you're given some. Just pretend to and I'll get...' Jessie broke off, as Edith was pulled roughly away.

During the afternoon and early evening, the screaming went on, but it slowly died down to sobbing and whimpering. Although Jessie and Edith had not resisted or fought back, they were still treated roughly. At one stage they had been tied down and given a savage beating.

When it finally ceased, night had fallen and they all had some more bread, cheese and tea. Although both would have given anything for a mouthful of tea, Edith remembered Jessie's warning and quietly spilt it, although she was still suspicious whether or not it was drugged.

Her doubts vanished as she saw the other women begin to fall asleep. So she followed Jessie's example, and let her head nod forward as she too pretended to fall asleep.

Once the women had been carried upstairs, by the men, they were bundled, unceremoniously onto their beds.

'Shagging makes me hungry,' guffawed one of the men.

'Quite a nice bit of meat amongst them though,' another chortled.

'That wasn't what I meant,' laughed the first man. 'Come on, let's go and get some grub, have a couple of drinks, get our strength back and get ready to start again tomorrow.'

Jessie waited until they had locked the door, then she listened to their footsteps fading along the landing, before she sat up. Although the other women were in a drugged sleep, it did not prevent several of them from whimpering.

'Edith!' she whispered.

Edith sat up, and quickly joined Jessie. 'You look awful,' she commented, on seeing Jessie's bruised face.

'I can't say you look so good, yourself,' grinned Jessie.

The short banter restored their confidence.

'Now we've got to get out of here,' whispered Jessie. 'Those bastards stole my hair pins, but I've got this.' She felt around in the hem of her dress and pulled out a piece of wire. 'Come on,' she called. 'But first, ruffle up those bedclothes and make it look as if we're still there. It won't fool them for long, but it might buy us a few precious seconds.'

Edith stood and gazed at the other drugged women, whilst Jessie fashioned another pick lock from the wire, she had found. Soon she had the door unlocked.

'Come on!' she instructed.

But Edith did not move.

'What about the others?' she said. 'We can't just leave them.'

'We've got no choice. Their best chance is for us to get away from here and get some help.'

'Who'll ever believe us?'

'Dr Whiting will. After all he only examined us a few hours ago, and now look at us.'

Edith was forced to agree. 'You poor cows,' she breathed. 'Hang on whilst we get some help.'

But like Jessie, she knew all their lives would be in danger until they could get to Dr Whiting.

Taking a last look at the other women, she stepped through the door, and waited. Once Jessie had relocked it, she followed her along the landing.

It was late afternoon when Robert left the American Embassy, and made his way back to Scotland Yard.

After he had identified Mordeccai Carew and Michael Concannon as being the same person, the Embassy man asked him many more questions, particularly about *The Society for the Proper Education of Fallen Women*.

'I think, Mr Andrew,' he had said. 'And please forgive me for trying to tell you, and your Mr Mayfield, how to do your jobs, but you need to take a very great interest in that particular operation. Our mutual friend, Concannon, has long been suspected of forcing girls into prostitution, and selling them abroad. What he's doing at the moment could be a perfect cover for doing just that.'

With the man's words echoing in his brain, Robert was dismayed to discover his brother-in-law was still at court. Robert gave his name, and agreed to return later. Meanwhile, he decided to go and have a look at the address which handled the leasing of the White House. He would check that out first and then send an electric telegraph message, now called a telegram, back to John. For a moment he thought about doing it then and there, but decided it could wait for just a little while longer, until he had more to report.

A cab took him to the immediate area, but not, as Robert requested, to the actual address. He was a little surprised to discover it was very close to the river, which ran at the rear of the premises. And that was not all.

Having expected to find a small office, he was even more surprised, and concerned, to find the address was a medium sized warehouse.

By now it was early evening, dark, and a fog was starting to rise from the river. He lurked, for a while, in the shadows on the other side of the road, and just watched. Once the fog had thickened even more, Robert decided it was safe to cross the road, and take a closer look at the building.

From where he had stood, Robert had already seen there was no name board anywhere on the front of the building, which aroused his suspicions. Several lights blazed away inside.

Just as he was about to cross the road, four wagons arrived at the front of the building, and one of the drivers went inside. He returned several minutes later, as a larger door, by the wagons opened, revealing a lit interior, which looked like a storeroom. Several men accompanied him. He immediately recognised one of them as being Mordeccai Carew.

They went to the first wagon, and the driver climbed up on to it, pulled back the canvas covers, and lowered the tailboard. He jumped back onto the road, and stood to one side. The first two men leant inside the wagon and pulled out a wicker basket, which Robert estimated was about the same size as a coffin.

The thought made him go cold. Were these some of the women whom Concannon was shipping abroad? He had to act quickly, and he turned round to head back to Scotland Yard.

'Not so fast, cully. Where be you going then?'

The voice came from one of two large men, who had stepped out from the shadows. In spite of the gloom, Robert saw they both carried thick cudgels, in their right hands.

They moved towards him, slapping their cudgels up and down on to their left hands. Robert looked anxiously about him, but there was nowhere for him to run.

'There's nowhere to run, cully, and no one to hear you. So what are you doing here?' said the first man, who now stood in front of Robert, whilst the other one went to stand behind him.

Robert moved backwards, but he was soon up against the wall of a building.

'I'm not going to ask you again, cully. What are you doing here?'

Robert started to act nervously.

For the most part, it was a genuine performance. He knew he was in trouble: real trouble, and did not fancy being tortured as Lake had been.

'You know how it is,' he replied nervously, licking his now very dry lips. 'I've got to make a living, and well, you know, people often leave things lying around.'

'Ah ha!' came the sarcastic reply. 'You're trying to convince us you're a thief are you? I think you're a crusher.'

Robert gave a forced laugh, and held up his left hand. 'With this?'

His questioner looked down at Robert's withered hand, and pulled at his curved fingers. There was no life in them and their flesh felt cold to his touch. Suddenly he was not quite so sure.

'Be that as it may, cully, but you've seen too much.' The first man spoke again and nodded at his companion. 'What do you think?'

'Yeah.'

Suddenly Robert felt a heavy blow on his head, and there came a roaring in his ears. He was vaguely aware of falling forwards, and then nothing more.

'What's going on?' asked Mordeccai Carew who had suddenly appeared. He nudged Robert's inert form with his foot, unable to see his face. 'Who's this? A crusher?'

'No. Just someone looking for something to steal, cheeky sod.'

'Are you sure it's not a crusher?'

'Oh yes.'

'Get rid of him,' instructed Mordeccai, pointing towards the river. He walked away without waiting for their reply.

The two men thrust the cudgels into their belts, then they reached down, and picked Robert up. They carried him across the street, went down a narrow alley to the river front, and put him down. After a quick glance around, they were satisfied no one could see them.

One of them took Robert's arms and the others his legs.

'On the count of three?' one of them suggested.

The other nodded.

They began to swing Robert's body.

'One…two…three!'

On the third swing they let him go, and Robert flew though the air. Seconds later they heard the splash as he hit the river's surface, and sank.

'Enjoy your swim, cully,' chuckled the first man.

'Amen to that, as the good Reverend would say,' laughed the other.

Still laughing they returned to the shadows on the other side of the street, and continued to watch out for unwelcome strangers. It would not be a long watch as two of the wagons were already empty.

Edith followed Jessie down the stairs. Both their hearts were pounding, but it was very obvious they could not stay at the White House. Luckily the snow had quickly thawed, but the bright moon shining through the windows indicated it would still be very cold outside.

'You're making enough noise to waken the dead,' came a voice to one side of them.

Turning in horror, their hearts sank as they saw Jane Howatt standing in the passageway.

CHAPTER SEVENTEEN

Tuesday

J essie and Edith stopped and turned towards her.
'This way, and for God's sake don't make so much noise,' hissed Jane
Howatt.

The other two stood still, unsure of what to do.

'Listen!' hissed Jane.

They heard the sound of footsteps coming towards them.

'It's up to you,' continued Jane, and she turned away.

This time they followed her into a small room, lit by a single candle. She
closed the door quietly behind them, and stood with her back to it, whilst the
footsteps passed.

'We haven't got very long,' said Jane. 'You have to trust me, or you
stand no chance at all of escaping from here.'

The other two held hands and nodded.

'In a few minutes they will have discovered your escape and all hell will
be let loose. It will be assumed you're heading into Warwick, so that is the
last place you can go. It'll be more sensible to head for Birmingham where
you can lose yourselves for a few days. It won't matter after the week-end,
because this operation is closing down.'

'Why are you helping us?' asked Jessie, still not completely sure of the
other woman.

Before Jane could answer, they heard the sound of running footsteps
coming back down the stairs, and passed the door.

'I suspect they've found out you've escaped.'

Jane led them across to one sides of the fireplace, where she bent down and twisted the bell push.   Seconds later, the fireplace slid silently to one side.

'The man who had this place built, wanted it to be like an old castle, so he had at least one secret passage made.   Come on, there's no time to waste.'

They followed her into the recess, and moments later, the fireplace slid back into its original position.   Jane led the way down some steps, lighting them with her candle.   Several steps later, they were on level ground, and Jane signalled for them to stop.

'We're just by the kitchens,' she said.   'And I know you must be hungry and thirsty.   Wait here.'

'How do we know you'll come back?' asked Jessie.   Edith nodded in agreement.

'If I'd wanted you to have been recaptured, I could have just left you walking along the passage, straight into one of the men.   Don't be so stupid. Or, if you'd rather, I'll let you out here and you can go your own way.'

'We're sorry,' interceded Edith.

Jane nodded and she was gone.

They waited for what seemed like an eternity for Jane to return.   In fact, it was only a few minutes.   When she reappeared, Jane handed them each a large slice of meat pie, some cheese and a bottle of beer.   She also gave them each a coat and a scarf.

'You'll need these for when you get out.   They're a bit on the large side, but it was the best I could do.   Don't eat the food too quickly, and wait for a moment before you do.'

She led them on for what seemed ages, before stopping in a small, but airy chamber.

'I'll leave you here, until tomorrow night.   Believe me you're safe for the time being.   Enjoy your food, and try and get some sleep.   Now, look up there.'

She pointed to the ceiling, where they could see a very small window, which let in some moonlight.

'If I'm not back by nightfall, it means I'm not coming.   So, make your own way out through that door over there.'   She pointed to a small door.   'It leads down on to the canal towpath. When you hit it, turn right and head towards Birmingham.'

Then she was gone.

Emotionally exhausted, the two women sat down, ate the pie, drank the beer and fell asleep in each other's arms.

Meanwhile back in the White House, a search for the missing fugitives had failed to find them. A search party had gone into Warwick, but it had found nothing. Other men were sent out on to the Birmingham Road, where they met with a similar result. Once the missing coats had been discovered, it was assumed they had left the White House and could now be anywhere in the countryside.

The fact they had not been found in Warwick was treated initially as a blessing. Nevertheless, armed guards were placed in and around the White House to warn of the approach of any police. Only later would someone question why the missing women had not been found by the dogs.

John was worried.

As Tuesday passed, there was still no news from Robert Andrew, who should have returned from London by now. Had he been delayed, John knew he would have sent a telegram to that effect. He knew Robert had intended visiting his brother-in-law at Scotland Yard, as well as going to the American Embassy.

Robert lived alone, never having married, as most women were deterred from having a long term relationship with him, because of his hand. Although John knew there was little or no point in having his rooms checked out, he did so all the same. As he expected there were no signs of him. Reluctantly he sent telegraph messages to the American Embassy and to Scotland Yard.

He received replies later in the day. Yes, Robert had been to the Embassy, but he had not seen since his last visit to Scotland Yard.

Gordon Mayne was now very concerned. As Robert had not been seen for nearly twenty-four hours, he had him officially reported as missing, and believed to be in some danger. There was nothing more he could do now, but wait. He sent a telegram to John, advising him of what he had done.

This gave John some time to think. He was already having worrying thoughts about the White House and Mordeccai Carew. And that meant wondering, just where did Madeleine fit into all of this?

Whilst he accepted she could not be held accountable for the actions of her brother, was it realistic to think she did not know what he was doing? Yet she was always very pleasant with other people, and had really helped him in his struggle to come to terms with Harriet's death. His men, and Silas, all liked her, as did his friends.

John stopped.

No, that was not strictly true. Emma Roberts had not been comfortable in her company. And Madeleine had been upset that night by Cornelius Lake. Perhaps he ought to go and see Emma. The more he thought about doing so, the more the idea grew. And there was nothing he could do just sitting in his office, and waiting for news from London.

He pushed his chair back, stood up and went into the charge office.

'Get the trap harnessed up, please,' he instructed Harry Barlow.

'Where are we going guv'nor?' asked Harry who was only too glad to escape from the office for a while, even though it was a cold night.

'Claverdon,' was his reply.

Harry Barlow was quite happy with that. The village was only a few miles out of Warwick, and it would be a reasonably short drive.

Some time later, Harry drew up outside Daniel and Emma's house. He waited whilst John rang the front door bell. It had been a cold but not unpleasant journey, in the early evening.

The door was opened by the butler, who greeted John, whom he knew, and ushered him inside the house. Less than five minutes later, a footman appeared and took Harry and the trap round to the rear of the house.

After un-harnessing, the horse was led away to a stable, and Harry was invited into the kitchen. Very soon, he was sat in front of a roaring fire, nursing a mug of tea, and rapidly demolishing a large bowl of stew. It did not take him long to start regaling the kitchen maids with some of his adventures in the police.

Meanwhile, in the drawing-room, John was being entertained by Emma. She had known John since he and her husband Daniel had been constables in the Metropolitan Police. Daniel had transferred to the Birmingham police, and had helped John out on more than one occasion.

Following his medical discharge from the police, Daniel had quickly become a partner in a very successful transport business. The company continued to grow, and was one of the largest transport contractors in the Midlands, with branches in other parts of the British Isles and elsewhere.

'How lovely to see you, John,' said Emma, and demurely shook his hand, as the butler showed him into the drawing room.

However, once the butler had left the room, she flung her arms round John's neck and kissed him. They were more like brother and sister than just friends. Whilst Emma had been upset by Laura's death, she was devastated when Harriet died.

Moments later, she had ordered a pot of tea for John, respecting the fact he was on duty, and sat him by the fire.

'I'm afraid Daniel's in Wolverhampton this evening,' she smiled.

'Actually, it's you I really wanted to see. I need to ask you a favour and I desperately need your advice.'

'How can I help?'

'It's about Madeleine Pascoe.' Even as John spoke, he sensed a change in her attitude. Somehow she had stiffened, and her nostrils flared. 'The favour I want is for you to be absolutely honest with me. Why don't you like her?'

Emma was silent for a while, and gazed into the fire. John waited patiently. At last she turned to him.

'As you may recall, we were in America shortly before the war started, trying to get into that market, working for the Federal government, and we were involved in transporting medicines, amongst other things.'

John began to feel cold.

'When the war started, we were owed a considerable amount of money by the Federal government, and they were finding all manner of excuses not to pay us. It had been a new venture, and I had gone over with Daniel, to supervise it ourselves. Benjamin stayed behind to look after things here. After a while we were approached by a man, who called himself Michael Concannon.' Emma paused, clearly unwilling to continue.

'He explained how he worked for an organisation called...'

'*The Voluntary League of Medical Helpers,*' answered John. 'They operated for both the Union and the Confederate armies. I've heard all about them from Silas.'

Emma relaxed considerably, and nodded her head. Both she and Daniel knew Silas was John's son. 'Concannon told us he had the authority of the Federal government to move medicines, blankets, medical instruments and so on, through the lines to the South.'

She paused and took a large mouthful of tea. 'Basically, if we wanted to get our money, then we had to take these consignments through the lines. We felt we had no option but to do as he wished. So we agreed.'

Emma shuddered.

'Initially he wanted me to stay behind whilst Daniel went with the supply column. But I refused. He absolutely terrified me.'

'And what did you bring back?' prompted John.

'Cotton, apparently it came with the blessings of the Confederate government. It was very easy, as both governments gave us safe conducts. We did about six or seven trips, and received some of our money back. Then we discovered that in with the medicines, we were smuggling firearms from the North into the South, for their army. So we abandoned what was left of our money and left everything behind, and caught the next boat home. It was a dreadful experience. If we had been caught by the Federals whilst smuggling those guns, we would have been hanged.'

John sat in shocked silence.

'I'm so sorry I asked,' he said.

Emma turned to him with a wan smile. 'Actually I'm glad I've told someone about it, and even more so it was you. I feel you've lifted a weight off my shoulders. But, you still want to know about Madeleine?'

John nodded.

'On one of our visits to Concannon, he was holding a recruiting drive for nurses. Your Madeleine was there, playing the part of a nurse.'

'Playing the part of a nurse?'

'Yes. Playing the part. She was not a real nurse.' Emma took a deep breath. 'With all the nurses I have seen, and who I got to know, when Benjamin was ill, and especially after Daniel was shot, I am fairly confident I know what a nurse does. Madeleine just did not fit that image. Yes, she was dressed the part. But that was all. She was just playing a part.'

'Perhaps she had only just joined up?'

'I'm sorry, John, but no,' Emma shook her head. 'She was dressed as a supervisory nurse, and not as a new entrant. And, she was encouraging other women to join her. I just felt it was all an act.'

'For whose benefit? Concannon's?'

'That I don't know. To be fair, although she acknowledged him when he came through the foyer, that seemed to be all.'

'Do you think she recognised you, that night at the ball?'

'No. And Daniel didn't remember her. We didn't speak to her in America. In fact I never knew her name until you introduced us that night.'

John began to feel more confident, and prepared to ask his favour. 'Speaking as a woman, and a long and very dear friend, should I ask her to marry me?'

'Oh John! That is the one question I cannot answer. All I can say is listen to your heart or listen to your head. The choice has to be yours. What would Harriet want you to do?'

'To be happy and not remain celibate, but also to be careful, and not to rush into anything, until I was completely sure of what I was doing.' Even as he spoke the words, the vision of Harriet suddenly appearing and stopping him from making love to Madeleine, came to mind. Was she trying to tell him something?

'That has to be your answer. Clearly you are not sure of what to do. So, if you have some doubt…Perhaps, leave it a little while longer. And I promise to try and be nice to her.'

'Thank you.'

'Forgive me for asking though, but wouldn't Silas's mother, Kate Whiting, be a better bet for you?'

He shook his head sadly. 'That's not possible. She has someone else now. Silas has told me there is a man in her life, and it just wouldn't be right for me to try and...' He broke off.

'I'm sorry, John. We got to know her quite well after the Cooper affair, and really liked her. Even before we knew about Silas, I know just how much you felt for her.'

They talked about other matters for a while, including his concerns for the missing Robert Andrew. Emma knew Robert, and she was sad to hear of his disappearance.

After drinking some more tea, John asked for his horse and trap. Several minutes later, Harry Barlow appeared and informed him all was ready for the return journey. John politely shook hands with Emma, having given her a hug just before Harry arrived.

She stood at the window, and waved until they vanished into the cold frosty night, and headed back towards Warwick.

Emma was worried about John.

Losing Laura had been hard for him, but not as hard as Harriet's illness and death. To be fair, Emma knew she was biased. She had liked Laura and understood John's guilt at never having found her killer. But Harriet had been someone completely different. Ever since John had first mentioned her, Emma had known instinctively Harriet was right for him.

But she could not say the same for Madeleine. There was something about her that bothered Emma. Her experiences in America were one thing: but there was something else, although she just could not say what it was.

The trouble was she knew John was very smitten on Madeleine, and from what she had seen of them together, had no reason to doubt the feelings were mutual. She had discussed them both with Daniel, but he could see nothing wrong with Madeleine. He was certain Emma had either misjudged her, or confused her with somebody else. Laughingly she had teased him with being influenced by a pretty face. He had shared the joke.

Perhaps she was just being over cautious, and slightly resenting another woman coming so quickly into John's life. And there was always the possibility she might have confused Madeleine with somebody else. Certainly Madeleine had not seemed to have recognised her.

But Emma knew she was right. She had definitely recognised Madeleine.

Emma shrugged. It was really none of her business. And, even if it was, could she really bring herself to ruin John's happiness, at the expense of their friendship?

It was a question she was unable to answer.

She drew the curtains once more, and went back to the fire. Looking at the clock, she hoped Daniel would soon be home.

It had been a long, cold and hungry day for Jessie and Edith. When they awoke, from a fitful sleep, it was still dark and they had no means of knowing the time. Gradually they saw the little window grow lighter, and a feeble amount of daylight was admitted into the room. After another eternity, the daylight faded and night fell once more.

Just as they were debating what to do, Jane reappeared.

'Go quickly,' she instructed. 'Go towards Birmingham.'

'Why are you helping us?' queried Edith.

'Don't ask questions. Just go! They think you're possibly still around, and they are sending out more search parties. Go!'

She opened the door and hustled them out into the cold frosty night.

Jessie and Edith went out of the chamber, and the door closed behind them. They quickly found the canal towpath, where they stopped. Birmingham. It was eerily quiet, and they could see a thin veneer of ice already starting to form on the water's surface.

'Jess,' said Edith. 'I don't want to go to Birmingham.'

'Me neither. Shall we go back to Warwick, and tell the crushers what we know? It's the only chance those other poor girls have got.'

'Yes.'

However, they agreed to keep off the roads, as much as possible. At the next lock gates, they crossed over the canal, to where there was no towpath. Climbing a gate, they went into a field and made their way, cross country towards Henley-in-Arden, which was well away from the Birmingham Road, although this would have been a shorter journey into Warwick.

Just as they were crossing the road, they heard a horse and trap coming. They debated, for a moment or two, whether or not to flag it down. In the end, they chose to run away from it.

Harry Barlow was startled by their sudden appearance, and had to pull the horse up, as the women ran out in front of them.

The sudden movement stirred John out of his reverie.

'What was that?' he asked.

'Don't know, guv'nor. Looked like two youngsters either having a bet, or else they were tired of living.'

'Strange,' replied John, looking at where they had disappeared into the hedgerow. 'I suspect they were up to no good. I wonder who they were?'

Jane Howatt opened the secret fireplace entrance, and climbed back into her room.

'Well! Well! Well!' She immediately recognised the dreadfully familiar voice. 'And just where have you been, I wonder? I think you've got quite a lot of explaining to do.'

Jane turned frantically to run somewhere, but it was no use. Strong hands grabbed her.

'Let's go to the cellar, shall we?'

CHAPTER EIGHTEEN

Wednesday

Jane Howatt was suffering, and she was in a great deal of pain. She was only vaguely heartened by the fact, that as yet, they had not used the hot poker on her. As if reading her thoughts, one of her tormentors went across to the fire, blazing away in the hearth, and inserted a thick rod of metal into the flames.

'Now Jane,' came her interrogator's soft silky voice. 'Let me ask you just one more time. Where have they gone? Now just think before you answer. I want the truth. It would be very easy to kill you. No doubt your employers would miss you.'

Jane started. 'But you're my employer. I just took pity on those two poor girls and helped them on their way.'

'Not good enough, Jane.' The voice retained its soft silky tone. 'I'm sure you will soon tell us who you work for, before very much longer. The pain you've received so far, will be nothing compared to the red hot poker. But we can avoid all this distress. Where have those girls gone?'

'I don't know. I just showed them a way out.'

'When?'

'Tonight. They'd been in hiding all day.'

'One more time, Jane. Where have they gone?'

The interrogator nodded to the man by the fire. Slowly, aware that Jane's terrified eyes were watching him, he took the metal rod out of the fire. It glowed a bright red. With an evil grin on his face he advanced towards the unfortunate victim.

'They've gone to Birmingham,' screamed Jane, although the rod was nowhere near her bare feet.

'Where have they gone?'

'Birmingham,' sobbed Jane.

She was not to know Edith and Jessie had ignored her advice, and gone to Warwick instead.

'We'll check it out. Meanwhile, you'll stay here.'

'What are you going to do to me?'

'I've been thinking about that. You see, we've known about you for a while now. All your specially coded messages didn't go anywhere, except on the fire. Nobody knows where you are, so there cannot be any rescue attempt.' The speaker paused.

'As for what will happen to you, that's a good question. We don't have time to break you in like the other girls, but you can go with them, as a little bonus. My customer can then enjoy breaking you in himself. It'll be a fate worse than death, especially for someone your age.'

Jane sobbed. Her future was bad enough - her employers would have assumed from her silence that she was dead, and there would be no help from there. And now she had betrayed the two girls who had trusted her. Although with a bit of luck, they might still escape. Thank goodness she had persuaded them to get far away from Warwick.

In another room at the White House, the interrogator sat with the other men, and planned what do.

'Do you believe her?' asked one of the torturers.

'No,' was the interrogator's reply. 'All the messages which we intercepted from her were all in a reverse code, and meant the opposite to what they actually said. I can see no reason for her to tell us the truth. And I think it's the same here. She's trying to send us in the wrong direction. They've not gone to Birmingham, but have returned to Warwick.'

'Will they go to the crushers?'

'Even if they did, do you think for one moment the crushers would believe them?' The interrogator replied.

The others shook their heads.

'And I think I know what they'll do. They only know one trade and I think the churchyard beckons.'

It was well past midnight when Edith and Jessie arrived back into Warwick. Surprisingly there were still several people around. By now they were extremely hungry, tired, thirsty and cold.

On the way they had discussed what they should do. Common sense told them they should go the police. But in their way of life, they had a grave mistrust of any figures in authority. Perhaps if they found the right crusher, he would believe them; but as for the others?

Dr Whiting was a good possibility, but neither of them knew where he lived. They had gone to the hospital, but the night porter quickly escorted them off the premises. Going home, they decided, was too risky. The only alternative was to stay out for the night, probably in St Mary's churchyard, and find the doctor later that morning.

'You go into the churchyard,' suggested Jessie. 'We can use Joe Garner's hut. He keeps the key under a flower pot, just outside the door. It'll be dry in there. I know as I've used it before.'

'Where are you going to go?'

'I'm going to the *Warwick Arms,* where hopefully, I can scrounge some food from Tom Benson, the night porter.'

Edith raised her eyebrows in mock disapproval.

'I've met his wife. She's a right dragon. Let's just say, I do him the odd little favour, and get paid in kind.'

They chuckled and parted company.

Edith was not very happy about going into the churchyard on her own. She was only too aware of what had happened to Lottie, in there. As a rule, Edith avoided churchyards.

Her grandmother used to tell her all manner of ghost stories, often involving churchyards, during the long, dark cold winter nights, when she was a small child. Even though she was now an adult, Edith remained very wary of churchyards, and she used them for business purposes, only if she had to.

For a while, she kept to the shadows, under St Mary's tower, close to Northgate Street. How she wished Jessie would hurry up and come back.

'Psst! Psst!'

Edith turned and peered into the churchyard, where she could just make out a shadowy form, which beckoned towards her. She hesitated, and wished again Jessie was back.

'Psst! Psst!'

The whispering, and beckoning, was now more urgent. Edith still hesitated, but only for a few seconds. After all the money would be useful, and she would have some company until Jessie returned.

Hoisting up her skirts, she walked into the churchyard and followed the shadowy figure.

Jessie was longer at the *Warwick Arms* than she had intended. There had been a late night function at the hotel, and the last guests were still leaving when she arrived. To make matters worse, Tom Benson was busy taking some late night drinks to three of the bedrooms. When all had quietened down, Jessie approached him.

Surprisingly, she found he was quite reticent. She was not to know how he had been interviewed by the police, after her last visit. But Jessie was an attractive girl, in spite of her bruised face, and she soon had his full attention. Several minutes later, she left Tom to get dressed again, and was on her way with bread, cold beef and some bottles of beer.

Now there was no one around. Going up Church Street, towards St Mary's church, she recognised Edith still loitering under the tower. Moving closer to the buildings, Jessie thought, mischievously, about creeping up on the poor girl, and pretending to be a ghost.

Then she saw Edith suddenly walk, purposefully, towards Northgate Street. As Jessie reached the tower, she saw Edith go into the churchyard, and laughed quietly to herself. The lucky girl had found a customer, even at this hour.

Jessie followed discreetly, crossing onto the grass, intending to go to Joe Garner's hut, and wait there for Edith. But, at that moment, the moon came out, and she stopped dead.

In front of her, Edith's customer had caught the other girl by her hair, and pulled it hard back. Before Edith could scream, a scalpel was slashed across her throat.

As Jessie saw her friend's blood spurt, she sank to her knees in terror. Dropping the food, she clasped her hands to her mouth in horror, but she could not take her eyes off her dying friend. Even before Edith's body had fallen to the ground, her attacker was slashing away at her body with the scalpel.

After what seemed a lifetime, Jessie saw the figure stop slashing, and stand up. She saw the figure's face was covered by a mask, which was then removed.

Jessie recoiled in horror, as she recognised her friend's killer, now clearly visible in the moonlight. Still clasping her hands to her mouth, she fell forward in a deep faint.

For some reason, Edith's killer had neither seen nor heard Jessie, and was unaware of her presence. The killer walked away, in the opposite direction to where Jessie lay.

When Jessie recovered consciousness, she sat, just staring at her dead friend. With her hands clasped around her knees, she continually rocked backwards and forwards. Now in a state of deep traumatised shock, she had no idea of what was happening.

Later, the doctors agreed that rocking continuously throughout the rest of the night, had stopped her from freezing to death.

Betty Lambourne, the vicar's wife, was on her way to St Mary's church, where she had agreed to oversee its cleaning for a few days. The verger, who normally did these duties, had been confined to bed with a fever. As the vicarage backed onto the churchyard, it was much quicker for both George and his family, to use their back garden gate as a short cut.

As she stepped through the gate, she met Nell Robbins, who had just come into the churchyard and stopped to gossip. It was not what Betty wanted to do, as she had several commitments that day. Finally, she managed to escape, but, she had only gone a few paces, when Nell called her back.

'Mrs Lambourne! Mrs Lambourne! Can you come? There's a girl here!'

Betty Lambourne suddenly felt cold, and hoped it was not going to be another body. For a moment she toyed with the idea of going back home to fetch her husband. But she knew he was at work preparing his sermon for Sunday. Resignedly, she went to join up with Nell.

She found Nell, a kindly disposed woman, squatting on her haunches, trying to talk to a young woman, who was sat on the grass, continually rocking. Betty was relieved to see this woman was alive, and she was not looking at another dead body. Her relief was soon shattered.

Looking over Nell's shoulder, Betty saw Edith's body lying only a few feet away. It did not take Betty long to see all the blood lying around, to know she had been murdered. Nell saw the change in her companion's face, and she turned to see where Betty was looking.

The moment Nell realised what she was looking at, her piercing screams echoed around the churchyard.

John was having a late breakfast.

He had not slept very well, and had given up trying at about 3 o'clock, when he had got up, and gone down to his study. He quickly persuaded the dying embers in the fireplace to come back to life, and threw some logs onto it. His actions were rewarded by a shower of sparks.

Once he was satisfied with the fire, John went into the kitchen, where he boiled a kettle, and made himself some tea. Once Mrs Simms, his cook, found out what he had done, she would be fussing all over him, like a mother hen with her chicks, making sure he was not ill. He could never convince her that he was not helpless, and was quite capable of looking after himself.

When he returned to his study, John went over all the points he could remember from his conversation with Emma the previous night. This time he wrote them down. To these he added other points which occurred to him. He was also brutally honest with himself, about his feelings for Madeleine and her brother.

Slowly, a pattern began to emerge. But it was a pattern he did not like.

Somehow, all the various tentacles kept linking Silas to the American murders: to the White House, and thus to Mordeccai and Madeleine. He was more than convinced Silas was innocent, and he was glad Robert agreed with him. And he liked to think Madeleine was innocent as well. But Emma's comments had bothered him greatly. What had she said about Madeleine?

She gave the impression of playing a part.

Yet, in their more tender moments, he could find nothing to suggest Madeleine was not as she seemed. When they failed to succeed in making love, the other night, it had been his fault, not hers. He was certain she had been as keen as he was. Everyone was saying how right they were for each other.

Except Emma.

To be fair, she would not commit herself. Also, she agreed it was possible she might have been mistaken, about meeting Madeleine in America. But in all the years he had known Emma, he had rarely known her to be wrong. In this respect, she was very much like Harriet.

The other tentacles which bothered him, all led back to the White House. He had hoped, after the Cooper affair, never to have had the need to go back there again. But it had not turned out as he had hoped.

'Oh Harriet,' he said softly. 'Can't you give me some guidance?'

At last he fell asleep, in the chair at his desk.

John dreamt of the time when he and Mathew had so nearly been killed at the White House. It was only thanks to Harriet they had survived. The dream brought it all back to him.

When he awoke, he recalled the dream vividly, and knew what it was telling him. The White House meant danger.

It was becoming increasingly obvious to him, how he would soon have to pay the White House an official visit. But to do the job properly, he would need a warrant plus some evidence to support it. As yet he had neither.

Where was Robert? If he could only prove Mordeccai and Michael Concannon, were one and the same person, then he had a chance of obtaining a warrant.

At the same time, he knew raiding the White House might well mean the end of his relationship with Madeleine. And that was another reason, he admitted to himself, for delaying the raid, until he had sufficient evidence.

He also knew that if it was to be a choice between love and duty, then duty would have to win.

Now John sat in the dining-room, having a late breakfast. As he had suspected, Mrs Simms had fussed over him, and she would not let him go on duty until he had eaten. John was just finishing his last piece of toast, when he heard a piercing scream coming from the churchyard.

Dropping his toast, and not stopping to put on a coat, John ran out through the kitchen, across the back garden and into the churchyard. He was closely followed by Seth Walters and several other male servants. Mrs Simms locked the back door after the last one had left. Then she and the maids huddled together in the kitchen, and waited fearfully.

John was soon at the scene, and he quickly saw what had happened. By now Nell had stopped screaming, mainly because Betty had slapped her smartly across the face. As John arrived, they had just succeeded in lifting Jessie to her feet. He immediately recognised her, in spite of her bruised face.

'Take Jessie into my house,' he instructed the two women, and one of his servants. 'Will you go with them George?' he asked the vicar, who had just appeared, after he heard the screaming.

John looked at Edith's body, and he did not need to be a doctor to know she was completely beyond human help. She had been killed the same way as Lottie Goodwin, and the other women in America.

Whilst he looked around the scene, John was conscious of Seth instructing one of the servants to run to the police station for help, and sending another to fetch a doctor. Another servant was detailed to go and fetch John's coat. A few minutes later, one of his servants appeared with the coat, and helped John into it. Then he handed him a scarf, gloves and hat. John was grateful for them.

In the next few minutes, policemen began to arrive. The first one cleared the growing number of spectators out of the churchyard. Soon afterwards Silas had arrived.

Kneeling beside Edith's body, he confirmed she was dead, but John noticed he was frowning. Silas moved John to one side.

'Something's very wrong here,' Silas said quietly to John. 'I only saw her on Monday, up at the White House. Then she, I think her name's Edith, and her friend Jessie, had joined one of those courses. Then she was fit and well, but now, look at the bruising on her face!'

John looked. He had noticed the bruising when he first arrived, and he assumed it had happened during the attack. He said as much to Silas.

'No!' Silas was adamant. 'That bruising is several hours old. I would say at least a day or more. Where did it happen?'

'Clearly she was attacked since Monday when you saw her. If I understand you, what you are saying, is if this bruising did not happen here, it probably happened at the White House?' John went cold. This suggestion, coming so close after all the work he had done in his study, was not welcome.

'Possibly. I'm beginning to wonder about that place. Their last lot of women have quickly been moved on. And...' He paused. 'I couldn't help but feel that Edith, and Jessie, wanted to tell me something, but they just didn't have the chance.'

'Did you say Jessie? Would that be Jessie Brampton?'

Silas nodded.

Quickly John explained how Jessie had been found at the scene, also with a badly bruised face, and she was now in his house. Silas went off to examine her, accompanied by one of John's servants. Meanwhile he made arrangements for Lawrence Perkins to photograph the scene, so Edith's body could be removed to the hospital mortuary.

'Guv'nor?' Harry Barlow appeared at his side. He was one of the constables who had volunteered to remove Edith, when the time was ready. 'That coat she's wearing. Do you see it?'

'Of course, I do. I...' His voice tailed off, as he realised what Harry was suggesting.

'Yes,' continued Harry. 'I'd stake my life that she was one of those two who ran out across in front of us last night.'

'You're right Harry. And her friend, who we also found here, and has gone to my house, was wearing a similar coat. She'll be with Dr Whiting now, but on your return from the hospital, go and have a look at her coat, will you, please?'

'Will do guv'nor.'

John was quiet for a moment, whilst he mulled over what Harry had said. He would have to have the area checked, where they had seen the two women. Strictly speaking it was policed by the Warwickshire Constabulary, and he would need permission to search there.

However, he had a very good working relationship with them, helped by Mathew's two sons, who were members of it. One of them was stationed at nearby Henley-in-Arden and knew it would not be a problem. With luck, they might even help in the search.

He knew, only too well, that by cutting across the fields from the direction the women had appeared, their paths could go back to the White House. It was beginning to look as if it was there, where they had been beaten.

And now, the nagging suspicions he had long felt about Mordeccai, and what he was really doing, were beginning to take a very firm, and unpleasant root in his mind. However, at the moment, his main concerns were for Jessie's well being and trying to find Edith's killer.

He would give it until the weekend to investigate all the possibilities, but if there was no news from Robert and, in the absence of any other evidence, he would raid the White House sometime on Saturday.

But then he had another thought.

Clearly Edith's murder was linked to those of Lottie, Cornelius, and the ones in America. So was the earlier attempt on Jessie's life. Edith's murder had a clear link to the White House, so what if the others did as well? He did not like the thought. What could Jessie tell him? Hopefully, she might well provide the answers.

He shrugged his shoulders. Even if he could not find enough evidence for a warrant, he would make something up. After all, it would not be the first time he had done so. By now he was more than ever convinced Mordeccai was the killer.

Whilst he had only met the man twice, on each occasion he felt there was something about him, which was not quite right.

For the first time since Harriet had died, John felt invigorated. He now knew what he was doing, and where he was going. The vague plan he had considered, during the night, became more certain. Now he had to find a way to unsettle Mordeccai, and that would have to be through Madeleine.

If he was wrong, it would remove his suspicions about the man. If he was right, then the case would be solved. Hopefully she would not realise what he had done: although the more he thought about that, the less likely it would happen.

Even if she did, John found it inconceivable she willingly supported her brother's criminal activities. John could understand how she might have no option, but to support him. After all, the man was a bully. Whilst he had explained at their meeting, in the *Warwick Arms*, about his distrust of policemen, John did not entirely believe that was the real reason for his hostility. He had encountered too many liars over the years.

At the time, he had been prepared to give Mordeccai the benefit of the doubt, but now he was far less sure. Once Silas told him about Edith's injuries having happened before her murder, the inference was they had happened at the White House. If that was so, then something was very, very wrong with the *Society* Mordeccai and Madeleine ran, up at the White House.

If he lost Madeleine, then John would grieve, but he strongly hoped she was just as much a victim as the other women. He always trusted his instincts, and they rarely let him down. *Do your duty and everything else will follow,* had always been his policy, and he saw no reason to change it now.

John was firmly back in charge once more.

But he had an immediate problem. How was he going to make Mordeccai take the bait he wanted to offer him?

CHAPTER NINETEEN

Later the same day

His answer soon came.

Just as Lawrence was putting his camera away, having photographed the murder scene, and Edith's body had been removed, John saw Madeleine talking to Nell Robbins. He knew she would waste no time in telling Madeleine what had happened, and give him the opportunity he wanted.

Minutes later, Madeleine strode up to John, carefully keeping her skirts out of Edith's blood, although Joe Garner, the grave digger, was already spreading sand over it.

'Isn't it awful?' she said on joining up with John.

John shook his head, almost in disbelief at what had happened. 'Even after all the years I have been a policeman, I still cannot see how any human being could possibly do that to another. I really can't.'

'Don't let it get to you, my love,' she clutched his right arm and hung on tightly. 'As it happened here, in the churchyard, do think I'm in any danger?'

'No. But I would suggest you don't use the churchyard as a short cut home, in the dark, until we've caught him.'

'Mrs Robbins was telling me, there was another girl here as well. Is that right?'

'Yes. In fact, you would have known both of them. They were Edith, I think her other name was Dennison. She's the one who has been murdered. Jessie Brampton was sitting by her. Dr Whiting only examined them at the White House on Monday.'

'Of course. But they didn't stay. I don't know why, but it does happen sometimes. What did Jessie say?'

'Absolutely nothing. She's in a terrible state of shock and won't say a word. Poor Jessie, she must have seen what happened to her friend. Who knows, she might even have recognised the killer!'

'Oh the poor, poor girls! Why didn't they stay with me?'

'I wish we knew. Perhaps Jessie can tell us, if she recovers.'

'When is that likely to happen?'

'I just don't know. Neither does Dr Whiting. I've read about similar cases where the person quickly recovered in a matter of hours, or possibly days and sometimes...never. We'll just have to wait and see.'

'Would it help if she came and stayed with me, either back at the White House or here at home?'

'That's very kind of you,' John smiled. 'But Dr Whiting wants to keep her at the hospital. He's very concerned that both girls had apparently been badly beaten up, only a short while before Edith was killed. He feels Jessie knows something about that as well, so I'm inclined to agree the hospital is the best place for her.'

'Beaten up? By who?'

'We don't know. Apparently both girls were fine when he saw them on Monday, but now this...' John's voice tailed away.

'That's terrible. I'm going to the White House now, and I'll get Mordeccai to make some enquiries. If any of my staff have done this, I'll see you know about it. Then you can deal with them however the law sees fit.'

'Just one thing; do you know when they were found to be missing?'

'I'm not sure. Sometime yesterday morning, I think, so it's possible they went on Monday night. I'll have to make some enquiries. Now let's change the subject. I don't suppose there's any chance of your coming round tonight, is there?' Madeleine pulled a face.

'I'm sorry my love. Unless we get a sudden breakthrough, which I think is highly unlikely, it'll be a late night. However, I could always come and see you out at the White House, as I ought to talk to the other girls there. What say you I mix a little bit of pleasure with business?'

'Oh John! Not today, and I've got meetings for the rest of the week. And I must find out about Mordeccai's trip to London. He went on a fund raising expedition, and only got back late last night. What's wrong?' She saw how John's face had clouded over.

'Will you ask him, when he was in London, if, by any chance he came across one of my men, Robert Andrew. He went there on Monday, and now it seems he has totally disappeared. To be honest, I'm very worried about him.'

'I know I shouldn't ask, but what was he doing there?'

'He'd gone to the American Embassy and was asking about the murdered man, Cornelius Lake.'

'Of course I'll ask him. Now I really must fly.'

Madeleine looked furtively about her. Only when she was convinced no-one was looking, did she stand on tiptoe and kissed John on the cheek. Then she was gone.

John went back home, where Silas was waiting for him. They went through into John's study.

'I'm sorry,' he said. 'But there's no change in Jessie. And I'm not sure if there ever will be. She's had a terrible shock...And there's just no telling.' He shook his head and held out his hands, palms upwards. 'However,' he continued. 'I was right. Just like poor Edith, someone has given her a real beating. And I'm getting concerned.'

'So am I if you're thinking about the White House. Now, I fear Edith was killed for a purpose, and not just to frighten the other street girls here in town. The fact that Jessie survived was, I think, an oversight, and not by design. That being the case, I fear the killer will strike again, and she will be the next victim. So I want her kept in a safe place for the next two or three days.'

John outlined his plans.

'You can't do that!' Silas was aghast at what his father had just told him.

"I'm confident we're getting close to arresting our murderer, but unless we catch him in the act, proving it will be difficult. So Jessie has to be released from our custody and put back in St Mary's churchyard, to act as bait.'

'No father! No! No! No! What if it goes wrong?'

'It's got to succeed, and I've already put the word out Jessie is in the hospital, but in fact I'll keep her here. I suspect some one will be making enquiries about her in the hospital later on today, but they'll be told she's already been moved to a secret location.'

'But remember what they did to your office. They'll stop at nothing, and if they are the same people I came across during the war, the *VLMH*, they are utterly ruthless.'

'And that is the reason why I shall put armed guards in the hospital, for the rest of today, and all of tonight. In the morning, I will announce she has run away, but has since been arrested, taken to the police station on suspicion of murdering Edith. Then I can put the next part of the operation into effect.'

Silas shook his head in a mixture of wonderment and disbelief. His mother had told him how *Mr Mayfield* was a law unto himself, and he was more than likely to make it up as he went along. He took chances, which, so far, had all paid off. Hopefully this case would not prove to be the exception. Silas agreed, finally, albeit reluctantly, to John's suggestion, and kept Jessie sedated for most of the day.

After Silas left, John called all his servants together and gave them their instructions. Mrs Simms was to act as nurse to Jessie, and Seth would arrange a rota of guards to look after her. Seth was instructed to carry a revolver at all times, until Jessie was out of the house.

John knew he was very fortunate in having employed Seth. No longer young, Seth was a widower, and a former sergeant – major in the army. He had been retired early, after being severely wounded at the Battle of Balaclava, during the Crimean War. Whilst he missed the army, and his wife, Seth enjoyed the irregularity of working for John, and he had been totally devoted to Harriet. Although he would never mention it to any one else, he had reservations about Madeleine.

To be fair, he admitted nobody could ever take the place of Harriet, and he would willingly have exchanged his life for hers, when she was dying. This was the way many people had reacted to Harriet.

Whilst he ran the house strictly, Seth was scrupulously fair in the way he treated the other members of staff. In their turn, they trusted and obeyed him without question. He always ensured their views were heard, even when he disagreed with them. The turnover of staff, under Seth's control, was very small. Over the years, he had been approached by other householders, offering him more money to come and work for them. Seth always turned them down.

Nobody was to be allowed entry to the house, until further notice, unless it was with John's special written permission, or else they were known to the servants. Even then they would need John's permission. He listed the few people who were permitted to enter.

As he would be out most of the day, it effectively meant there would be very few admissions to his house. The servants would all have been briefed by Seth, and John knew he could not leave his house in better hands.

On several occasions, Seth had been sworn in as a special constable, if circumstances required extra staff. This often happened at certain trials at the Quarter Sessions, and the Assizes, especially the controversial ones. Likewise, John often needed extra staff at public executions.

Apart from being a first class organiser, Seth was a large man, who, in spite of his earlier wounds, was still more than capable of looking after himself in a rough house.

John went back to the police station, to a flurry of activity.

As expected, a search of the churchyard had found a bloodstained scalpel, and apart from the food and drink Jessie had dropped, that was all. It was the work of only a few seconds to establish the beer had come from the *Warwick Arms*, and Harry Barlow had been despatched there to make enquiries.

Luckily, Inspector Edward Harrison, one of Mathew's sons, was posted at the County Police Station in Henley-in-Arden. He was now having the area searched where John and Harry had seen the two women, not that John expected them to find anything. They would also question any narrow boatmen or other labourers, and itinerants whom they happened to find.

Acting on John's instructions, Caleb instructed two reliable constables to go to the hospital, and stay there until they were relieved, even if it meant staying all night. They were to sleep in turns, with always one of them on guard, to assist the hospital porters. Although John felt it unnecessary for such precautions during the day, when the hospital was busy he was not prepared to take any chances. If any attempt was to be made, then it would happen in the dark. Both constables were issued with revolvers.

Other men were making general enquiries, but so far, they had not discovered anything of importance.

In the early afternoon, Harry Barlow appeared, bringing with him a reluctant Tom Benson. Harry brought the unfortunate porter straight to John, who was sat with Mathew.

'I believe you know Mr Benson, guv'nor,' said Harry. 'It seems he gave Jessie the food and drink.'

'Gave them to her?' queried Mathew.

'Shall we say, they came to an arrangement,' grinned Harry.

'Please don't tell me wife,' pleaded Tom.

'What about your employer?' John asked mildly. 'I don't suppose he'll be too happy, about you paying for your sexual adventures, with his food and drink. Eh?'

Tom needed no persuasion to explain, truthfully, what had happened when Jessie visited him the previous night. Just as he had finished, Silas arrived, with the results of the autopsy he had carried out on Edith.

Tom was sent back to the *Warwick Arms*, with Harry, to check on his story. John asked Sam and Caleb to join him and Mathew.

Silas began by stating how Edith had died as a result of the injuries to her throat. He went on to talk about the bruises to Edith's face.

'Also,' he continued. 'She had plenty of other bruises all over her body. I also believe that where some of these injuries happened, it means she was systematically raped several times. And it is a similar story with Jessie, except she's alive, but still in a state of shock.'

'I know it's asking a lot,' said Sam. 'But firstly, can we get those injuries photographed? Lawrence will do Edith, and Lucy's quite happy to do Jessie.'

Silas agreed.

'Secondly,' continued Sam. 'I know I'm asking a lot, yet again, but is it possible to say when they were beaten?'

'It may not stand up in a court of law, but I am no stranger to dealing with bruises and worse, and I can prove it, so I am willing to testify they were inflicted, no later than Monday evening.'

'Madeleine thinks that was when they probably went missing, so we still can't prove they were received at the White House,' replied John.

'Could they have been the reason for their running away?' asked Caleb.

'That I can't say,' answered Silas. 'But there is something else. Edith had eaten very little food for about thirty-six hours and I'm willing to bet the same applies to Jessie.'

'Which would explain why Jessie went to the *Warwick Arms* for food,' observed Mathew. He explained about their recent interview with Tom Benson.

'I hate to say it, John,' continued Mathew, breaking their unspoken agreement to only use their rank, when they were on duty. 'But the White House keeps cropping up. Just what is going on up there? God knows I thought we'd seen the last of that place all those years ago.'

'Let me tell you,' replied John.

He explained his thoughts, and how Jessie was not in the hospital, but he declined to say where she was. They did not ask him. Only he and Silas knew, and John wanted to keep it that way for a while longer.

Later that evening, Police Sergeant Albert Newman, of the Thames Division of the Metropolitan Police, was parading his men for their tour of duty. He read out the day's orders, including any special messages, which had filtered down from Scotland Yard.

'Lastly,' he intoned. 'The detective branch, want us to look out for a missing cove called Robert Andrew. It seems this cove works for the Warwick Police, God knows who or where they are, and he was down here on official business.'

Newman took great delight in stressing words like *detective branch* and *official business*. As he had anticipated, there was a snigger from the men standing in front of him. Generally speaking there was no love lost between the uniform and detective branches.

'Quiet now,' Newman intoned. 'Here's his description, so take it down.'

He ran though Robert's description and then stopped. 'Oh,' he continued. 'It seems this cove has a withered left hand.'

'Can you say that again, sergeant?' asked Constable Sidney Hotton.

'Why?' sneered Newman. 'Are you going deaf in your old age? You know what they say?'

Once the laughter had subsided, Sidney Hotton tried again.

'That sounds like the cove we pulled out of the drink the other night. He had a withered hand.'

'Right!' Newman was all business like. 'Get yourselves to the Yard and ask for Inspector Gordon Mayne. It says here he can be contacted day or night.'

At about the same time, Trevor Larwood, night porter at the Harriet Foxton Hospital in Warwick, heard the bell ringing at the front door. Whilst it was not the recommended time for visiting, people often arrived late. He waited until Eddy Chadwick, one of the police constables, joined him, before going to see who was knocking. Eddie followed, but kept to the side of the door. He took out his revolver, and nodded to Trevor.

The night porter pulled back the small inspection grille and looked out. He saw a small man, heavily wrapped in a cloak, standing on the other side.

'Yes?' asked Trevor.

'I want to see me sister, Jessie Brampton,' came the reply.

'Just a minute, and I'll have a look at the register.' He closed the grille, and, as arranged with Eddie, walked into his small office, and made a pretence of checking the register. After a few minutes, he returned to the grille and opened it.

'I'm sorry,' said Trevor. 'But there's no-one here by that name.'

'Don't mess me about! I know she's here.'

'She was. But she's run away. It was just before the crushers came looking for her.' Trevor chuckled quietly. 'And I can tell you, they weren't happy about it.'

'Did they have any idea where she might have gone?'

'If they did, you don't think they'd tell the likes of me, do you? But I heard one of them say she might have gone to somewhere in Leamington, but they didn't know where.'

There came a muttering from the other side of the door.

'Poor lass,' continued Trevor. 'She's said nothing all the time she was here. Didn't speak or anything. I hope she gets on all right. Do give her our best wishes.'

Moments later, the visitor walked away, and Trevor shut the grille.

'He's gone,' Trevor said unnecessarily to Eddy. 'Did I do all right?'

'You certainly did. The stage lost a good actor when you came here.'

Trevor happily returned to his office, where he offered Eddy a mug of tea, which was gratefully accepted.

CHAPTER TWENTY

Thursday

John was just about to sit down to his breakfast, when the front door bell rang. Moments later, Madeleine was shown into the dining room.

'How nice to see you, my love,' he smiled, standing up to greet her. She kissed him tenderly on the lips.

It was a pleasant domestic scene, which, deep down, he knew might soon be over. Once he exposed Mordeccai for the murderer John believed him to be, his romance with Madeleine could only go one of two ways.

Either she would be grateful to him for releasing her from Mordeccai's evil influence. Or, she would never forgive him. He wanted her love, and not her gratitude. Whatever happened in the next two days would decide their future: be it together or otherwise.

'Would you like some breakfast?' he invited.

'I thought you'd never ask.'

They enjoyed a pleasant meal together.

'How's poor Jessie?' Madeleine asked, at last. 'Has there been any change in her condition?'

'I don't know. It seems she ran away from the hospital sometime yesterday, and we don't know where she's gone. There's a possibility she might have gone to Leamington, and I'm having enquiries made there.' John paused.

'As for her recovering, who knows? Dr Whiting says it could be at least another week before she recovers or even longer. Or she might never recover her wits. And that causes another problem. Even if we find her, the hospital refuses to have her, as they are concerned about their other patients.'

John took another mouthful of tea before continuing. He took the opportunity to study Madeleine over the rim of his teacup. There was no obvious reaction to his words, which gladdened him.

'Actually I am inclined to agree with them,' he continued. 'So I'm planning to have her arrested, as soon as she is found. I think she knows all about Edith's murder, and she may even be involved herself. If I'm lucky, it will shake her out of her so-called shock. I'm not convinced it's real, but then I'm only a policeman and not a doctor.'

'What makes you think she's gone to Leamington?'

'Someone answering her description was seen heading that way, and it's all we've got to go on, but I'm very confident we'll find her soon.'

'Where will you keep her, when she's found? The police station?'

'Yes. In fact I'm hoping once she's been arrested that it will encourage the killer to come after her. If he does, then there'll be quite a reception waiting for him. All my men will be heavily armed, and I have some soldiers there as well.'

'And if he doesn't come?'

'Then I'll have no option but to release her, probably late tomorrow night, and she'll have to take her chances.'

Suddenly Madeleine looked at the clock and gasped. 'Is that the time? I'm so sorry my love, but I must go.' She stood up, kissed him and moved to the door.

'Madeleine,' he called. 'I don't suppose Mordeccai saw anything of Robert Andrew in London, did he?'

'I'm sorry, my love.' Madeleine shook her head, blew him a kiss, and then she was gone.

He felt slight qualms of conscience for having lied to her. Jessie was still sleeping upstairs, under the watchful Seth and Mrs Simms.

Later that morning, anyone watching the police station, would have witnessed the sudden arrival of a figure, in manacles, being rushed into the police station, surrounded by several policemen. Hopefully, the watcher would have passed on the news that Jessie Brampton had arrived back in Warwick. In fact, the heavily escorted figure was one of John's men, wrapped in a cloak.

Now all John had to do was to wait. Hopefully Jessie would be safe in his house for the next few hours, before he could put the next part of his plan into operation. She would not be removed to the police station until much later, the next day.

It was a long day, during which John and his men made very little progress in their investigations. They knew John was working to a plan, but they were kept in ignorance of it: he would tell them when all was ready. At last John left the station and made his way home, where he had a visitor waiting for him, under Seth's watchful eye.

The man was waiting patiently in John's drawing-room. As soon as John had removed his coat, he went to meet him. His visitor's name meant nothing to him.

'Mr Mayfield? I'm Willie McEwan,' the stranger held out his hand, and John shook it, giving him time to study his visitor.

He judged Willie to be only a few years older than himself. At first glance, the man the looked quite kindly with a scholastic look about him, accentuated by a shock of grey hair, whiskers and a beard. But John was not fooled by his initial appearances. A closer examination showed the man was lean, and he looked physically fit and muscular. To John's experienced eye, he gave the distinct impression of having had a military background.

Being of a similar height, he looked straight into Willie's steel grey eyes and saw himself. This man was not the kindly scholastic person he appeared to be. And John knew this was not just a social call. He was glad Seth was hovering in the background, as he always did when John received any strange visitor.

'You can relax, though I can see my name means nothing to you,' smiled Willie. 'I used to be in the army and was stationed at Walvis Bay. One day whilst on patrol, we came across a shipwrecked English woman with lovely red hair.'

'Of course!' cried John. 'Sergeant Willie McEwan! How could I have forgotten your name, after all you did for Harriet. What brings you here?' At the same time he clasped Willie's hand in both of his.

'I was just passing through and thought I would see how Harriet was doing.' His face fell. 'I'm so sorry to hear she is no longer with us.'

John was silent for a moment. Although he did not feel threatened by this man, he also knew Willie was not telling him the truth.

He soon established Willie had nowhere to stay and offered him a bed for the night, which was quickly accepted. Likewise, Willie was happy to stay for supper. Seth served them some wine, then satisfied John was in no danger, went to arrange their supper, and have a bedroom prepared for the unexpected visitor.

Willie told John about the uncut diamonds Harriet had given him, and the rest of his platoon. Once his share of them had been realised, Willie left the army. However, it did not take him very long to become bored. Having money was all very well, but he missed the military life.

After his wife died, Willie drifted across to America, where his sister and her husband lived. Then the Civil War had started, and Willie had been happy to enlist in the Union army. Sadly, his brother-in-law joined the Confederates, and was killed at Shiloh.

It did not take the army long, to discover how Willie had a talent for working behind enemy lines. He was soon involved in all manner of clandestine operations, at which he excelled, although he did not give John any great details about them. When the war ended, Willie was no longer wanted by the American government, and he now indulged himself in travel. Money was no problem, as he had his own private income, plus what he had saved during the war.

'And so, finding myself in England,' he explained. 'For the first time in more years than I care to remember, I thought I would come look Harriet up, and to really say thank you for the diamonds.'

They had a pleasant meal together and John found himself telling Willie about the murders, Cornelius Lake and the *VLMH*.

'The *VLMH*!' Willie interrupted him. 'You be very careful when dealing with them. I don't think I've ever come across such a ruthless and evil lot of bastards in all my life. They're thought to be behind some real bad murders in America, both during and after the war. They have connections in all manner of land frauds, and terrorising the negroes. If you've got them here, then you've got real trouble. If they think for one moment that you are a problem to them, they'll kill you, without giving it a second thought.'

John was taken aback by the vehemence of Willie's words. Yet when he thought about it, it seemed obvious, and merely strengthened John's views that he was dealing with an evil group of people. He would need to take very great care tomorrow night.

They were on their third glass of cognac, and John was seriously thinking of going to bed, when an ear-piercing scream was heard coming from the churchyard.

'Please God, not again,' prayed John as he leapt to his feet, and rushed for the door.

Willie was right behind him as John led the way through the kitchen, and into the back garden. Seth and another male servant joined them.

Without giving a moment's thought, John pulled open the back garden door, which led into the churchyard. As it opened, Willie caught sight of a slight movement in the churchyard, and without hesitating, he pushed John to one side. Even as he did so, there came the crash of a rifle, and a bullet thudded into the gate, where John had been standing only moments before.

Willie slammed the door shut, and he helped John to his feet. Nobody said a word as they all trooped back through the kitchen, and into the drawing room. Seth sent a servant to the police station, and then he poured two more cognacs. John insisted he and the other servant, who had been with them, had a glass as well. They did not demur.

Before the other glasses had been emptied, there came a frantic ringing of the front door bell. Seth went to investigate and found a sobbing Madeleine standing on the doorstep.

'Tell me it's not true!' she cried, with tears rolling down her cheeks. 'John hasn't really been killed, has he?'

'No, my love, I'm fully alive,' replied John, as he came into the hall. 'Whatever makes you think that I'm not?'

'I heard the servants saying you'd been killed, just after that shot was fired.'

John saw the look of genuine heartfelt relief on her face and he was glad. He moved her towards his study, following behind. Looking over his shoulder, he saw Willie creeping quickly upstairs.

For a while John held Madeleine until her sobbing subsided. Finally he kissed her tenderly and took her gently to the front door.

'Much I would love for you to stay the night, I must report this attack on me and I fear there will be little or no sleep for me tonight.' He shook his head. 'And I've got a very busy day ahead of me tomorrow.'

For a moment she stood, hugging him on the doorstep, unwilling to let go. 'Dare I ask,' she queried. 'Have you found Jessie?'

'Yes. But she's still saying nothing, in spite of being locked up.'

'Has anyone tried to get at her?'

'No. It looks like I've got that one wrong, but I'm still keeping the guards there, for tonight and tomorrow. I don't doubt the Watch Committee will complain about the cost. But, if nothing happens within the next twenty-four hours, then we'll have to turn her loose and she'll have to take her chances.'

Even as they spoke, the police horse and trap arrived and an anxious Sam Perkins climbed down. He was less worried once he saw John. Sam waited discreetly whilst John said goodnight to Madeleine and watched her go indoors.

'That was close Sam. If the man had shot a fraction earlier, then you could have been promoted tomorrow!'

CHAPTER TWENTY-ONE

Friday

John had not even tried going to bed. He had been kept busy after the shooting, and when he finally returned home, it was nearly 4 a.m. Yet he was not at all surprised to find Seth waiting up for him.

They shared a pot of tea together, and reminisced about their respective military service. When Seth finally went to bed, John retired into his drawing-room. For a while he sat at the table, and discussed his plans for the coming hours with Harriet, just as he always did when she was alive. After he finished, he looked longingly at her portrait, and was certain she was smiling her approval.

Even after all the months her portrait had hung there, he never stopped admiring the way Lucy Perkins had captured her. She was so life-like.

It still seemed incredible that he would never see her again.

He awoke with a start as a maid came into the room to clean out the hearth, and lay a new fire. She became all flustered at finding him there. He smiled at her, and made his way upstairs to his bedroom. Further sleep was now out of the question, so he washed, shaved and changed his uniform. After an early breakfast, he went on duty.

John was pleased to see that two wagons, each minus their wheels, had been placed in the road, on either side of the police station. They effectively prevented any other wagon, possibly loaded with gunpowder, from getting too close. As an extra preventative measure, each wagon was also guarded by some of John's men, each of whom was armed. Hopefully, these measures, which were crucial to his plan, would deter any attack on the police station. He needed the killer to be able to strike elsewhere.

His office had not yet been fully repaired after the fire, and the whole building smelt of fresh paint. He had taken up temporary residence at the rear of the building. Harry Barlow soon appeared with a mug of tea, and a large cloth bound parcel.

'This arrived for you, guv'nor, a short time ago. The man said you were expecting it.'

'I am indeed,' smiled John. This package was crucial to his plans for later that night.

Harry Barlow realised John was not going to enlighten him, so he left.

The morning passed slowly, with the only interruption being the arrival of Jessie Brampton, wearing extremely old clothes, unconscious, and thrown over Harry Barlow's shoulder. Anyone who came any where close, reeled at the smell of alcohol coming from her. To all appearances, she was dead drunk.

She had been smuggled out of John's house in a laundry basket, which ultimately arrived at Thomas and Sarah's. Soon afterwards, Redman had sent a servant to find a policeman, to remove a drunken woman from their back garden. The plan had worked.

John was glad when it was 2 p.m. and time for his special planning meeting. Mathew, Sam and Caleb arrived together. Soon afterwards Willie joined them. After the necessary introductions had been made, John outlined all the information they had accumulated to date. They all agreed how Mordeccai clearly was their main suspect, both for the murders in Warwick and America.

John explained to them about the concerns Silas had raised, regarding the injuries Jessie and Edith had sustained, so soon after he had medically examined them.

'I don't suppose there's any change in Jessie's state, is there?' queried Mathew.

'Not really,' replied Sam. 'I've only just come from her. However, she is now eating and doesn't cringe in a corner. But, as for speaking...then no. She's still saying nothing.'

'May I ask a question?'

'Go ahead Willie,' answered John.

'With this girl, Jessie, being unable to talk at present, how can you use her to identify Mordeccai as being your killer?'

'A good question.' John was silent for a moment.

They all waited, expectantly, for his answer.

'At about 11 o'clock tonight, Jessie will be released from custody, and she will take a walk in St Mary's churchyard, where I hope Mordeccai will be waiting for her.'

For a moment nobody spoke.

'Guv'nor you...'

'You can't do...'

'No. No...'

'I don't believe this...'

Everyone spoke up together, but John only smiled, then he held his hands up. 'Don't worry, she'll be well protected. I want every entrance and exit to and from the churchyard covered. Also, there will be men inside the churchyard itself. We know where he's likely to strike. And there's something else, which is where I will need your help, Willie.'

John went on to explain the next part of his plan.

'No guv'nor!'

'That's absolute madness...'

'What if it goes wrong?'

The three policemen voiced their concern and looked at Willie to support them. But they saw he was grinning.

'I like it,' he chuckled. 'I like it. It's a damned good idea, and if it works, we'll catch Mordeccai in the act.'

'Thank you Willie,' said John, looking him straight in the eye. 'Now, please don't get me wrong. I'm truly very grateful for your actions last night, otherwise I would not be here today. But what are you really doing here in Warwick?'

'Like I told you: it's just a coincidence. I was passing through, and decided to come and visit Harriet.'

'In this job, we don't believe in coincidences.'

John was aware how the atmosphere had changed, in the office. He also saw Sam had stood, and moved to stand in front of the door.

'You're quite right.' Willie looked abashed.   'Yes I came here deliberately, on behalf of the American government, who still employ me. We really would like to see Mordeccai Carew, or to give him his real name, Michael Concannon, brought to justice. The late unfortunate Cornelius Lake was on the right track, but nobody told him just who he was mixing with.' Willie paused.

'We have an agent in Pinkerton's who passes on all manner of useful information to my department, so we knew, sooner or later, Lake would end up here. Regrettably, he blundered into something which was too big for him. And knowing of his reputation, the chances were he kept quite a fair bit of information to himself. And I like to think if Pinkerton's had known of his heart problems, he would not have been sent.'

'That oversight, coupled with him not telling us everything, almost certainly cost him his life,' added John. 'However, his abductors were just a little bit too clever, when they tried to put the blame onto Dr Whiting.' John paused and looked straight at Willie.

'But let me ask you again. What are you really doing here?'

'The Embassy had a visit from your man, Andrew, on Monday, which resulted in him positively identifying Concannon to me. We were quite happy to leave it to you, as you have a good reputation, and if possible, we wanted to keep the American angle out of it.' Willie sighed.

'But when we discovered Andrew had gone missing, then I was instructed to come and give you all the help I could, albeit unofficially. My knowing Harriet really was a coincidence, and one, which I must confess, I used to get to you.'

'Do you know where Robert is?' asked Mathew.

'No. Regrettably we don't. He should have gone to meet with his brother-in-law, but he never made it. After leaving us, he disappeared.'

Satisfied with Willie's explanation, they discussed the forthcoming evening for some time, repeating the plan several times. At last John called a halt.

'We've been over it enough times. But if something goes wrong, or which we haven't planned for, we'll deal with it as best as we can.' John looked at his watch.

'It's just on 5 o'clock now. I want everybody in position by 9 o'clock. Only those who have to come here are to do so, otherwise they are to go straight to their positions. And I know they are all trustworthy, but it's absolutely vital they keep a very low profile, once they are in position.'

The others left to brief their men, and make their final arrangements for the forthcoming night's work. Whilst having several reservations about John's plan, they knew nothing else was likely to succeed. Sam had been tasked with acquiring some other articles which John wanted, and he hoped Lucy would help him in another way.

Back in his office, John went through the plans yet again, as the minutes ticked slowly away. He hoped to God he was right about all this.

Was he letting himself be led the wrong way because of the personalities involved in the affair, and his relationship towards them?

Was he letting his animosity towards Mordeccai influence his thoughts? Was he letting his love for Madeleine deflect him from the correct path?

Taking up a pen and paper, he wrote out three short lists. These were the main characters in the whole affair. Even before he started to write down their names, he knew what his list would tell him. And there would be names which appeared in each list.

AMERICA	WARWICK	WHITE HOUSE
Mordeccai	*Mordeccai*	*Mordeccai*
Madeleine	*Madeleine*	*Madeleine*
Cornelius	*Cornelius*	*Edith*
Silas	*Lottie*	*Jessie*
	Edith	*Cornelius?*
	Jessie	*Silas*
	Silas	

At first glance, Lottie was the odd one out, not having been in America, but she was linked to Cornelius and Silas by the scarf. And now with confirmation from Willie that Mordeccai Carew and Michael Concannon were one and the same person, the link was there.

When he wrote down the White House, John's thoughts strayed back to the time when it was owned by James Cooper, all those years ago. He had hoped never to return to it, but ironically, Madeleine worked from there. Suddenly a thought struck him. Surely, after all these years, this business wasn't connected with Cooper?

He tried to dismiss the thought.

But another one quickly took its place. What had Robert said about the house being owned by a company in London? Standing up, he went into Robert's small office, and looked in his filing system. He was right. It was in London, and, as he knew from his earlier days there, it was by the side of the Thames.

What if Robert had gone there to make some enquiries? What if he had seen something, but had been discovered? Knowing the type of people they were now dealing with, he knew it was highly likely he would never see Robert again.

The very least he could do was to send a telegram to Robert's brother-in-law, Gordon Mayne and get the place raided. Then he remembered it was late on Friday, and the telegraph office would have closed for the week-end.

And so he waited as the minutes slowly ticked away.

Just after 11 p.m. there was a commotion in the police station. A gentleman passing by, with his lady, was appalled to hear the shouting and screaming coming from the building.

'**YOU BASTARD CRUSHERS!**' screeched a high pitched female voice. '**BASTARDS! BASTARDS! BASTARDS!**'

The same gentleman saw the police station doors open and a slightly built female figure was pushed out into the street, and the cold clear night.

'Any more of that sort of language, Jessie Brampton,' snarled a police constable, 'And you'll come back in, and go before the magistrates. Understand?'

The female figure gathered herself, and blew a raspberry at the back of the retreating constable. Shrugging her shoulders, the figure blew another raspberry at the gentleman and his lady, before strutting off towards the Market Place.

'Well really!' puffed the gentleman. 'Whatever is the town coming to?'

On leaving the Market Place, the female made her way to the Old Square. She was seen to pass by a shop doorway, slow down and go into it. Several minutes later, she emerged, straightening her dress, and was accompanied by a sturdy, and well-dressed man. It was obvious, to any bystanders, what the couple had been doing in the doorway, although nobody actually could remember having seen the man before.

He took her by the arm, and they walked into Church Street, heading towards the Court House. She leant on his arm, but as they reached the second entrance into the churchyard, she whispered something in his ear. The man embraced her, they parted company, and she made her way into the churchyard.

She had only gone a few steps, when a dark figure appeared before her, in the moonlight.

'Psst! Psst!'

The figure beckoned to her, and she followed it further into the churchyard.

Although the attack was expected, it still came as a violent surprise.

Suddenly the dark figure grabbed the female's hair, and at the same time slashed towards her throat with a scalpel. The attacker was momentarily confused, when the hair came off the intended victim's head. It was a wig.

At the same time, the female lurched backwards and stumbled over a gravestone. Whilst the scalpel missed her throat, it cut deeply through the dress, which fell open before slicing upwards, through her right cheek, which began to bleed profusely.

Undoubtedly, had the intended victim not tripped over the grave, it could have been a fatal slash, except the attacker had felt a hard jar, as the scalpel hit the victim's chest, which had not been expected.

'**Mathew! Sam!**' shouted the female figure as it fell.

On hearing the voice, now immediately recognisable as that of a man, the attacker hesitated for a few seconds. The delay gave Mathew and Sam time to tackle the figure in black.

Sam's staff descended heavily on the back of the hand holding the scalpel. Meanwhile Mathew had closed with the figure, and kicked his legs from underneath him. The figure fell and Sam dropped onto its back with all his weight.

He and Mathew soon had a set of manacles on the figure, as more running policemen arrived on the scene. In spite of being manacled, the figure still fought hard, and kicked out. Harry Barlow grunted as one kick hit him on the shin. He kicked back, and was gratified to hear the grunt from his victim, as his boot struck hard.

Moments later, they had leg irons on the figure in black, thereby restricting his movements further.

Mathew was helping John up, from where he had tripped. Blood was flowing freely down his cheek. He tore up part of the dress John was wearing, and quickly formed a pad, which he instructed John to hold against his face.

'Have we got the bastard?' John asked between gritted teeth.

'Oh yes, we have indeed. Thanks to you, but don't you ever dare do anything like this again. If you hadn't fallen over that grave, it might have been too late for you.'

'I don't intend to. Thank God for the armour I borrowed from the Earl of Warwick, although I suspect he won't be too happy about the scratches. And I owe Jessie a new dress. And thank God for Harriet's grave, which I fell over.'

John was silent for a moment, as the enormity of what had happened sunk in, and he realised just how close he had been to being killed. It seemed Harriet was still protecting him, even in death.

'Thank you, my darling,' he whispered.

'Are you going to unmask him, guv'nor?' asked Sam.

'No. Let's all go back to the station, and we can draw lots for who has that privilege. Well done everybody!'

They all moved off, with their captive, into Church Street, where Eddie Chadwick waited with a closed carriage. The captive was bundled inside it, and John, Mathew and Sam followed. Eddie drove off, and the carriage was escorted by the other policemen.

Several minutes later, they were all back in the police station, where John was treated by Thomas Waldren, who had been on stand-by for the whole evening. He quickly put a few stitches in John's face.

'It needs looking at and stitching up properly,' said Thomas, as he worked. 'To be honest, I've seen some of the work Silas has done and I know he'll make a far neater job of you than me. But I think you'll still have quite a scar.'

Meanwhile Willie came into the office.

'You don't make a very good lover,' he grinned. 'Perhaps the scar will make you more attractive.'

'Well you don't exactly choose the most romantic places to entertain a girl, do you?' John replied. 'I ask you…a shop doorway? And you might at least have had a shave before inviting me out.' He winced, as he tried to smile.

The atmosphere in the police station was one of immense relief, and satisfaction following a job well done. They were all still high on adrenaline, and reaction had not yet had time to set in. Acting on Mathew's instructions, Sam had written out all their names on pieces of paper, which he folded and put into a police helmet, ready for the draw to be made.

In the charge room, there was great euphoria and excitement. Harry Barlow, a one time drummer in the army, had hold of two wooden rulers, which he was using as drumsticks and beating out a tattoo.

…tumpity tum: tumpity tum: tumpity tumpity tumpity tumpity tum…

He was accompanied by Eddie Chadwick, who had been a bugler. Now he was miming playing a bugle and giving a fanfare

…dah…di…dah…dah…di…dah…dah…dah…dah

Sat very still, on a bench, heavily manacled, was the masked figure in black.

Sam came in, shaking the helmet, containing the names. He continued shaking it. Mathew came in with John and Willie. A chorus of cheers and whistling greeted John, as he stood amongst them, still dressed in the remnants of Jessie's dress. They all wanted to shake his hand.

Thomas declined to attend the unmasking. 'No John,' he had said. 'It's you and your men's celebration. I'm not part of it.'

Mathew looked askance at John and then the two musicians.

'Let them be,' said John. 'It's celebration time.' He tried not to wince, as his face began to throb.

Sam offered the helmet to Willie, who made a big show of pulling out a piece of paper. He opened it slowly, turned it upside down, then he put on some spectacles, and peered closely at the name. His audience loved it, as he milked the moment. They cheered all the more, whilst the masked figure sat deathly still.

'And the winner is...Let's have a big roll of drums...'

Harry Barlow obliged.

'The winner is... Caleb Young!'

There came an even greater roll of drums and fanfare as Caleb strode over to the figure, and he slowly peeled back the mask.

The drums and fanfare rose to a crescendo, then stopped suddenly, as the mask was peeled away from the figure's face.

In horror, everyone turned to stare at John.

CHAPTER TWENTY-TWO

Later

M athew reacted first, and he ushered John out of the charge office and back to his own.

'Sergeant Perkins,' Mathew instructed on leaving. 'Have the prisoner charged and put in the cells.'

'Yes sir.'

'I don't have to tell any of you, just how dangerous this person is. When you have to make a visit, you will not go alone. Is that understood?"

A chorus of *yes sirs*, answered him.

All of a sudden, the jovial atmosphere of only a few moments before had gone. How desperately sorry they all felt for John. He had been adamant their murderer was Mordeccai, but only to discover he was not.

Willie was also shocked.

He too had believed, in fact he had wanted Mordeccai to have been the murderer. It would have made matters, and his specific assignment, so much simpler. Now this was shown not to be case, he would have to rethink his own strategy on how he dealt with Mordeccai: and replan it quickly.

There would be little time in which to act. If the police did nothing, he would have to do something on his own.

Willie shrugged. Perhaps he was not really surprised how matters had not gone according to plan. In his experience, quite often if a thing seemed just too easy to be true, then it often was. He would need to wait, although not for too long and see what happened next. Just give the crushers a few minutes to sort themselves out.

Thomas was horrified to see how ashen his friend had gone. He knew the loss of blood would not have helped, but from the sudden silence, in the charge office, he knew something had gone terribly wrong.

'Would I be correct in assuming it's not Mordeccai?' He asked.

Mathew nodded his head miserably.

'Then in God's name, who is it?'

The Warwick bound train from London had broken down, somewhere on the Oxford side of Banbury. Although Inspector Gordon Mayne had tried pulling rank, it seemed nobody was interested in helping him and his small party get to Warwick.

Likewise, no one could give him any estimate of how long it would take to make the necessary repairs, and continue their journey. To make matters worse, until the breakdown was repaired, no other trains could pass them.

Speed was now drastically important. Gordon knew they had to get to Warwick in time to intercept the convoy with the women on board, preferably before it started. Whilst he had another plan, he really wanted to rescue the women as soon as was possible. The weather had turned very cold again, and the thoughts of them being transported in open wagons, with little or no warmth, and in a drugged condition, made him far from happy.

But what really galled him, was the fact he had all the information at his fingertips, but the Warwick telegraph office was now closed until Monday, and that would be too late. There had been no alternative but to come up himself, with a few of his own trusted staff.

Now, their train was broken down in the middle of nowhere, and God alone knew when they would get going again. Walking into Banbury and hiring transport was not a viable option. They would just have to wait.

In Warwick, the six wagons were travelling along the Birmingham Road, prior to turning through the gates of the White House. Here they were met by one of Mordeccai's men. After the tired horses had been unhitched, fresh teams were attached, and then the drivers went to have some food. After they had eaten and taken a brief rest, they drove their wagons round to the front of the house, and waited for the order to load up the women.

Before Mathew could answer the obvious question Thomas had just asked, there came a long piercing scream from the cell block.

Mathew ran out to see what had caused it.

Meanwhile, John just sat with his head in his hands.

'I just can't believe it. I can't believe it. I can't believe it.'

'Tell me, old friend,' said Thomas gently. 'What can't you believe? Who is your murderer?'

Thomas was aware of the office door opening as he spoke, and a man entered. Looking up, he put his finger to his lips. The visitor nodded, said nothing and waited.

John raised his head, and stared at Thomas.

'This must be a nightmare. Tell me I'm going to wake up soon,' he pleaded.

'I'm sorry, John. It's for real. Waking up won't help. Tell me, who have you arrested?'

Thomas could not think who the murderer was, other than it had to be someone who John knew. But here, the choice was endless. Perhaps it was a local dignitary.

Finally the train was moving again, albeit slowly. Once it arrived at Banbury, it stopped, and all the passengers were transferred to another train.

After a further delay, the new engine got up steam, and moved out of the station.

'Madeleine,' John replied at last. His voice was so quiet, that Thomas had difficulty in hearing him.

'Madeleine?' Thomas could not believe what he was hearing. 'You say Madeleine is the murderer? I can't believe it! Surely there must be some mistake?'

'I'm afraid it's true, Thomas,' said Silas, who had been waiting quietly in the office.

The door opened again and they were joined by Mathew and Sam.

'Father,' said Silas urgently. 'Jessie has recovered her memory. Seeing Madeleine under arrest did the trick. She has told us how she saw Madeleine kill Edith, and I'm sorry, but there can be no doubt about it.'

'But that's not all, John,' said Mathew. 'Jessie's told us it's a white slavery racket they're running at the White House, and the girls are being moved out tonight. We've got to stop them.'

John sat for a few seconds as he absorbed the news.

'Right, this is what we'll do.'

The others breathed a sigh of relief. John was back in charge again.

For the next few minutes, there was a flurry of activity.

One constable was sent to commandeer several cabs. Another was sent to John's house to bring Seth, certain of his servants, and two saddled horses round to the police station. On the way, they were to collect Redman.

When Seth arrived, he and Thomas set about rousing several other local men, who would be sworn in as special constables. Meanwhile John wrote two short letters to the neighbouring Leamington Borough Police, and the County Police at Kenilworth. He asked for some assistance from them in policing Warwick, and being prepared to join him at the White House, if necessary. The two nominated servants, now sworn in as special constables, mounted the horses and departed with the letters.

The cabs began to arrive, as did Redman and several of John and Thomas's servants. In his role as a magistrate, Thomas quickly swore them in as special constables, and they were tasked with guarding the police station until John returned. Redman would also direct the next detachment of special constables down to the White House, once they had arrived. Another magistrate had been roused from his bed, and he now joined them at the police station.

Within twenty minutes John had assembled his party of men, both regulars and specials. He had also changed out of the remnants of Jessie's dress, and taken off his breast plate. Now he was dressed in police uniform once more.

'This is what we are going to do,' John addressed his men. 'Leave your coats and helmets behind. Just take your manacles and staffs. These people are hard, and they will not hesitate to use extreme violence to resist arrest. So, we hit them first: and we hit them so hard they go down and stay down. Understood?'

They all nodded.

The men climbed on board the cabs, which set off at a quick trot along the Birmingham Road. When they arrived at the White House, the men climbed down from the cabs and waited. Once they were all down, the cabs went back to the police station for the next contingent of men.

The gates to the White House were open, and once John and his men were through, Eddie Chadwick closed them, and locked them with a set of manacles. He had already left a spare key for them at the police station.

John led the way following the gravel drive, but keeping to the grass to minimise the risk of them making any noise. Quietly they reached the last of the bushes, and peered through them.

Jessie's information had been quite correct.

There was a bustle of activity outside the front of the house, and they saw several wickerwork baskets being loaded onto the wagons. Four of the wagons looked already full, and the fifth was getting that way.

The atmosphere amongst the men loading the wagons was fairly relaxed. However, John noticed two men, each armed with a shotgun, generally patrolling around the perimeter of the house and lawns. He also saw Mordeccai going from wagon to wagon, making last minute checks. Unlike the others, he was clearly agitated, and on edge.

Seeing Mordeccai still at liberty, brought back the overwhelming misery of Madeleine's betrayal to John. But he quickly had to push it to the back of his mind. He would have to cope with that at a later date. Here was his priority for the moment. Undoubtedly Mordeccai was wondering where his sister was.

For several moments, John was tempted to shout out how she was in custody. But common sense prevailed. They needed as much secrecy and surprise as possible.

Gordon Mayne was the first off the train when it arrived at Warwick. Surprisingly there were no cabs to be had, and so his party had to walk quickly into town, and to the police station. Although it had turned midnight, he was further surprised to see many of the houses were still lit.

'Is the town normally this awake at this hour?' he asked.

'No,' replied his immediate companion. 'There must be something going on.'

When they arrived at the police station, Gordon was surprised to find the door was locked, and the shutters securely fastened, although there were some lights inside. He knocked loudly and waited. After what seemed an eternity, a small inspection grille in the door opened and an old face looked out.

'Yes?' queried the face.

'We want to see Mr Mayfield.'

'He's not here. So go away'

'Redman, is that you?' asked the man stood alongside Gordon.

'Is that you, Mr Andrew? We all thought you were dead.'

'I nearly was. Now please will you let us in, and tell us what's happening.'

Moments later the bolts were drawn back, and the door opened. Inside Robert, Gordon and his companions were confronted by a motley collection of men, each armed with a weapon of some sort. They visibly relaxed as they recognised Robert. Quickly Redman explained what had happened.

They were soon joined by the magistrate. Gordon explained how he and his five companions were police officers from London, who did not have any powers to act as such in Warwick. The magistrate nodded knowingly, and he quickly swore then in as special constables.

By now the first of the cabs had returned to the police station. Gordon's little band, including Robert, quickly piled into three of them, and they made their way to the White House. Sometime after they had left, Redman realised he had forgotten to give them the spare key to the manacles on the gates.

As they arrived at the White House and found the gates were locked, there came several blood curdling cries from inside the grounds.

John despatched Seth and Willie, being the two most experienced military men, to take care of the two armed sentries. It did not take them long. A sharp blow to each of their heads quickly rendered them unconscious. Two gags and sets of manacles completed the task.

Once they had returned to John, he gave the order to slowly advance, intending to get as near to the men as possible, before being seen. They were nearly fifteen feet away, when a man coming out of the house saw them.

'HEY!' he shouted. 'WHO ARE YOU?'

'NOW!' screamed John.

He led the charge, screaming at the top of his voice. The others were close behind him, also screaming. Their screams worked, and the police were amongst Mordeccai's men before they had time to react.

Staffs rose and fell, and several of Mordeccai's men went down. But all too soon the initial surprise was over, and his men fought back ferociously. John was now aware of some of his men falling, and they were forced to retreat. As they did so, John saw another group of six men running towards them from behind. He turned to shout a warning, but he was surprised to see they did not stop, but ran head on into Mordeccai's men.

These new helpers gave John's men fresh heart and they resumed their attack. But by now Mordeccai's men had recovered, and they were beginning to fight back with a fierce desperation.

Suddenly there came the sound of horses on the gravel drive as several more cabs arrived. Men leapt from them even before they had stopped. They were a mixture of special constables, plus some regulars from Leamington and the County forces.

John found himself facing Mordeccai, who glowered at him with undisguised hatred. Taking John completely by surprise, Mordeccai dropped his shoulder, charged and knocked him to the ground. Before John could react, Mordeccai had kicked him hard in the ribs. John both felt and heard some of them break. As he gasped for breath, Mordeccai kicked him again. He wished he had kept the Earl's breastplate on. But it was too late now.

Before he knew what was happening, Mordeccai was kneeling over him.

'Now I'm going to kill you, you bastard. And do you know why? Not for spoiling my plans here, but for shagging my wife.'

'Your wife?' gasped John, genuinely puzzled.

'Yes. Madeleine's my wife! Not my sister.'

John winced at yet another betrayal.

'But I didn't...' he began.

'I saw you, when you were in the summer house, in the snow, only the other night. I should have killed you then.'

'In the end I couldn't make it,' coughed John. 'We never made it.'

'Too bad: and now you die. It's a pity she can't be here to see it happen. Where is she?'

'Locked up for murder, and with luck you'll join her on the gallows.'

Mordeccai stopped for a moment, as he absorbed what John had just told him.

'You bastard!' Mordeccai banged John's head on the ground. 'This is where you die. It's not like the last time you fought here, is it? No doxy to come to your aid, eh?'

Just at that moment John did not really care. His body was a mass of pain from where Mordeccai had kicked him, and he ached elsewhere. But his physical hurts were nothing compared to his mental pain.

Not only was Madeleine the woman he thought he loved, a killer, but she was also married, and had been all along. How right Emma was about her *having played a part*. He was almost glad to feel Mordeccai's hands go round his throat. Then he heard a faint swishing sound, immediately followed by a grunt of pain from his attacker.

Before Mordeccai could react, Sam Perkins was running up to him. Over the years he had not lost his skill and deadly accuracy, when it came to throwing his staff, and other items, at people.

'We're not finished yet, Mayfield!' snarled Mordeccai, as he got to his feet. 'I'll seek you out, wherever you are, and then I'll kill you.'

Leaving John on the ground, Mordeccai ran off towards the rear of the house. He had always considered the possibility of things going wrong, and planned accordingly. At the end of the rear garden of the house was a field, which led down to the railway track. On the other side of the track, he had a horse already saddled and waiting for just such an emergency.

Initially he did not see Sam running after him. Neither man saw Willie also running in the same direction.

Slowly Sam began to gain on Mordeccai, as they left the garden and moved into the field. When Mordeccai looked behind him for the first time, and saw Sam following him relentlessly, he was not too concerned. He had another plan, which should work, although it would need very precise timing. As if to remind him, he heard the whistle of an approaching train.

Sam also heard the approaching train and he had visions of Mordeccai trying to get on board. It was common knowledge, how the Birmingham bound trains had to slow here, and then gather up steam to get up the Hatton incline. Putting on an extra spurt, he began to steadily close the gap between them.

Still out of sight, Willie also heard the train and reasoned the same as Sam, but he also knew he was probably too far away to do much about it.

Sam was only a few yards behind Mordeccai as they approached the railway track, and it then he noticed his quarry was running parallel to the track, heading towards the oncoming train, and letting Sam catch him up. Sam realised what Mordeccai was planning to do.

At the very last moment, Mordeccai would jump across the track, in front of the train, which would be too late for Sam to follow. As it was a goods train, Sam knew it would be a long one. By the time it had cleared, Mordeccai would have long been gone. Sam carefully watched every move he made.

When the train was just a few yards away Mordeccai took a last look at Sam. Moments later, he leapt in front of the train and onto the other side of the track. As he landed he turned to smirk at his pursuer, only to find Sam had also jumped over the track. His next move took Sam by surprise.

Turning on his heel, Mordeccai started to jump back over the track. But, as he did so his foot slipped, and he fell onto the rails immediately in front of the train.

Sam could only watch in horror, as the train ran over the screaming Mordeccai.

The driver put his brakes on, but it was far too late. Once the train had finally screeched to a halt, the white faced engine driver and his fireman ran back to Sam, quickly recognising his uniform.

'There's nothing for you to worry about,' Sam told them gently. 'I was chasing him, and he fell whilst trying to get away. Believe me, there's nothing any of us could have done. It was entirely his fault. And the world is now a much better place for his passing.'

'And I also saw it all happen, just as the sergeant said,' endorsed Willie, as he approached them. 'None of you could have stopped it.'

It was some time before Sam was able to return to the White House.

When he did, he found it to be fully in control of the police.

CHAPTER TWENTY-THREE

Execution Eve

John sat quietly in his office, and watched the minutes tick away ever so slowly, as the early evening progressed into night. How he wished tomorrow would come and go. Then perhaps, just perhaps, he might get some rest. God knew how he needed it.

At 8 a.m. tomorrow, Madeleine Pascoe or Concannon, which was her correct name, would keep her appointment with the hangman.

As he sat there, John relived the events of the past few weeks, which had started with Edith's murder, and his growing suspicions about Madeleine's involvement. Then as if the betrayal of her being the killer was not enough, it had transpired she was already married to Mordeccai Carew alias Michael Concannon.

Every time John looked in the mirror, he saw the scar on his cheek and relived, yet again, that terrible night. Thomas was right about Silas's skill with a needle, and he had sewn up his father's cheek as a labour of love. Consequently, the scar was nowhere near as livid as it might have been.

When Sam and Willie had returned with the news of Concannon's death, although John could still only think of him as Mordeccai Carew, he was relieved. Whilst there would have to be an inquest into the man's death, it would now be a much lower key affair. The coroner agreed, and he played it all down, in view of the forthcoming trial at the Assizes.

Thomas and Silas had worked hard on the injured policemen, after they had tended to the rescued women, whom John had insisted were treated first. As the night wore on, two other doctors were called out to assist. Both Lucy and Lawrence Perkins came with their cameras, and took numerous photographs of the scene.

At one stage, Willie came over to John, with a woman hanging on his arm. John recognised her as Jane Howatt, whom he had seen at the White House, when he visited there with Mathew. In fact neither man had liked her.

'John, let me introduce you properly to Jane Howatt.'

'We've already met,' came John's stiff reply.

'No, you haven't. You met Jane Howatt, one of the gang. Let me now introduce you to the real Jane Howatt, who is a special agent employed by my department in Washington. She did what she could to help Edith and Jessie escape. But, apparently Madeleine already knew she was one of my agents, and treated her quite badly. She'll tell you all she can, but she won't testify in court.'

John started to protest.

'No John. The last thing she needs is publicity. Her life would be in danger, and she would not be of any further use to us.'

Deep down, John knew he had no option but to agree. He also knew there would be no shortage of evidence to use against this gang.

During the course of the next few days, the White House began to give up its grim secrets with Jane's help. Four bodies were recovered, from where they had been buried. Jane identified them. They had succumbed to the beatings they had received.

Gordon Mayne was introduced to John by Robert Andrew, who had quickly told him what had happened. Leaving the two men talking, Robert went to start making a record of the arrested men. He left two of them to the very end, when he found an excuse to be left alone with them. They were both manacled and in leg irons, and so posed no threat. The two other constables were happy to leave Robert alone with them. It gave them a chance to go and smoke their pipes.

The two captives recognised Robert. To be more accurate, they had recognised his withered hand.

'Thought you'd got rid of me, didn't you cully?'

Robert had a long metal bar in his good hand, which he tapped against his bad one. It was a similar gesture to the one they had used on him.

'It wasn't personal mate,' whined one of them. 'We was just doing our job. Please don't hit us.'

For a long moment Robert looked at them.

'I know what I'll do,' he said at last. 'I'll spread the word round in the gaol that you don't like women, and have your minds set on men only. That'll give you quite an interesting time, if you live long enough that is. Just think of all those sex starved men in clink. Oh they'll have great sport with you.'

Turning on his heel he walked away from them. Deep down he knew he would say no such thing, but they would not yet know that.

As the days progressed, John and his men plus all their helpers became the toast of the town, and for the next week they never had to buy a drink. Whilst John's First Battle of the White House, in 1840, had long been celebrated, the Second Battle, which had involved many more people, quickly overtook it.

Being more than true to his word, John bought Jessie not one but three new dresses, to replace the one which he had been wearing when Madeleine slashed it. He also replaced the one Lucy had lent Jessie.

At the same time, Jessie's trade increased dramatically. In early 1868, she became the long term mistress of a Leamington businessman, and was able to give up the street life.

Strictly speaking John's injuries kept him at home for several days, officially off duty. However, he spent much of that time at the White House. Gordon Mayne stayed on for a while, and kept him company.

John learned the full story concerning the attempt on Robert's life, and how he had been fished out of the Thames by the two policemen. They decided he had tried to take his own life, and Robert was put into a mental institution where he stayed until Gordon had managed to get him released on the Friday morning.

Thanks to the information Robert had given him, and armed with a search warrant, Gordon had raided the warehouse by the river, and the captive women were rescued only hours before they were due to be shipped out of the country.   There was no trace of what had happened to all the other women, who had fallen into the clutches of the *VLMH.*

After leaving one of his sergeants in charge, Gordon, five of his men, and Robert had headed for Warwick. They had arrived at the White House just in time to give John some much needed support, after having climbed over the gates.

Using John's sick leave as an excuse, Mathew had taken charge of all the paperwork involved in putting the case together for hearing at the Lent Assizes. This way, it was Mathew who formally charged Madeleine with murder, and not John.

Much to everyone's surprise, especially John, she pleaded guilty to Edith's murder.   At the end of the hearing, she remained absolutely emotionless as the judge put on his black cap, and solemnly sentenced her to death. Several other members of the gang received similar sentences.

John had sat with Willie, behind her in the court. If she had been aware of their presence, she did not acknowledge them.

After the trial, Willie took John for a farewell drink at the *Warwick Arms.*

'Willie, who are you?' asked John.

'Let's just say, I really do represent the American government, or to be more accurate, certain members of it, in particular the Irish faction. You see, Concannon or Carew as you called him, always said he operated on behalf of the Fenians.' Willie paused and took a sip of his drink.

'Believe you me, the Fenians would not want to be associated with any of his activities. And, as I have said, he made many enemies in America. We lost track of where he was, suspecting that Jane's letters were being intercepted. Your uncovering him, or rather Robert uncovering him, changed matters drastically.' Willie took another drink.

'Quite simply, my orders were to make sure he stopped being an embarrassment: and I was to do whatever it took, to ensure he caused no more trouble.'

'So you would have killed him?'

'If necessary, yes.'

'And was his death really an accident?'

'Oh yes. Have no doubts on that score.'

They had another round of drinks.

'Tell me John. Just for Harriet's sake, is there anything you would like me to do before I go? I shan't stay for the hanging.'

John thought for a moment.

'Actually there is.'

During the course of the next round of drinks, they were observed talking very quietly and secretively.

Willie finished his drink, shook hands with John, and left. John had another drink, and then went back to his empty home.

Sometime during the night, the White House was found to be on fire. Although they tried, the town's fire brigade, even with help from their colleagues in Leamington and Kenilworth, failed to extinguish the fire. It seemed to have broken out in every room at the same time. Shortly before it started, a man who answered broadly to Willie's description, was seen leaving the area, and heading towards Birmingham.

When that information reached John's ears, he insisted in searching the London side of town, which was in the opposite direction. None of his men queried his instruction.

No-one was ever arrested in connection with the fire that totally destroyed the White House. It would be many years before it was rebuilt.

John's thoughts were interrupted by a knock on his office door.

'Excuse me, guv'nor,' said Harry Barlow. 'But Warder Johnson is here to see you.'

'Come in, Charles,' called John. 'How's the leg?' he enquired as he shook the warder's hand.

'Fine, Mr Mayfield, sir. Fine. Yon American doctor did a good job. I've come at Governor Mitchell's request.' He stopped and chewed at his lips. 'The prisoner Concannon has asked to see you.'

John was stunned. He had not spoken to Madeleine since before her arrest, and he had always kept out of her sight when she appeared at court.

'Mr Mitchell says it is entirely your choice, and he would not seek to influence you one way or the other. However, if you agree to see her, I have a carriage outside and we can go now.'

At first John was inclined to say no, but then he thought better of it. Minutes later, he was sat alongside Charles Johnson as he drove to the gaol.

Warwick Gaol had once been conveniently situated within a short walking distance of the police station. That all changed in the early 1860s, when the transportation of felons to Australia ceased. Consequently, convicts were now sentenced to varying terms of imprisonment in England. Along with many other places, Warwick's original gaol was no longer big enough, and a new one had been built just out of town, in the area known as the Cape.

'The town's getting busy,' remarked Charles. 'There are more people around than when I came to collect you.'

John had also noticed the growing crowds. He knew there were three main reasons for their macabre interest in the forthcoming hanging.

Firstly there was the notoriety attached to Madeleine. The other members of the gang, who had received death sentences, had been hanged the previous week. Madeleine would have the gallows to herself.

Secondly, tomorrow's execution would be the last public one to take place in Warwick. After many centuries, public executions in England were due to cease in the next few weeks. Whilst they would still take place, they would occur inside the prisons, with only a few official witnesses.

Both men also knew the third reason for the early gathering of the crowds, although it was only 8 p.m. with another twelve hours to go. But viewing points, at the new prison for watching executions, were limited: only the early arrivals would be able to see what happened.

Fifteen minutes later, John had arrived at the prison where he was shown into a visiting room. After a short wait, Madeleine arrived dressed in formal black prison dress, accompanied by a wardress, and looking very pale. He thought how she had aged dramatically, and her once attractive face was now lined and drawn. There were large shadows under her eyes. John felt glad he was not the only one who was not sleeping.

'Thank you for coming John,' Madeleine said as she sat down.

'How are you?' said John, as he sat down. 'Sorry, that was a stupid question.'

'Will you...will you be there tomorrow?'

'Yes.'

'Thank you. At least I won't feel completely alone.'

They sat in silence for a moment.

'Is that why you wanted to see me?' John was beginning to feel annoyed.

'No,' she replied. 'I felt you deserved an explanation from me. I have written it all down, which you can have after tomorrow and use it as you will, but I wanted to tell you myself.'

'Why did you do it?'

'For revenge.'

'For revenge? Revenge on who?'

'You!'

John was completely lost for words. Had he heard her properly? All these killings were to get her revenge on him? For what reason?

'Me? Why?'

'Because you were responsible for the death of the love of my life,' she continued. 'You didn't kill him with your own hands, but you had him killed, on the gallows here in Warwick. I have always held you responsible for the death of my beloved Charles.' She paused and waited for her words to register.

John sat back in his chair, and he quickly went through, in his mind, people who had been hanged here, during his tenure of office, who had the name Charles.

There was only one.

'Charles Pearson?' he asked quietly, almost disbelievingly.

'Yes: my beloved Charles.'

'But he committed murder in front of numerous witnesses. He got no more than the law of the land demanded.'

'That's as maybe. But if you hadn't started interfering in his business affairs, it would not have happened.'

Yet again, John was lost for words. This meeting was not going anything like he had expected it to.

'Why did it take you so long?' It was the only thing he could think of asking.

'Oh I started soon after his death. The Whiting bitch lost her husband and son. She thought it was cholera, but it was one of my poisons. The trouble was it gave me a taste for killing. Next I turned my attentions to you. I don't think your Harriet liked the play I wrote.'

The silence in the room was electric. How well he remembered what little he had seen of that play. It had driven Harriet away from him, and yet, in doing so had probably saved her life.

Suddenly he felt deathly cold, as he sensed which direction this conversation was now taking.

Madeleine took a deep breath and continued. 'Her being lost at sea was a bonus, and it saved me a job. You see, I was determined to make you, and the Whiting bitch suffer, before I killed you both as well.'

'So, it was you who killed my Laura, and our unborn child?' John's voice was very quiet and full of menace.

CHAPTER TWENTY-FOUR

Later

Madeleine nodded her head. 'Yes,' came her quiet reply.
John felt totally stunned, and numbed. This woman…This woman,
sat in front of him: a woman whom he had begun to love, was not just a
murderer. She had murdered his Laura and their unborn child, all those years
ago. And to think, he had been contemplating asking her to marry him! No
wonder Harriet had stopped him making love to her.

He became possessed by a hard rage and the veins stood out in his face
and neck.

'By God!' he snarled. 'I'll save the hangman a job.'

He jumped suddenly to his feet, knocking his chair over in the process.

'Easy sir!' cautioned Charles Johnson, as he laid his hands on John's
shoulders. 'Don't sink to her level.'

For a moment John remained taut, but he slowly relaxed as the warder's
words sank in.

'You're right,' he replied, and turned to leave.

Madeleine had remained calm throughout John's rage. 'Stay a moment
longer,' she pleaded.

John made no further attempt to leave, but he did not resume his seat.

'Make it quick, as I am not sure just how much longer I can bear to be in
the same room as you.'

His words struck home, and he saw tears appear in her eyes. 'I do not
expect you to forgive me, but there is one thing you must believe. Although
I came back to Warwick expressly to destroy you, I found I couldn't do it.'

She paused, and gave a deep sigh, before continuing. 'You see, although I was married to Michael, I genuinely found myself not just liking you, but falling in love with you.'

She brushed the tears from her cheeks with the back of her right hand.

'When I found out Harriet had survived the shipwreck, I set out to kill her,' she continued. 'But when I arrived here, I learnt she was already close to death, so I let her be. By a stroke of good fortune, the house next to you was empty, so I took on the lease, and staged my arrival just as your funeral party was leaving.'

John slowly absorbed her words. What had Emma Roberts said? *I just felt it was all an act.*

'Our, or rather my intention, was to get you to propose to me. If you didn't, then this is a leap year, and so I would make the proposal. Originally I was going to leave you standing at the altar. However Michael came up with a better idea. He would stop the wedding ceremony by stating I was already married to him. The scandal would have finished you.'

John continued gazing in horror at this woman.

How could he have been so taken in by her? Obviously she had exploited his weakness, just after Harriet's death. She was a cold, hard calculating woman, the likes of which he had never met before. He shook his head in total disbelief. How had he ever fallen for her charms?

'I did not want to do that. I decided to just fade quietly out of your life, when we wound up the White House job. That would have been punishment enough for you, and I would have been satisfied.' She paused.

'But Michael had seen us that night in the summer house and he assumed the worst. I told him what had really happened, but he did not believe me, and that was when he decided to kill you. I was truly relieved when he missed.'

Both John and Willie had agreed how she had seemed genuinely relieved he had escaped.

'And that was when you gave your game away,' said John. 'None of my servants had said anything about me having been killed. You assumed Michael or Mordeccai, or whatever his name was, had killed me. But he had missed thanks to Willie McEwan.'

'I realised my mistake too late, but I still had to carry on. We knew we couldn't leave until the following night when the wagons arrived. And it gave me more time to find, and silence Jessie. She and Edith knew too much, and they had to be silenced. Once Lake appeared on the scene, and I recognised him, in the *Warwick Arms* with you, then we knew our days at the White House were numbered.'

'When did you buy it?'

'It was soon after Charles had been buried. I used some of the money he had left behind, which I ensured you lot never found.'

'And you made other mistakes too. Why tie Silas Whiting's scarf round Lake's neck to make it look it had been strangled?'

'To put the blame on him, as I tried with Lottie Goodwin. I knew it was his scarf. I thought it would be a lovely touch. You, the Whiting bitch's friend, being responsible for the execution of her son. How poetic. I had tried during the war, with those other whores, but Lake was either too clever, or too stupid not to make the connection.'

'He was actually too clever for you, especially in death. In reality, in spite of the *VLMH,* you knew very little about medicine. Had you had that knowledge, you would have known a post mortem examination would reveal he died of a heart attack. Unlike you, he was not determined to have Silas hanged at any price. You see, you made mistakes over there. The nurse who you killed at Gettysburg was not a whore. Also, Silas was not at the scenes of the last two killings. He had been hospitalised. Lake's appearance panicked you, didn't it?'

She nodded.

'One last question John. Will you think about forgiving me? I'll ask you tomorrow, and I'll die accordingly.'

He did not answer her. His mind was still in too much of a whirl.

'This really is the last question, John. Do you know who Silas Whiting's father is? I know it can't be the Whiting bitch's husband, because he was already dead.'

'Yes. He's my son.'

Madeleine's hands went to her face in horror.

John turned his back on her, without another word, and left the room with Warder Johnson. His mind was still reeling from her confession.

Charles led John away from the interview room. But instead of going back out to the carriage, he escorted him to Governor Stephen Mitchell's office.

'Mr Mitchell would like to see you sir, if you don't mind.'

John nodded absently, as he struggled to fully understand the enormity of Madeine's confession. She had killed all those people, just to get her revenge on him. He remained in a daze, as Charles took him to Stephen Mitchell's office. Just as they arrived, Stephen's previous visitor left. He nodded to John as he passed.

The man was George Smith, often known as *Topper* Smith or *Throttler* Smith. He was the hangman who would be performing tomorrow. John knew him by sight, but he made no effort to return the nod.

'I'll be waiting outside for you sir,' said Charles as he escorted John into the office.

'Thanks for coming, John,' greeted Stephen Mitchell, as he stood up to shake John's hand. 'Are you feeling all right?'

Not having seen John for a few weeks, he was shocked to see how gaunt and drawn his guest looked.

'As well as can be expected under the circumstances,' replied John, accepting the proffered seat, by the fire. He only now realised how cold he felt. Moments later, he was telling him about Madeleine's confession.

'She killed your wife Laura?' Stephen was appalled. 'It was before my time here, and I never had the privilege of knowing Laura, but I know how her death, and your failure to find her killer, has haunted you all these years.' He crossed over to his sideboard.

Bending down, he opened a door, took out two glasses and a bottle of cognac. He poured two generous measures, and handed one to John.

'I know your rule about not drinking on duty. As you know I have a similar one. But as of now, both of us are off duty. And I won't take no for an answer.'

John did not argue, but he accepted the cognac gratefully. It was a good drop and he did not object to a refill. For a while they talked of general matters, but John kept coming back to Madeleine's confession. Stephen was a good listener and he let him talk.

John declined a third drink, and stood up to go.

'Stay a moment, John. You know, you don't have to come tomorrow. Everybody will understand. I'm sure Mathew or one of your sergeants would come in your place.'

'Thank you for the offer. But no, I'll be there, both from a duty point of view, and I promised her I would be. And I think I need to be there, just to put the whole sorry affair to rest. To be honest with you, I think she's completely insane.'

'You may well be right. But she was examined by various doctors prior to the hearing. They all agreed she was fit to stand trial. And in any case, it's too late to do anything about it now.'

'Oh I know that, and to be honest with you, I don't think I would be at all happy for her to be confined in an asylum. It wouldn't be the first time such an inmate has escaped, and murdered again. And when I think of the horrors those women experienced at her hands, not only the killing and the rapes, but being sold into slavery, then I think it's best she hangs.'

'I'm sorry you had to see Smith just as you arrived. He was late getting here because of the crowds. As we all know, he's not the cleverest of hangmen. But I have told him, in no uncertain terms, if he bungles tomorrow, then he'll never have another job in this prison. Personally, I for one will not be sorry when capital punishment is abolished altogether, though I know it won't be in my lifetime.'

'Just at this moment in time, forgive me if I find it just a little hard to agree with you. But doing away with the public spectacle of public executions, is a step in the right direction.'

'I agree. After tomorrow, there will be no more public hangings here in Warwick. And very soon, the same will apply all over the country. Thank God.'

The two men said good night to each other, and Charles Johnson drove John back to the police station. Very conscious of how his passenger must be feeling after hearing that terrible confession, he made no attempt to engage John in conversation. However they both noticed how the crowds had grown considerably whilst John had been in the gaol.

'I'll be with you at half-past five tomorrow morning,' Charles advised, as he dropped his passenger at the police station. John nodded his appreciation, and went inside. He was not surprised to find Mathew and Sam already there. Taking them both into his office, John told them the gist of Madeleine's confession.

They were horrified about her revelation concerning Laura, and hoped John would derive some comfort from the knowledge. He had already decided not to go home, and they left him alone in his office.

For a long time he sat, just staring into space, as he went over and over in his mind what Madeleine had told him. His mind went back to the notes he had made on that terrible Friday when his world had totally fallen apart, yet again. He remembered thinking then, that James Cooper might still have figured in it somehow, and how he had dismissed the thought. Opening a drawer in his desk, John found his old notes, which he took out, and spread on his desk.

AMERICA	WARWICK	WHITE HOUSE
Mordeccat	*Lotite*	*Mordeccai*
Madeleine	*Edith*	*Madeleine*
Cornelius	*Cornelius*	*Edith*
Silas	*Mordeccai*	*Jessie*
	Madeleine	*Silas*
	Silas	

That was how he had read it at the time, firmly convinced that Mordeccai was the common link, not wanting to believe Madeleine or Silas were. To make matters worse, he had gone against his own golden rule, and thought it was just coincidental that the White House was the real hub of the secret.

He knew now how he had been blinded by his love for Madeleine, believing she was an innocent party. Consequently, he had kept her abreast with how his enquiries were progressing, just as she had intended he would. However he took some comfort from the fact her plotting had worked against her in the end.

God, what a lovesick fool he had been. If only he had followed his intuition, and added the names of Cooper, Pearson and Katherine to his notes, perhaps he might have seen it sooner. Taking up a pen, he dipped it in the inkwell and added Katherine's name to all the three columns. Next he added Cooper's and Pearson's names to the **WARWICK** and **WHITE HOUSE** columns.

Katherine and Silas were the common personal links to himself. He excluded Cornelius. Why, oh why hadn't he seen it before? John did not know just how long he sat there, staring at the paper on his desk.

Slowly he became aware of a tapping on his office window, which since the fire was now situated at the rear of the building. Puzzled, he stood up. Crossing the floor, he pulled back the shutters and opened the window slightly.

In the clear moonlight, he saw Madeleine, still dressed in her prison black, standing there. She looked the same as when he had last seen her, but her face now seemed harsher and more strained.

'John you must help me,' she pleaded. 'I've escaped from prison. Please don't send me back there. Please help me. If you really loved me once, then please, please help me now.'

Unsure of what to do, he opened the window, reached out into the back yard and started to help her inside. Then she screamed, and he felt a hand on his shoulder.

'Guv'nor! Guv'nor!' came Harry Barlow's urgent voice.

CHAPTER TWENTY- FIVE

Execution Day

John woke with a start, to find Harry gently shaking him by the shoulder. He was amazed he had even slept. Undoubtedly Stephen Mitchell's generous glasses of cognac had helped. Although he could have done without the dream he had just been having.

'What's the time?' he asked.

'I'm sorry, guv'nor; it's only half-past three, but Charley Johnson is here already. Mr Mitchell sent him early. You just won't believe the thousands of people who are in town at the moment, and every train brings more.'

Whilst Harry was speaking, John took off his tunic, and shirt, and he began to shave in the hot water Harry had brought him.

'Mr Mitchell feels if you don't go now, you'll just never get there,' Harry continued.

'What's the mood of the crowds like?'

'Fairly friendly, but Mr Harrison has alerted the Yeomanry to be ready if necessary. Hopefully they won't be needed.'

John mentally thanked Mathew for thinking about taking such a course of action, without bothering him.

'Where is Inspector Harrison?' John asked as he changed into his best tunic.

'Um…I think he and Sergeant Perkins are out in the town somewhere.'

John did not comment on Harry's vague answer. Minutes later, he climbed into Stephen Mitchell's carriage. As he did so, he became aware of two men already in it, sitting in the gloom.

'Morning John,' said Mathew. 'Sam and me thought we'd better come along in case you needed us.'

'We've left Caleb in charge,' added Sam.

John's initial reaction was one of annoyance, but he very quickly recognised the good sense of their being with him. It also explained Harry's vague answer, because he knew where they were.

'Thank you,' was all he could say, as he felt a lump come into his throat. How lucky he had been with these two men, both as his subordinates, and also his friends.

The journey to the prison took them nearly two hours, such was the crush of people who were in town for this particular execution. It was only thanks to the warder's skilful driving they were able to get through the crowds, and finally into the little known rear gate of the gaol. They would never have made it on foot.

Several minutes later Charles ushered them into Stephen's office. He came across to greet them. The three new arrivals looked around at the men already gathered there.

In addition to various prison officials, including the doctor and chaplain, there were also the Lord-Lieutenant of Warwickshire and the County Sheriff. Both men acknowledged the policemen. There was also another man, whom they did not know, and who rushed over to them.

They saw he was aged in his late twenties, short, well built, untidily dressed, and with a shock of brown hair. Mathew saw Stephen grimace, as he moved forwards trying to head him off: but he was too late.

'Well hello,' cried the stranger in a loud and excited voice. 'I say, which one of you was shagging the doxy who we're going to hang this morning?' The man took a notebook out of his pocket.

A sudden embarrassed and hostile silence greeted his outburst.

'Oh! Have I said the wrong thing?'

The silence became even more hostile.

'Gentlemen,' announced Stephen making great play on the word. 'This *creature* is a Mr Bryant, and he is here against my wishes. He is a newspaper reporter from London. It seems that, with the exception of

London, we are to have the dubious distinction of being one of the last places to hold a public execution. The Home Secretary has insisted he be here.'

Stephen made no attempt to introduce him to John and his companions. In any case, they ignored the reporter, and mingled with the other persons in the office.

The time dragged slowly on, until the chaplain made his excuses and left to prepare Madeleine to meet her maker. Not that he was very hopeful, as she had shown little interest in religion so far.

At half-past seven, Stephen called for silence.

'Gentlemen, I am going to leave you now, as I have certain duties I must attend to. Warder Johnson will come for you in twenty minutes time. At exactly five minutes to eight, he will lead you out onto the scaffold, having first informed you where to stand. This will be new to you, Mr Bryant?'

'Good Lord no. I've been to hundreds of hangings.'

'As I was saying,' continued Stephen. 'Once you are in position, there will be a slight delay. Then, as the prison clock begins to strike eight o'clock, the prisoner will be led out onto the scaffold. Before the clock has finished completely striking the sixteen chimes, she will be in position. The clock will commence striking a further eight times. By the time the last one has struck, it will all be over. Are there any questions?'

'That'll be the sign for breakfast, will it, once the doxy's dead?' asked Bryant.

'Mr Bryant,' snapped the Lord-Lieutenant. 'In approximately half-an-hour, we are going to commit murder, albeit legal murder.' He paused and poked Bryant in the chest. 'Just remember that!'

'I thought executions were legal?' smirked Bryant.

'Be that as it may,' answered Stephen quietly. 'Nevertheless, we are still deliberately taking someone's life.'

'Perhaps she should have thought about that,' retorted Bryant.

'Mr Bryant,' said Stephen very coldly. 'If I have another word out of you, I will have you locked up in a cell, until the execution is over. You will miss it, and therefore will not be able to write about it. And if that happens, then I suspect your editor will not be impressed.'

Bryant opened his mouth to reply, but clearly thought better of it.

'Gentlemen, and Mr Bryant,' continued Stephen. 'May I suggest you make use of the privy whilst you wait for Warder Johnson, to come and collect you.'

Stephen left the room.

John said nothing whilst he waited for Charles Johnson to appear. Everyone else in the room respected his not wanting to talk. Even Bryant had gone very quiet. He was beginning to look a little pale, and a thin sheen of sweat had appeared on his cheeks and upper lip.

After what seemed an eternity, the door opened and Warder Johnson came into the room.

'If I may have your attention please gentlemen! In a moment we shall make our way out onto the scaffold. I would be obliged if you would line up in the following order. Thank you.'

He read out their names, starting with the Lord-Lieutenant and ending with Cedric Bryant, who had now gone extremely quiet. When they had lined up, he led them out of the office, to a nearby closed door. At exactly five minutes to eight, he opened the door and led the way out onto the scaffold.

A roar of approval greeted their appearance, which none of them acknowledged. However, when John appeared, flanked by Mathew and Sam, there came a silence, broken only by several people calling.

'There's Mayfield.'

'Look! It's Mayfield.'

His relationship with Madeleine was well-known, and in fact, many people felt desperately sorry for him.

John took his place on the scaffold, and waited.

The crowd fell silent, and all eyes were fixed on the prison clock. At last, it began to strike.

Ding, dong, ding, dong!

Double doors opened and the chaplain appeared, followed by Madeleine and two warders. There came a gasp from the crowd, as she stepped onto the scaffold.

Ding, dong, ding, dong!

Madeleine was led to where *Throttler* Smith waited for her.

Ding, dong, ding, dong!

She stepped onto the trapdoor, whilst *Throttler* pinioned her legs. At this moment Bryant ran across to one side of the scaffold, leaned over it, and was violently sick onto the people standing below.

Ding, dong, ding, dong!

Throttler offered to put a hood over Madeleine's face, but she shook her head. Passing the hood to one of the warders, he put the noose over her head, and tightened it.

There came a dull thud as Cedric Bryant fainted. Nobody paid him any attention.

Dong!

Madeleine turned her head and looked at John

Dong!

'Can you forgive me?' she mouthed at him.

Dong!

'Yes,' he mouthed back at her, and nodded his head.

Dong!

Madeleine smiled.

At the same moment, *Throttler* pulled the lever: the trapdoor sprung open with a crash, and Madeleine fell through the gap.

There was a roar from the crowd.

Dong!

John realised, with a growing horror, how *Throttler* Smith had been looking at him, when he nodded to Madeleine. He had taken it as the signal to operate the trapdoor.

It was over.

Dong!

John saw the rope still swinging from the gallows. Only now it seemed as if he was looking at it the wrong way through a telescope, and all the figures looked very small and far away.

Dong!

The sound of the clock, and the roar of the crowd, now seemed to be very far away. All he could hear was a roaring sound in his ears which was growing louder, and his knees began to buckle.

Dong!

John never heard the clock's final strike. Neither did he feel Mathew and Sam's strong hands grip his belt, and keep him upright. The Lord-Lieutenant, Sheriff, Chaplain and Charles Johnson realised what had happened, and they quickly stood round him. Nobody in the crowd saw what had happened.

When John opened his eyes again, he was aware of something very pungent, being wafted underneath his nose. The doctor was looking anxiously at him.

'How are you feeling?' he asked.

John pulled a wry face. 'What happened?'

'You fainted.'

'Fainted? Me? Fainted?'

'Don't worry: everyone rallied round you, and they were the only ones to see what had happened. Here, drink this.'

The doctor thrust a mug of tea into John's hands. He drank it greedily, and went to stand up.

'No, don't try it,' the doctor advised. 'The tea contained a powerful sleeping draught. You're not going anywhere for a while.'

Several minutes later, John was deeply asleep.

When the doctor rejoined the others in Stephen Mitchell's dining-room, he saw they had already started breakfast. He was also interested to see Sam deep in conversation with Cedric Bryant.

'It was your first, wasn't it?' probed Sam, gently.

'Yes,' agreed Bryant. 'And I missed everything.'

'What are you going to do? Make it up?'

'Yes, it's all I can do, and just hope my editor never finds out.'

'I can help you there.'

'Can you?'

'Yes. I won't tell your editor what happened, and in return, you make no mention of my guv'nor's involvement with the woman who was just hanged. Agreed?'

Bryant nodded miserably.

Sam went across to the breakfast buffet, and soon came back to Bryant, carrying a plate with a cover on it.

'Here you are. Just to seal our little bargain, I've brought you some breakfast.' Sam was conscious how all the other diners were watching him.

With a flourish, Sam took the cover off the plate. 'Look!' he instructed, with a grin. 'I've got you devilled kidneys: pickled oysters, curried pig's trotters…'

Sam did not get any further as Bryant jumped up, put his hands over his mouth, and ran from the room, much to the amusement of the other diners,

'That was cruelly done, Mr Perkins,' said the Lord-Lieutenant, in between his laughter. 'Though I must confess, I couldn't have done it better myself. Well done, sir!'

A general roar of approval greeted the Lord-Lieutenant's comments, who then took Sam on one side.

'Will Bryant make an issue of John's involvement with the Concannon woman?'

'No, sir. We've reached an understanding. If he breathes one word about it, then I will see his editor knows what really happened. He will soon discover how Mr Cedric Bryant's account of the execution, will be fictitious.'

'Well done.'

After breakfast, Sam offered to stay with John, until he was fit enough to return home, whilst Mathew went back on duty. There was still the problem of the vast crowds who were slowly dispersing.

The doctor showed Sam where John was, gave him some instructions and left them.

Sam made himself comfortable at the table in the room, opened the small case, which he had brought with him, and removed a pile of reports. He had anticipated something like this happening, and he was more than happy to stay. With luck, he should have most of the day, free from interruption, in which to catch up on his paperwork.

CHAPTER TWENTY- SIX

Mayfield's last case...Four months later

As St Mary's clock struck noon, John put down his pen, collected his hat, and locked his office door. Passing through the front office, he saw Harry Barlow.

'I'm going now, Harry, for a few hours,' he said. 'I'll be at home if anything happens.'

'Leave it to me guv'nor.'

Harry watched John leave the station, and he shook his head. He would not have believed it possible to see just how much the man had aged in recent months.

It was so unfair. Just as it seemed he was coming to terms with the death of his wife, and had found another woman, it had all gone terribly wrong. Even now, he could still see the look of horror on their faces, when Madeleine had been unmasked as the killer. No wonder his poor guv'nor had suffered so much.

John walked home, fortunately without seeing too many people he knew, who might have wanted to stop and talk. By the time he had reached St Mary's church, he felt another giddy attack coming on. He quickly went into the church, where he sat in one of the pews, and waited until the attack passed.

These attacks were becoming more frequent, and he knew he ought to speak to Thomas or Silas about them. But deep down he knew they would probably only tell him something he did not want to hear. So, he made yet another excuse for keeping quiet.

Once he had recovered, John made his way through the churchyard to his back garden. As usual, he stopped by Harriet's grave, and told her about what he had done that morning. Stooping, he removed a single weed, which had grown at the foot of her headstone.

Going indoors, he went straight up to the dining-room, where a plate of cold meat and bread waited for him. Seth soon appeared with a pot of tea. Like the rest of the servants in John's house, and those in Thomas and Sarah's, he was appalled to see just how ill John looked. In fact, he had already told Thomas about John's state of health. As he expected, it was also a cause for concern for both Thomas and Silas.

John thanked him for the tea, and he sat down. In doing so, he looked in the mirror, and saw there was another person in the room, whom he did not recognise. Then he realised.

The gaunt, haggard and lined face, with sunken bloodshot eyes, was in fact his own reflection, looking back at him.

He could not remember when he had last enjoyed a full night's sleep, without experiencing the recurring nightmares of Harriet's death, and Madeleine's betrayal. John refused to take any sleeping draughts, and so he rarely slept for more than four hours during the day. And that was never in one go.

Having finished his meal, he adjourned to the drawing-room. With any luck, he would sleep there for an hour or so, in one of the chairs. But first he took a large book from out of his desk drawer, and began to write.

It had actually been Sarah's idea, how he ought to write up his memoirs. Initially he had not wanted to do it, but she had insisted. Much to his amazement, he found it helped him. He now wrote a few pages every day, and it encouraged him to have a short sleep, which was usually dreamless. John felt it was only this short sleep each day, which kept him going.

However, this afternoon, when he took out the journal, his hand accidentally touched the butt of the revolver he kept there. Almost sub-consciously, his hand clasped it, and he pulled the weapon out of the drawer. Whilst it was kept unloaded, the bullets were in the same drawer. He knew it would take but a few seconds to put a bullet in it, and end his misery.

The more he thought about it, the more the idea appealed to him. Without any more thought, he loaded the weapon. Then turned for a last look at Harriet's portrait. Her lovely face would be last thing he would ever see.

But was that a terrible look of reproof on her face? Or was it his imagination? He remained totally undecided, and unable to take his eyes off her, or pull the trigger.

Suddenly there came a loud, regular ringing of his front door bell. It was an official sounding ring, which could only mean he was wanted.

Relieved, he unloaded the weapon and put it away. As he closed the drawer, there was a discreet knock on the door, and Seth showed Harry Barlow into the room.

For the past few days, building work had been taking place in Friars Street. The plan was for several new houses to be built on some open land. Before the building could actually start, the chosen site had to be levelled. Only then would the trenches be dug to hold the necessary footings.

Davy Round could never be described as being the hardest working of labourers, either on this site, or anywhere else. Whenever he thought the foreman was not looking, he would rest on his spade. At every possible opportunity, he would find an excuse for not working, which did not endear him to the rest of the crew.

Today was no different to any other.

So, it was a cruel twist of fate, that when he brought down his spade, part of the trench wall collapsed. On its own that was not a problem: but the difficulty was caused by what the fall unearthed.

Davy just stood and stared.

Protruding from the side of the trench wall was what appeared to be a large boot, albeit not in very good condition. Alongside it part of another one just was just starting to appear. Davy put down his spade, and looked around. Nobody appeared to watching, so he carefully felt around the boot, just in case there was something valuable to be found.

He was horrified to feel what felt like a leg, still inside the boot.

'OVER HERE!' he shouted. 'OVER HERE!'

Cursing, Max Jenkins, the foreman, put down the plans he was studying, and made his way over to Davy. Other labourers, always glad of a chance to down tools, were already on their way. Max had to push his way past them to get to the trench. By now he had fully made up his mind to sack Round. The man was a total idle waste of space.

'Look gaffer!' instructed Davy. 'It's a body!'

'Well cover it up then, and pretend you never saw it.'

'I can't do that gaffer. I'd be breaking the law. All bodies 'ave to be reported. And, ain't there a reward for 'im 'oo found it?'

The other workers muttered their support.

'Let's have a closer look then,' said Max, and he slithered into the trench.

Carefully he moved some more soil, and his worst fears were realised. The man was absolute right. It was a body, and now he had no option but to report its finding to the police. He only hoped they would not take long with it, and let him get back to work.

Knowing he was defeated, Max beckoned to young Bobby Long. 'Go and tell the crushers what we've found and, then come back here straight away. And make sure you run there and back. If you're too slow, then you'll lose some wages!'

'Yes Mr Jenkins,' came Bobby's squeaked reply.

Harry Barlow gave John the gist of what Bobby had told him.

'Sergeant Young's already on the way, and I've sent for Dr Waldren. And I have the trap outside, guv'nor.'

John followed him out of the house and climbed into the trap, where Harry soon joined him. Moments later, Harry turned the trap round, and had the horse trotting briskly towards the scene.

As they passed by Thomas's house, John looked to see if there was any sign of him, but there was none. However, he noticed the front door was open, and Redman was overseeing the carrying of several parcels, and a trunk, into the house. It seemed Sarah had been having a shopping spree.

Less than fifteen minutes after Harry Barlow's arrival at his house, John was climbing down from the trap, when it arrived at the building site. He saw Thomas was there already.

As he stepped down a wave of giddiness spread over him, and he rocked on his feet. Harry took his arm.

'Easy guv'nor,' he whispered.

After a few deep breaths, John moved onto the building site. He saw Caleb waving and went to join him.

'The doctor's in the trench,' said Caleb. 'Use the ladder.'

John climbed down into the trench. At the bottom of the ladder, he was hit by another wave of giddiness. He put his hands out, on the side of the trench, to steady himself.

'It's time we talked about that,' said a stern voiced Thomas. 'We can do it tonight, when you come round for supper.'

'Oh, I don't think I'll be able to do that: at least not tonight. It looks like I might have another murder to investigate.'

'Ha!' snorted Thomas, derisively. 'You have a body: yes. He's come to a violent end: yes. But as for finding out who killed him...' Thomas laughed. 'You stand no chance. I don't think you'll even identify him. Come!'

Thomas led the way over to where the body had been uncovered.

John saw it was just a skeleton, encased in some rusting armour, in which there was a large hole.

'In my estimation, this poor fellow's been dead for about two hundred years: probably during the civil war period. You'll have to inform the coroner, but after that, it's a job for the museum, not the police. See you tonight.'

With that, Thomas left the trench, and John made his way slowly back up the ladder. He had really not wanted to have supper with Thomas and Sarah. A murder would have given him the perfect excuse, but not any more.

He would have to go.

It was almost half-past six, when John stopped writing up his memoirs, put the journal away, and stood up. Standing in front of the mirror, he straightened his cravat, and brushed the shoulders of his coat. He was still appalled at how old and ill he looked.

Although he did not want to go out tonight, John knew he really had no option, and he was not looking forward to the medical examination he knew would be coming. He suspected, rightly, how Silas would be there as well. Ruefully he squared his shoulders and looked up at Harriet.

He stopped in amazement.

It seemed to him how she was really smiling, especially with her eyes, just how she used to whenever he had succeeded in a very difficult task. After her death he had thought he would never see that smile on her face again. And yet, here it was: even if it was only in his imagination. Perhaps the medical examination would not be as unpleasant as he thought it would be?

He soon discovered his hopes, at least in that quarter, were ill-founded.

Redman showed him straight into the drawing-room, where he was greeted by Thomas and Silas. Sarah sat a little to one side, engaged with some embroidery. Clearly she had been advised to let matters take their course, and to keep out of the way.

Thomas thrust a glass of sherry into John's hand, and offered him a chair.

'I'll come straight to the point, John,' he said without any preamble. 'We are all desperately worried about your health. We have all been watching you for a while, and have noticed the giddy spells. They're getting more frequent, aren't they?'

John nodded his head, knowing he had no alternative but to agree.

'Basically, from a medical point of view, neither Silas nor I think there's anything terminally wrong with you.'

John felt relieved, and yet slightly disappointed at the same time. He also felt a twinge of guilt, especially as he had thought about taking his own life only a few hours earlier. Was this why Harriet was smiling?

'However we are both convinced if you go on as you are, without getting very much sleep, you will kill yourself.'

Thomas let his words sink in. All three men took a sip of their drinks and waited for a reaction.

'I appreciate what you are telling me, but the only way I can get any decent sleep is if I take laudanum, or something similar.' John shook his head. 'And I will not do that and become dependent on drugs. In any case, the drugs do not always stop the nightmares of Harriet's death, Madeleine's betrayal and her execution.'

'When did you last have a real dream free sleep, not just an hour or so in a chair?' asked Silas.

'It was that long ago, I just cannot remember.'

Silas nodded. 'It was so often the case with many of my patients during the war. They only recovered once they were discharged from the army, and had moved away from that way of life. What you need is to do the same.'

John started to protest as he realised what Silas was suggesting.

'No, John, listen to me,' Thomas spoke firmly, and confirmed his worst fears. 'We think the time has come for you to retire from the police…'

CHAPTER TWENTY - SEVEN

Later the same evening.

'**N**o! I can't do that!'

'Why not? You don't need the money. Remember I was an executor of Harriet's will, and I know just how much she invested on your behalf. Even if the interest rate halved, you would still never be short of money.'

Thomas let his words sink in, before continuing.

'Even you must realise it is only a matter of time before your force is swallowed up by the County Constabulary. It's happening all over the country. I don't give you more than five or six years, at the most. Then you'll have to retire, because the County won't want you! You'll be too old.' Thomas was being deliberately brutal.

John knew that to be true.

'Now here's the deal. If you agree to retire on ill-health, it is guaranteed Mathew will succeed you. The promotion will do his standing a lot of good. I know how Harriet provided for him and Margaret. But he's been a loyal deputy, and a good friend to you. It would be a nice ending to his career.'

Silas said nothing, as he was not on the Watch Committee.

'A similar deal exists for Sam and Caleb. Your establishment is going to be increased, and there will be room for two inspectors: Sam and Caleb fit the bill a treat. Again I know their financial circumstances through Harriet's will. But it would also be a fitting end to their careers. And the County won't want them for the same reason as you. Sam will move into Lucy's photographic business, and Caleb will join Robert.'

'What about Robert?'

'As you know, Harriet made sure he's well provided for. And we'll give him all the help he needs in setting up the bookshop he has always wanted. In any case, with his hand, the County would never contemplate giving him any employment.'

'You have got it all worked out, haven't you?' There was a bitter note in John's voice. 'But what if I say no?'

'Then you will be retired, on medical grounds all the same, and outsiders will be given the superintendent's role plus the other inspectors' ones.'

In his heart, John knew Thomas was right. And what was being proposed was very generous. But he still needed a little more time, to absorb what Thomas had said. 'When will this all happen, that is if I agree?'

'Whether you agree or not, it will be with immediate effect.'

'What do you think, Silas?' John asked.

'It's taken me a lifetime to find you. The last thing I want now is to lose you. As you know, I am thinking of getting married, and I dearly want a grandfather for my children.'

John felt a lump in his throat, and he was almost too overcome to speak.

'Very well,' he whispered. 'You win.'

In his mind's eye, he could see Harriet's smiling face, as he had seen it, just before leaving home. Was this why she had been smiling? Surprisingly, now he had agreed to retire, it did not seem so bad.

Thomas led John over to his desk, and produced a letter for him to sign. Briefly, it stated how he wished to be considered for early retirement, on grounds of ill-health. Next Thomas signed two other letters. John saw one was addressed to Mathew, and the other one to Sam.

'Caleb's promotion will be in a few weeks time, you may rest assured on that. But it cannot happen until we have the increase in manpower. The Watch Committee will publish the advertisements later this month,' explained Thomas.

Moments later Redman appeared, in answer to Thomas having rung a bell. He took the letters.

'See these are delivered at once, please, to the persons named, and obtain a written receipt for them!' instructed Thomas. 'And let me know when it has been done.'

John guessed it was confirmation of their immediate promotions. Although he felt a little sad at the knowledge he would never investigate any more crimes, he knew Mathew would do a very good job. And, he had to admit, all those affected by his retirement would well deserve their promotions.

For a while they discussed what he should do with his time. A visit to the Swiss Alps for the benefit of his health was recommended, and Silas offered to go with him. Out in the hall, the grandfather clock struck and Thomas refilled all their glasses.

Throughout the exchange, Sarah had kept very busy with her embroidery. Now she smiled at the men in her life, and raised her glass to them. They returned the gesture. As they did so, Silas saw the drawing-room door open, and he wondered who it could be.

He soon found out.

Mathew was just on the point of going on duty, when his letter arrived. He was puzzled and not a little concerned, especially as he had to sign a receipt for it. After a moment's hesitation, he opened the envelope, took out the letter and read it.

Briefly it instructed him to take over command of the Warwick Borough Police, with immediate effect, pending John's imminent retirement.

'What is it?' asked Margaret, concerned as to why her husband was still at home.

He handed her the letter, which she read.

Excitedly she gripped his arm. 'Superintendent Harrison! I like it. But poor John! How ill is he?'

Mathew told her what he knew. 'But as the letter states, I have to report to Thomas Waldren tomorrow morning, when I will be told everything.'

It was a similar reaction in the Perkins household. Inspector Sam Perkins also had to report to Thomas Waldren in the morning.

Back at the Waldren's house, conversation was brought to a sudden stop, as Silas was the first to recognise the unexpected visitor who had just arrived.

'Mama!' he gasped.

'Hello John,' said Katherine Whiting, as she entered the room.

Silas put down his glass, stood up and walked towards her. But then he stopped, when he saw his mother only had eyes for John, and nobody else.

'Oh my dearest, dearest love,' she gasped. 'You look absolutely dreadful. Why, oh why, didn't you send for me, like I said you should?'

By now John had also stood up, still with his glass in his hand, which had begun to shake. Katherine had obviously aged a few years, but she was still the attractive woman he remembered.

Whatever was she doing here?

Could he dare to hope?

Although Thomas had no idea what was going on, he had the forethought to take John's glass from him. He glanced at Sarah, but one look from her was enough to stop him asking any questions.

'Silas said there was a man in your life, and I didn't think it right to come between you after all these years,' replied John.

'Oh my love! My dearest love! Silas was right. There is a man in my life.'

John's heart sank.

'He's the man I first met here, all those years ago, when he came to set up the town's new police force. He's the same man I fell deeply in love with in London. He's the same man who's the father of my...of our son. It's you, my dearest John. You're the only man in my life.'

There were no more words, as they both met in the middle of the room, and held each other's hands. For several long seconds the two of them just gazed into each other's eyes, as the years melted away, then they fell into one another's arms.

Silas studied John and Katherine with mixed emotions.

He was seeing something he never thought he would ever see: both his parents together, in each other's arms, and clearly still very much in love with each other.

The realisation hit him.

He was now part of a real family.

On the other hand, he cursed himself for not having seen the truth before.

His mother's secret lover, whom he never saw? The scrapbook of articles from the *Warwick Chronicle*, supposedly gathered initially to remind her of where she was born? That story was changed later in her letters to him, to it being a record she had kept of his father's deeds. But it was none of those. She had kept it for herself. As a doctor he was a failure, Silas reasoned, when he could not even diagnose a case of love sickness.

Slowly the truth penetrated. Thanks to his having misread the signs, he had caused all this unnecessary suffering to his father, although he might also just have saved his mother's life in the process. His mind was in turmoil.

Sarah watched the lovers intently. And because she was watching and hoping, she was the first to see it happen.

John had his head resting on Katherine's shoulder, with his eyes shut, just enjoying the moment. Her embrace had still been as electrically charged, as it had first been, even after all these years.

In his mind, John saw Harriet, but she was smiling happily, and was encouraging him. Suddenly he knew everything would be all right. A huge weight seemed to lift from his shoulders, and the tension of the past months began to flow out of his body.

And he felt incredibly at peace.

As she watched, Sarah saw two large tears appear in John's eyes, which slowly trickled down his cheeks, and were soon followed by others. Still watching, she saw his shoulders heave, as a strange strangulated sound came from him. Then his body began to shake. Moments later John was sobbing loudly, with the tears running unchecked down his cheeks. Katherine was crying too.

Sarah raised her eyes towards the ceiling. In fact she was looking towards Heaven. 'Thank you God,' she prayed silently. At last John had given way to all the grief and emotion he had been carrying since Harriet's death.

Putting down her embroidery, Sarah took Mathew and Silas by an arm each, and steered them out into the hall. She was not surprised to find Redman standing there, with a worried look on his face. The sound of John's agonised sobbing could be clearly heard, continuing unabated through the closed door.

'Redman!' she instructed. 'There will only be three of us for supper tonight.'

'Very good, madam.'

'And,' Sarah continued. 'No-one, and I mean no-one, is to go into the drawing-room without my express permission. Is that clearly understood?'

'Yes, madam.' Redman paused. 'May I ask, is Mr Mayfield all right?'

'Yes, Redman.' Sarah smiled. 'I think it can safely be said Mr Mayfield has not felt so well for a long time, and certainly not since Harriet's death. In fact I can truthfully say Mr Mayfield has started on his long road to recovery.'

Supper was a desultory meal, with all three of them wrapped up in their own thoughts. Sometime after nine o'clock, Katherine came into the dining-room. Both men rose, and Silas went across to her.

'I never realised, mama. Oh what have I done to you both?'

She kissed him, and put her finger on his lips. 'It doesn't matter any more. I should have told you long ago, but I'm here now.'

'I must apologise for how I look,' she said to them all.

They all saw her hair was dishevelled, with tear stains down her face, and all over her dress.

'The poor love's totally exhausted. He's sound asleep now, and sleeping like a baby. What have you been doing to him?'

'Would you like something to eat?' asked Sarah.

For a moment, Katherine was tempted to decline, but hunger made her change her mind.

'Perhaps I could just have something on a tray, which I can take into the drawing room, and still keep an eye on John.'

'No, mama,' instructed Silas, who was still on his feet. 'You stay here and eat. Thomas, may I have another glass of your excellent port, please? Then I will go and sit with papa.'

'What an excellent idea that was Silas,' said Thomas, as he filled all their glasses. 'Bringing your mother over here, is just what John needed.'

'But I didn't do it,' replied Silas. 'I thought you had done it.'

Both men looked at Sarah.

She looked at Katherine.

'Men!' she smiled.

EPILOGUE

Warwick ...late March 1869

Extract from the Warwick Chronicle:

*W*E *are pleased to report on the recent marriage, at St Mary's church, between Mr John Mayfield, our recently retired Superintendent of Police, to Mrs Katherine Whiting, a widow. Readers will remember that Mr Mayfield retired last year, for health reasons. Today we are very pleased to report he has almost returned to full health, following a long sojourn in Switzerland, and a sea voyage to America.*

The bride was given away by her son, Dr Silas Whiting, who wishes to be known in future as Dr Mayfield. His mother is a successful American business woman. The bride was attended by Mrs Sarah Waldren and Mrs Emma Roberts, from Claverdon. Mr Mayfield's best man was the recently retired Dr Thomas Waldren, whose medical practice has been taken over by Dr Mayfield.

As the happy couple left the crowded church, they were greeted outside by a large throng of well-wishers, and a guard of honour, provided by Superintendent Mathew Harrison, Inspectors Samuel Perkins and Caleb Young, and other members of the Warwick Borough Police.

We wish the married couple every happiness in their future life together. They intend to spend half the year in Warwick and the other half in America.

There were two other incidents that day, which the *Chronicle* did not report.

As Katherine and John were greeted by the crowds outside the church, she found herself separated from her husband. It was at that moment, when an old withered woman pushed her way forward and caught her arm, cackling as she did so.

Katherine went cold, as she recognised Phoebe Morris, her tormenter from the time when she had lived in Warwick before. Still cackling, Phoebe took hold of Katherine's empty hand, opened her fingers and pressed something inside it.

'I promised you this when you made good,' Phoebe whispered. 'But I missed you after the trial. You earned it many years ago for the way you sorted that bastard Cooper out. If only I'd known. I'm sorry.'

Katherine opened her hand, and felt the warm tears fill her eyes, as saw her mother's silver crucifix lying there. Phoebe had snatched it from her many years ago.

She went to thank Phoebe, but the old woman had gone, although Katherine thought she could hear her cackling.

'Are you all right, my darling?' asked her worried husband when he saw her tears.

'I'm fine, my dearest love. Look!'

She opened her hand, and showed him the crucifix. Instinctively he knew what it was, and knew the story behind it.

'Phoebe Morris has just given it back to me.' She smiled and wiped her tears away.

★ ★ ★

Later that evening, as the sun was beginning to set on what had been a gloriously warm and still day, Katherine crept out quietly out from the reception, that was being held in John's house, and which was now their house. She went downstairs into the kitchen.

'Oh! There's nothing wrong, is there Mrs Mayfield?' asked a worried Mrs Simms, who was talking to Seth.

'Of course not, Mrs Simms. You've worked absolute wonders today. I just don't know how to thank you both enough for looking after John so well in those difficult days.'

Katherine touched her arm. 'But there's a little job I must do. So, if anyone comes looking for me, you haven't seen me. I promise I'll be back in a few minutes.'

Mrs Simms watched as Katherine went out of the back door, across the lawn, through the gate and into the churchyard. Katherine was totally unaware that Seth was following her carefully, determined she should come to no harm.

Going into St Mary's churchyard, Katherine went straight to Harriet's grave, where she stood silently for a while.

'Rest easy now, Harriet,' she said. 'John's back in safe hands. I know in life we were once rivals, but you were always number one in his heart, and I will never ever try to replace you there.'

She stooped and laid her wedding bouquet on the grave.

'I promise to look after John in life and in death, if necessary, just as you did. Will you trust me to do this?'

After standing still for a few moments, Katherine turned and walked back towards the house. As she did so, a sudden warm, gentle breeze sprung up, rustled through her hair, and stopped just as suddenly.

Katherine turned back to the grave.

'God Bless You, Harriet. And thank you. I won't let you down.'

Katherine turned and went back into the house to rejoin her new husband.

HISTORICAL NOTE

As in the other Mayfield books, this is a work of fiction, although set in Warwick, which is a real town. Wherever possible I have called places by their modern day names. However, some locations are figments of my imagination.

You will not find the White House, the Harriet Foxton Hospital, or where John and the Waldrens lived. Warwick Gaol has long since gone, but in 1868 it existed in the part of town known as the Cape.

Public executions ceased in England in 1868. Although capital punishment would remain on the statute book for many more years, they were then performed in private.

For the medical service in the American Civil War, it was a steep learning curve. Many doctors had less then two years' training with little or no practical experience, and there was often animosity between the regulars and the volunteers. Initially new doctors had to seek advice from civilian doctors who had little or no experience in treating war wounds. And they were not permitted to embark on any form of treatment until they had done so. This ridiculous state of affairs did not last long.

When the war started, the entire medical staff for the whole of the American army consisted of one Surgeon General, 30 surgeons and 83 assistants. Of these, 24 defected to the Confederates. In due course, hundreds of humanitarian volunteers flocked to both sides. Nurses became the true angels of the battlefields.

71% of all the wounds suffered by the troops were on their body extremities, with gunshots being the most prevalent. Three out of every four injured limbs resulted in amputation, as being the quickest, and often the safest way of dealing with wounds.

These injuries were treated first, as body and head wounds tended to be fatal. Risk of infection was a very serious worry, and disinfectants were not always available until too late to be of any use. Chloroform, opium and ether were widely used, but many patients succumbed to nervous exhaustion.

Generally speaking, conditions both in the camps, and the hospitals, can best be described as insanitary. Latrines rarely had any drainage facilities. Many users preferred to go out of camp when necessary, rather than use them. Their actions only added to the insanitary conditions.

More than 600,000 soldiers would lose their lives during this war, and not just from wounds. Many died from disease.

Needless to say, speculation and corruption were rife, on both sides, in the pursuit of wealth. Officially the smuggling of chloroform to the South was declared illegal, by both governments. Not that it made any difference as many blind eyes were turned, often in return for tobacco and cotton from the Confederate States. However the *Voluntary League of Medical Helpers* is a figment of my imagination, and they would not have been wanted by the Fenians in their struggle against England.

The Fenians did attempt to invade Canada in 1867, but it was a doomed venture. Likewise there were some Union officers who wanted a war with England, in retaliation for the support given to the Confederates during the war. Common sense prevailed, and there was very little support for such a venture. However Fenian activity in England, and Ireland, would continue for many years to come.

Back in England photography had been used since its invention in 1839, and in time would be used for criminal evidence purposes. John Mayfield was forward thinking in his use of photography.

George Smith, also known as Topper and Throttler, was a real hangman who operated during this period. He obtained his nicknames from wearing a top hat when performing his official duties. His other nickname had to be connected with the way he performed his trade!

CONSPIRACY OF FATE

(This is Graham Sutherland's next novel, which is set in England and Europe between 1846-1848. It is a tale of murder and intrigue, at a time of great popular unrest, in the run up to the Year of Revolutions. Young Richard Fielding is cast into this maelstrom, because he has something various people want, and they will stop at nothing to get it. His only ally is Police Inspector Daniel Roberts, who has been tasked with arresting him for murder).

Sophie Henderson heard the wheels rolling up the gravel drive at Loxley House. She leapt up, hurried to the windows and looked out. All she could see in the gloom were the silhouettes of two people in the gig, and hoped they were Richard and Will Collins.

She knew about Will's mission to bring Richard back to Warwick, and had been worried when they had not arrived. Her anxiety increased when the gig stopped, and she saw the visitors were two big men, neither of whom she recognised. A groom ran out to greet them.

Instinctively she knew they spelt trouble.

Watching from the window, she saw them climb down from the gig. By the groom's lantern she saw the driver wait for his passenger, before they both strode purposefully towards the front door.

There was just enough light for her to see the driver was the older of the two, and he had a hard look about him, whilst his companion had a kinder face. Then they were lost to her view.

Nervously she sat down, composed herself and waited to discover who they were. Soon there came a discreet tap on the drawing-room door.

'Excuse me, Miss Sophie,' announced a footman, as he entered the room. 'There are two policemen to see Sir Felix.' He made no attempt to disguise the sneer in his voice, as he said *policemen.* 'I've told them the master's in London, but they insist on seeing you.'

Sophie swallowed, and her throat had gone dry.   Whatever could policemen want at Loxley House? 'Show them in, please!'

The footman withdrew, closing the door behind him. Forcing herself to sit still, Sophie waited for her visitors. Nervously her fingers strayed to her throat where Richard's locket hung. She prayed nothing had happened to him.

After what seemed a lifetime, she saw the door open, and put her hands in her lap, hoping no one would see how they trembled.

'The policemen, Miss Sophie!'

Again she heard the sneering tone in the footman's voice. She would speak to him later about that. Once the door was closed, she looked at her visitors.

'Good evening, miss,' announced the younger man.   'I am Inspector Roberts, and this is Sergeant Wilkes.'

'We've come from Birmingham,' added Wilkes.

Sophie said nothing for a moment. Her heart was pounding. Clearly it had to be a serious matter for these two men to have come from Birmingham.

'Please sit down. What do you want here?' She licked her dry lips and watched them sit down.

The inspector sat confidently in his chair, but the sergeant perched nervously on the edge of his. How she wished her father was here, or even Mallory. But he was not due for an hour or more.

'We've come about a Richard Fielding,' said Daniel. 'I believe you know him?'

'Of course I know him!' Her fingers went to the locket. 'Has something happened to him?'

'Not as yet,' answered Wilkes grimly.

'What do you mean?' Her voice was so quiet, she wondered if they had heard her.

'I have a warrant for his arrest.'

Sophie stared at Daniel, who seemed to be far away. 'A warrant? What for?'

'For the murder of a Duncan Gowrie, and another man.'

She sat very still. Surely she could not have heard him properly? 'Murder? Richard?' Her voice was no more than a whisper, and she felt herself swaying, and the floor began to ripple.

'Are you all right, Miss Henderson?' Daniel stood up, a genuine look of concern on his face, as he made his way towards her. Quite clearly she was shocked by the allegations.

Sophie swallowed and nodded. 'Surely there must be some mistake?'

'I don't think so.' Daniel shook his head. 'We have a very good witness who saw what had happened.'

Yet, even as he spoke, Daniel's misgivings returned. He had quickly taken in the surroundings at Loxley House, and the young woman sat before him. Normally he was a considerate man, but he had been deliberately brutal with her to judge her reactions.

She was genuinely shocked.

'No! No! I can't believe it! I won't believe it! Your witness is lying!'

'Why should he do that?'

Sophie thought for a moment. 'Obviously to get Richard into trouble. He's not a violent man. He just wouldn't do a thing like that.'

'Why not, miss? Perhaps he lost his temper?' Wilkes took up the questioning, using the information they had been given at Warwick Police station before coming on to Loxley House.

'He's never used violence towards anyone in temper.'

'That's not true, Sophie: and well you know it!'

They all turned to look at the speaker, who nobody had heard enter the room.

'And who might you be, sir?' asked Daniel.

'Permit me to introduce myself, gentlemen. I am Miss Henderson's betrothed, Mallory Kempe. And I am afraid she has been misleading you.'

'Mallory! How can you say that?'

'My dear. You remember Christmas and the way he assaulted me. How can you say he's not a violent man?'

Her shoulders sagged, as she remembered the incident only too clearly. No doubt so would many other people. She nodded dejectedly, as her fingers clutched at the locket once more.

Mallory related the details to the listening policemen, unaware they had already been told about it by Robert Andrew. Daniel made notes, as it was the kind of information he needed.

'That's very interesting, Mr Kempe, but I don't know how I could use that sort of evidence in court?'

In reality he did, but all of Daniel's instincts were warning him against this man. It was obvious the man hated Richard, and he was interested to see where it would lead. He soon found out.

'That's not a problem,' Kempe smiled. 'I'm a barrister, and no doubt it can be arranged for me to prosecute Fielding on behalf of the Crown, when you catch him. I'll see it's brought to the jury's attention. If Fielding's guilty, and I have no doubts that he is, I'll help you hang him.'

Sophie sprang to her feet. 'How could you Mallory? I...I...' She broke off, unable to say any more.

He stepped closer and put his arm round her shoulders. Angrily she threw it off, and ran from the drawing-room. Only Daniel saw the tears pouring down her cheeks. Kempe went after her.

The two policemen waited in silence. They could hear Sophie crying and shouting in the distance. When Kempe returned, his face was white and pinched.

'I must apologise for her behaviour, but I fear it has all been too much for her.'

The other men nodded.

'What else can you tell us about Fielding?' asked Daniel breaking the silence.

Kempe told them.

The two policemen left Loxley House about an hour later. It was a raw, cold night.

'What's happened to your rain, Sergeant Wilkes?'

'It'll come sir. It'll come.'

Lightning Source UK Ltd.
Milton Keynes UK
UKOW051412220212

187721UK00002B/28/P